AND THEN THEY RUINED EVERYTHING

BOOK TWO IN THE DEATH OF ROCK 'N' ROLL SERIES

A NOVEL BY DUNCAN MILNE

ISBN 978-1-943492-14-5 (hard back)
ISBN 978-1-943492-15-2 (soft cover)

WWW.ELMGROVEPUBLISHING.COM
San Antonio, Texas
www.elmgrovepublishing.com

What readers said about Duncan Milne's first book ***The Death of Rock 'n' Roll, The Impossibility of Time Travel...and Other Lies:***

"If you love a dry wit and share the author's love of (good) music then this is the book of the year... did I mention it was funny too?"
— David

"What a great and delightful read... great job in developing the characters and piecing together the history of rock n roll..."
— Andrew

"A coming of age novel that has an encyclopaedic knowledge of rock and roll! ...Duncan Milne provides a lot if insight into the human condition. It reminds me of Black Swan Green by David Mitchell. I recommend this to anyone who enjoys adventure, angst, or a fast paced narrative."
— Cemery

"What a wonderful read. The incredible descriptions transport the reader 'right there' and anxious for the 'next crossing.'
— Lois

"Duncan Milne has written a very interesting read here about Rock 'n' Roll and traveling through time to see rock shows... very well researched and accurate."
— Julie

"If you dig Chuck Klosterman's superb work in rock literature, if you felt a kinship with Cusack's character in High Fidelity, or if you just want to grab a slice of pizza and travel through time to some great gigs, you'll be highly entertained. Looking forward to the next one!"
— Steve Dodd

"One man's anthology of rock 'n' roll with fun characters that take you on their journey through society now and in the past. Keep pen and paper handy so that you can take notes about which songs you'll want to download later!"
— Janette

Also by Duncan Milne

Novels:
The Death of Rock 'n' Roll,
The Impossibility of Time Travel and Other Lies

Short Stories:
Grizzly
Any Day
Hard Nine
The Halloween Meeting
Measured By Your Weight
The Departure
Interstitial

To all who try to make the world a better place, regardless of their reason. Especially when such kindness is done unexpectedly, without provocation but simply with a view to leaving the world better because that's where they live.

In addition, to Nicole and Spencer, who constantly remind me to see the world in a better light. They inspire me to be kind and find a voice for something I would be proud of.

There are heroes everywhere, if you can't find one; be one.

Thank you.

The Story So Far

This is a story about time travel.

This is a story about rock 'n' roll.

This is a story about life and art, and is now the second book in a series. Literature like life, music, art, or time travel, it doesn't really matter where you start, just so long as you do. Welcome.

If you are starting here, this is a story in which two friends have discovered a means of traveling through time utilizing the video game Guitar Hero, coupled with a mixing table affectionately, maybe sardonically, called Louie Louie, a reference to the Kingsmen classic and Satan, the latter to whom DJs have often been compared.

Starting as a lark to attend gigs throughout time and space, the device allows Kenn Ramseyer and his best friend to enjoy a richer rock 'n' roll experience. However, before long they discover that certain situations need a nudge to return to the correct path. Sometimes more than a nudge is required, such as when they have to kidnap a British prime minister to restore the natural order of things.

Although typically painfully awkward around women, both of the boys find themselves infatuated by different women at the end of the first novel. The real trouble begins there, which is where the story resumes.

Contents

PROLOGUE:

Hell City, Hell

Good evening, this is Sid Itious, guest DJ at WNYU 89.1 FM. I love a good prologue. It's the equivalent of watching the roadies set up for a band. It builds anticipation, but sometimes it goes too far and feels like hell.

Even better than a prologue is being here with Kenn in New York. I now understand why people don't own cars here: finding parking is hell. In fact, it's what I really expect hell to be like—having to circle the block with a cumbersome, squealing, borrowed Oldsmobile that's running low on gas, the AC isn't working, and you can't roll the windows down to see where the curb is. You're late for an appointment and you need to park, so you have to keep circling. I envision people pointing and laughing as I pass for the gajillionth time.

OK, let's get the hell theme going. Up next is a lovely little collaboration with Zeke picking up with the Supersuckers hitting "Hell City, Hell." Let's go!

FCC transcript WNYU 89.1 FM 11.25.2017 0103

File as: "Occult"

Unbidden. Trespassing as an unwanted guest was how I felt moving through my life, at least most of the time. My outlook on life wasn't quite that stark perhaps, but it was certainly lacking a clear view as to the meaning of life or what I was destined to become.

Being dismissed by Kenn was bizarre, frustrating my clarity. Sure, friends clash, but this was different. Events had taken an uncanny turn, and I was now facing something never seen before, a standard that for us was higher than other people we knew.

My best friend Kenn and I no longer had a benchmark for the unusual. Although it was autumn of 2013, the event leading to my expulsion was a gig from 1988.

Through the convenience of time travel, we had returned from seeing a Tracy Chapman show in San Francisco to our hometown in Oregon within moments of leaving, without the aid of anything other than our love for music.

Time travel certainly started as odd for us, but we had been doing it for so long now that it had become more nuanced than strange. Naturally, benchmarking the unusual had become difficult. One such nuance was that we could only cross into gigs and couldn't control when we returned home.

We had tried to extend our journey past rock 'n' roll into sports betting, patent discoveries, and entry into the stock markets. Even with knowledge sure to profit us, it was not to be; inexplicably time travel never lived up to our dreams. It was a force of nature in its own right, one that would grant us access only to music. Ultimately music was enough for us and led us to meeting our heroes and others we didn't expect.

Meeting a girl in a bar who changed our lives was unexpected, and things became increasingly strange from there. Unbeknownst to me, the conflict with Kenn and the challenges we would face were still gathering energy.

Despite the multitude of challenges that I had with finding friends, or fitting in, or getting along with my parents, at least I could take solace in knowing that Kenn and I were friends and that we'd always be there for each other. But even that didn't last forever, and the trouble with time travel is that I can't really say when things fell apart between Kenn and me. I would say it was sometime between 1988 and the present day, but closer to the present. Maybe that's always the way: the past is always closer than it seems.

"Yeah, I'm good," he said with a detached coolness. "I can clean myself up. I'm good. I'll see you tomorrow. You should just leave."

"Nah, it's OK, Kenn. I'll call in some pizzas and set up a record. Maybe a little Joy Division to start things off?" I offered.

"Actually, just leave. Leave now." And with that, for the first time in our friendship, I was dismissed. Excused. Unequivocally told to leave.

Is that what hell was like? You might think searing fires of molten sulfur or waves of freezing rain fraught with pestilence and plagues. Whatever your imagination came up with, you could be certain that suffering would be involved. But being cast off from Kenn was the deepest cut. I suppose at the same time, being around him was never easy.

Kenn always had a conspiracy. He had asked, "You know why the government is so eager to prosecute obscenity in music?"

"Kenn, stop it," I would often find myself saying. "Dude, look, can we just take our coffee and talk about this somewhere that isn't so busy?" It was as though he were physically incapable of recognizing that the weight of people's glares wasn't a reflection of the whetted anticipation of hearing his views but rather the scorn from those who didn't understand us. In a crowded café, derisive glares would cause me to squirm. It was bad enough that we skirted around the margins of society, but being overheard only served to gain the unwanted focus of others.

Undeterred, he would continue, always. There was always something with Kenn. "It's the same as the War on Drugs. The government isn't really after a solution; they're not even worried about it. They just want some high-profile arrests and lawsuits so that when American voters heave themselves out of their La-Z-Boys during halftime, they can hear sound bites that their government is effective. People are stupid." Kenn motioned his arm across the café, gaining momentum and passion. "Look at everyone else around us; do they really give a hot flash for what's going on? Do you really think that they spare a second's thought to their freedom, or what's happening with the economy? Nope. As long as they can see some easy points go up on some clever-sounding stand for morality in music, then, like a cow with its cud, they're happy."

I never was particularly popular, unless you considered being a target for school bullies, but being Kenn's friend never helped. Kenn had a precise view of life. His was a view that included a vast array of theories to explain certain facets of life. Conspiracy theories that often included reference to a ubiquitous "they" or "them." Control was always being exerted by "the Man" at the behest of "the government." Kenn considered these theories to be explanations, and I suppose I should concede that sometimes they even proved to be right.

I've given considerable thought to the conditions of hell in my time. My liberal arts education, a scholarship teeming with works such as *Faust, Paradise Lost*, and the writings of Joseph Conrad, informed my views of the conditions that the damned faced. Other works such as *Moby-Dick* or *The Lord of the Rings* placed me in greater proximity to torments that seemed never to end.

Hell wasn't limited to bearing witness to Kenn's antics; no, for me hell seemed to be everywhere.

"What do you mean you're not going to law school?" my father, or maybe it was my mother, would start. "You mean next semester. Right? You're not going next semester, but you're going after that, right? Seriously. You're wasting your life. And after all the school that you've completed, what? Are you just going to throw it away?"

It was sort of a fair question. I didn't know what I wanted to really do, which was hell enough, but in trying to discover the missing piece, I had dallied through college, taking any number of courses that seemed interesting but easy. But what did I really have to show for it?

"Maybe he just needs to move out," one of my parents would say to the other, initiating the sort of amorphous conversation in which their voices and views became inseparable. My indifference mirroring their contempt for my choices, eroding any bond that might have existed between us. Like letting go of a tether during a space walk, bodies in motion drifting apart without any reason or particular direction.

My parents threatened me with all sorts of punishments aimed at attacking my liberty. It was the usual battery of threats for the usual transgressions.

"You know, he's just not being serious enough at school."

"Well, you know he's just wasting our money on [insert "beer," "pot," or "rock 'n' roll"]."

"It's not like he has any friends."

"At least no decent ones."

Being friends with Kenn. Not assuming my expected role. Not moving out of the house soon enough. Moving out of the house too soon. Not being a lawyer. Or an accountant, or a —.

My American parents. Patriots who vocally supported the fundamental freedoms incumbent to America, but yet somehow justified engaging in tyranny to abridge my freedoms.

"You know the Constitution says I don't have to live under tyranny."

"The Constitution doesn't say you have to live here."

"If you continue to threaten my liberty, I could offer your names to the congressional Committee on Un-American Activities." What often seemed well strategized merely resulted in greater reprisals. I tried to plead my case, I tried to utilize the formal logic that I had been taught in my philosophy courses, but my parents were impermeable to such tactics. Hell was like that.

Threats and expectations became the materials from which my parents built my own personal Sisyphean existence. Depeche Mode had a Personal Jesus; I lived in the bespoke conditions of damnation, but for an occasional hall pass into the world of rock 'n' roll.

Dante visualized hell as a place of personalized torment; not only did this concept of hell engage my imagination, it sort of appealed to me. I thought it actually might be my kind of place. You know, with members of all the best rock bands, the Ramones, the Cramps, the Beatles, the Divinyls, and really anyone who was remotely interesting paying for their sins, sins that I would later gladly die for. In fact, I was betting on the concept that a fitting punishment for these bands could result in an eternity of great gigs. But maybe not. Because for such a result to occur, I would have to be rewarded while the others were being punished, unless playing gigs was a reward, so then the Ramones would actually be in heaven. But why?

All of my philosophical inspiration came from the closing view of Dante's *Paradiso*, where all the rewarded souls are gathered in a catatonic-like state of grace; I knew where I wanted to go. At least at first. As always, I wanted to be amid the smoke, haze, and noise that hell and rock shows share.

The problem arose from the ashes of the urban legend about the answer to a final physics exam question: "Was hell an exothermic or endothermic system?" A student answered by applying Boyle's Law and the fact that he'd slept with someone who'd claimed that she would only put out once hell froze over.

Without knowing what either system was, an awareness of the exothermic/endothermic paradox dawned upon me as I was considering my own mortality. If Dante was right, then hell would be neither exothermic nor endothermic but rather characterized by a lack of order, except as required for the purposes of tormenting souls. Thus, any of the obsessive personalities such as lawyers or engineers who found themselves in hell would discover they were beset with randomness and unpredictability: clocks that functioned poorly, demanding schedules that were impossible to meet, and rules incapable of being complied with.

Conversely, all the anarchists would find unity and conformity at every turn, queues upon queues where their existence was choreographed to the second for the rest of eternity. These condemned souls would be free to act and behave however they wished but would be met with tolerance, understanding, and accommodation to such a degree that frustration would be overtaken by mind-numbing despondence.

Sometimes I merely thought that hell was just specific moments in my life. Being with Kenn was sometimes like that. But not always.

The latest of these experiences happened in 1988 in San Francisco, but the impact upon today was unmistakable. Kenn and I had crossed to see a gig and then remained caught in the past for a while, a while that ended up with him falling in love with a girl who was equally aggressive with her upright bass and her Taser. It was a remarkable sight. It was another example of how close we always seemed to hell, but also to a state of grace.

Always missing the bigger picture, I reached these conclusions while I was preoccupied by the fear that Armageddon and Judgment were at hand. I should have been considering the pending crisis with Kenn, my relationship with Pyrah, and the significance of my record collection, but it's often the smallest details we overlook that lead to the larger crisis. The truth was that Armageddon, Judgment, Kenn, Pyrah, and my record collection were all related. As strange as that might be, the importance of my radio show also played a role.

I wanted to be like the guy in Paul Westerberg's song "My Road Now"—you know, brave, so that people wouldn't call me "chicken"— but instead Kenn and I became like the pair in David Bowie's "Heroes." Maybe this was fitting, because while I thought that parts of my life, or at least episodes of it, were hell, and while I didn't know what the meaning of life might be, I understood that Kenn and I would endure Armageddon. We would face our Judgment. We would host radio.

How did it all start? Well, it started on very familiar territory for me: being thrown out of somewhere. Unbidden. But this time it was different; this time Kenn dismissed me.

He met a girl, and with Kenn's words reverberating around my cranium as I walked away, I realized that I was truly unbidden.

PART 1

ISOLATION

Isolation:

A noun referring to the state of being separate from other like things;
A sense or state of being or existing alone; and
A form of punishment or deterrent used to control actions or emotions.

Isolation was a way of life, living in a small college town in Oregon.
Isolated from larger centers, we were distinguished by what we
    didn't have.
"Isolation": a song by Alter Bridge from the 2010 album *AB III*.
"Isolation": a song by Joy Division from the 1980 album *Closer*.

1

Unbidden

Radio is a metaphor for my life. A narrative with a sound track, an empty discourse that may or may not be shared. Ripples radiating from the station perhaps affecting someone along the way. Do my interventions really mean anything to anyone? At least the music is good.

I'm going to start the next set with some monster rock. The Forbidden Dimension, all the way from some two-bit Canadian town. Here's "Unbidden." May it send shivers down your spine.

FCC transcript KQOO 90.9 FM 07.04.1996 0149

Operator's Comments: "Station ID fail"

Unbidden? I walked home shocked. Stunned. Never before had I seen Kenn like this. For years, Kenn and I had been of like mind and singular in purpose. Sure, we had arguments and heated discussions, but these, more often than not, were simply part of the repartee that had always been a pillar of our relationship. Ways of challenging each other and enlivening the discourse around the discovery of rock 'n' roll— it was more than what we did to pass the time; it was the connection between us. But now . . . now things were different.

My body felt like it had been thrown on a pile of rocks. Abandoned and aching with that sort of jarring pain that seems to resonate from the marrow of your bones, and Kenn's voice echoing in me like the sound of breaking glass in an abandoned church. The conclusion was clear: Kenn had changed.

No question; anyone would expect that having mastered time travel would change a guy. How could it not? Time travel itself was a concept at the pinnacle of fantasy. Not only could Kenn and I time travel, we possessed the Holy Grail of science fiction. Ours was an unparalleled accomplishment, used unselfishly to make the world better. But it was also strange because Kenn and I couldn't share it with anyone else. It wasn't like there was a focus group for time travelers or anyone that we could tell.

I mean, really, the only people that Kenn and I could confide in about time travel were each other. It had been years now since Kenn had spoken with his parents, and mine wouldn't listen to anything that I had to say anyway. And what? You're going to tell a friend or parent, really? What would you say? "Hey, guess what! Kenn and I—yeah, you know my buddy Kenn, the one you think is an idiot, yeah, right, him. Well, as it turns out, we're not wasting our time together; we're time traveling. That's right, he's blurred the line between genius and idiot, and as a result, he and I have been traveling through time to see rock bands. Look, we're going to go see T. Rex sometime this week. You want us to get you a T-shirt?" You'd be loaded into a padded room before you finished your explanation.

Originally, Kenn discovered that playing the Guitar Hero MC5 module hurtled him through time into the gig. Unfortunately, that discovery was limited to only the gigs that MC5 were a part of. Later, after a series of trials, we discovered that by processing the Guitar Hero video game through a mixing table we could move through time into any past gigs. All we needed was a recording of the band we wanted to see. Kenn called the mixing table Louie Louie, because of his view that DJs are devils, but tolerated its imposition since it facilitated combining MC5, Guitar Hero, and any other music we wanted. The history of rock 'n' roll was unlocked and laid before us.

I suppose it was to be expected that becoming heroes was going to be lonely, but I didn't expect this isolation to extend to Kenn.

It was more than the vacant and discarded feeling of being unceremoniously thrown out of Kenn's house. He was now distracted and distant. Kenn was changing; now, suddenly, he was smitten with a girl, and ironically a girl who had also smote him. Sure, she was some girl, but still, a girl? Kenn's theory of rock 'n' roll and girls was well developed and fiercely held; now I started feeling like Peter Hook must have, watching Ian Curtis being led astray from his wife—and even worse his band, Joy Division—by Annik Honoré.

Maybe Kenn was right. Girls were merely set on the destruction of rock 'n' roll. Refusing to explain the exceptions, like Poison Ivy, Cat Power, Feist, L7, Kirsty MacColl, or Ann Magnuson of Bongwater, as anything other than merely outliers. I thought something else was at play. Maybe it was better to judge on the merits of the person, rather than her gender, religion, race, or belief. But with girls, Kenn was having none of it. This wasn't even a discussion that we would have had on prior occasions—another challenge that Kenn presented.

Kenn would always challenge me, but now, after these crossings, it was more than that. Like he had to be Batman and I had to be Robin. But I didn't know what it was that he needed to prove. Why now? Maybe I wasn't even Robin; maybe I was just Alfred, Batman's butler.

Without immediate plans for crossing and now suddenly exiled from Kenn, I felt my mind start to drift. My thoughts were a dried leaf on an autumn breeze, something that once had purpose but was now on the cusp of ruin, floating between freedom and abandonment. But this was a good thing. I would have time for myself, my radio show, for lectures from my parents, for . . . for Pyrah. Shit! How had I forgotten about Pyrah? As I kept my world with her apart from Kenn's and mine, the details were falling through the gaps. Although my heart now raced with thoughts of seeing her again, I couldn't remember how long it had been since we had been together. Days? Weeks? Hours? Time travel had left my world disjointed and confused. History was present and the future malleable.

As I reached into my pocket, my phone, as if confirming my decision to call Pyrah, began to vibrate and ring, the ringtone from the Stone Roses' "She Bangs the Drums." I thought, *I wonder if I should change that to "Love Me" by the Cramps*. All the same, Pyrah had reached out to me first.

"Hi. Do you know who this is?" she asked demurely. "Got some time for me?"

What could I say to such a clear sign from the cosmos that we were destined to be together? My heart leaped as my isolation was being dispatched. "Hey, I was just thinking about you. Funny, I had just reached for my phone to call. Of course I've got time. Should I come by? I could pick up pizza."

"Well, I guess we're thinking the same thing. I'd love if you'd come by. Sure, bring pizza. I've got a box of white zin' in the fridge."

Within moments, my apprehension and anxiety had been shed like a heavy jacket with the first warmth of spring. Pyrah was happy just talking to me; it was as though virtually no time had passed since we had last spoken; suddenly the details didn't matter.

The conversation continued without much substance or depth but had a palpable effect upon me. Pyrah's manner, at once both reserved and enticing, electrified me. It was like every ounce of her being was focused on me. I loved it. Within a few moments, the abrupt dismissal from Kenn was forgotten and we made plans for dinner, or a movie or something. Whatever it was, it involved Pyrah and me being together.

That night became the morning after, which then became breakfast, coffee, late lunch and another dinner, drinks, and then magically it all repeated. Soon we had drained the week of its days like the wine boxes cluttered around her recycling bin. I was coming and going from Pyrah's apartment as though it were my own. I would go to work, or call in sick, as the case might be, all from the sanctuary of Pyrah's home. I would plan my radio show and search for new music using Pyrah's laptop. Everything that I did, I did in close proximity to Pyrah. Our relationship blossomed, awakening unanticipated feelings in me. Sure, I had been close to Kenn and shared a bond, maybe even a kinship, but this was different, a different kind of intimacy that lacked the challenge that things with Kenn always held. I was happy. Content. All because I had Pyrah with me, and strangely I thought very little about Kenn and my unceremonious dismissal.

While at first I was concerned about what Kenn might think, I actually convinced myself that it would be OK. In fact, I resolved to tell Kenn about Pyrah—soon—just not now. First I had to work my way back to talking to Kenn, but I was sure that was going to happen, not only because we had been friends for so long, but also because of how electrified he had been about the bartender/bass player. It would be all right. Everything made sense, because this, too, was rock 'n' roll. Kenn would not only understand but also welcome the broadening of our horizons.

I didn't know when I would talk to Kenn about Pyrah but suspected that soon enough we would be sharing pizza and Frank's RedHot and a few beers and talking about rock 'n' roll. Maybe even planning our next crossing. Soon enough, if I only knew, but for now things just continued around and around like a record being played, and as always when a record was spinning I was content.

My contentedness was reinforced with the ringtone of my cell phone announcing, "Do You Remember Rock 'n' Roll Radio?"

"Kenn, how you doing, buddy?" I was trying to sound like nothing had happened.

"I'm good. Where have you been, Dick? I've got a couple of pies being delivered—a Hawaiian and a Kitchen Sink. Why don't you grab some beer and we'll go see the Stooges tonight."

I cast a furtive look toward Pyrah, and without needing more explanation she motioned, "Go, go."

"I'll be over in ten. Still got some Mountain Dew in the fridge? So I just need to grab beer?"

"Yeah, that's what I said. You'll be here in five? I'm not waiting on the pizza for you."

Of course he wouldn't wait; it was never about anyone other than Kenn.

"That was Kenn, he wants me to come by."

"You should go. Have fun. I've been spoiled by your affections, if you're not careful, I might grow accustomed to it."

"Thanks, Pyrah. I might be late; you wanna do something tomorrow?" I asked, pulling her close for a long embrace.

Walking toward the door with me, she said, "Of course. You haven't seen Kenn for weeks, and I'm not really the same to talk about music with." Handing me a key, she continued, "I've got to go out for a while anyway. Let yourself back in when you're done with Kenn. Don't worry if you're late; I'll be in bed. Wake me up and you'll be glad you did. In fact, now you've got a key you can wake me anytime you want! Maybe you can call in sick to work again tomorrow."

Pizza, live music, and seemingly assured sexual congress; I was holding a winning trifecta ticket. My life wasn't hell; I was in a state of grace.

Letting myself into Kenn's, I called out, "Hey, man, gonna grab a Dew. Want one? You've got mail." I grabbed the handful of mail that had been blowing around Kenn's front door and headed toward the music.

"Didn't hear you," Kenn said. "What's going on?"

"Highlights: I'm here; afternoon of music, pizza, and beer; here's your mail; your copy of *Rolling Stone* looks like the mailman tried to eat it." I was referring to the most significant piece of mail that I had picked up for Kenn: the January 2014 issue of *Rolling Stone*. "You had shit blowing all over your yard. You gonna put cars up on blocks next?"

"I don't read *Rolling Stone*. It's a rag."

"What?"

"*Rolling Stone* is a waste of time; it's a rag. I don't read it. Do you need a picture? Get it out of my house."

"Kenn, what are you talking about? When did this happen? I've got your copy right here. You've subscribed for years."

"Canceled. It's shit. I'm not reading it. Not after the Rollins interview."

"You mean his rant about not following the music featured in *Rolling Stone*?"

"Maybe."

"Kenn, I get that he's a hero of yours from way back to the Black Flag days—"

"The guy's an icon. A rock 'n' roll legend."

"Sure, but do you really think that he needs you to take a stand for him against major publications?"

"It's a fact. People are vulnerable to the media. If the common man doesn't stand up for what's right by rejecting publications that prey on the vulnerable, there is nothing to check their actions. Look at the *Duck Dynasty* guys who were threatened with the ax from A&E for expressing their views. As far as I know, we still enjoy free speech in America. The swing taken at Rollins was just as bad as the paparazzi preying on Suri Cruise. It has to stop, and the only way it will is if the little guy stands up."

"Listen, I'm not sure you're ever going to convince anyone that Henry Rollins is vulnerable, or at least as vulnerable as Suri Cruise."

"It doesn't matter. It's the same as Snowden: if people don't take a stand against the Man, society is going to go to hell in a handbasket. I do what I do because it's right. Rollins deserves respect. If he said 'hi' to us when we were walking down the street, we'd both lose a big load in our adult incontinence shorts."

"Kenn . . . imagery I don't really need. But sure, Rollins is a big deal—bigger for you than me, but still it would be pretty cool to talk to him."

"Big deal? Rollins is a rock god. He shouldn't have to justify himself to *Rolling Stone* or anyone else for that matter. Rollins has done more for music than the entire boreal forests of America have for carbon dioxide exchange."

"Agreed, but he could have reached a little further in that article. I mean, stating that David Bowie's album *The Next Day* is brilliant? Come on, what's the next big reveal? That fish live in water? Of course, a Bowie album that people have been waiting ten years for is going to be brilliant. Reznor said the same thing days earlier."

"I don't watch TMZ and I won't read *Rolling Stone*. Rollins is a legend," Kenn stated. "Leave it alone."

I agreed, but still eager to antagonize Kenn, I said, "So I suppose we're not listening to Daft Punk tonight."

"What are you doing about the pizza? You just lookin' at, it or are you havin' a piece? Throw out that fucking rag before I become ill."

Falling back into our normal banter—eating pizza, listening to music, drinking beer, and otherwise forgetting about San Francisco—rock 'n' roll regained the day.

That night we saw the Stooges in Germany, and everything, at least for a while, seemed to make sense. Life was going our way, but we didn't dwell on it. After all, it was too much fun soaking in the gigs; that's just who we are.

2

Who We Are

The rules of society form us. They direct us and control not only how we act, but the context that we understand our world in. This is Sid at KQOO 90.9 at 1:35 a.m.

It's the context and our experiences that inspire our views and our expression. That last set was finished off by Arcade Fire. Can you believe that they managed to get David Bowie to collaborate with them? Talk about making it big. OK, let's listen to Imagine Dragons and consider "Who We Are."

FCC transcript KQOO 90.9 FM 09.05.2014 0135

Search Term: existential

Operator's Comments: redacted

Who we are? I always thought that I knew, and maybe I did. Or at least maybe I knew who Kenn was and lied to myself only about who I was. If I didn't always know who I was, I at least usually knew *what* I was.

I was hot and sweaty, as though I had the flu or was watching one of the late-night offerings from Showcase with Pyrah. As the sensation of discomfort and disorientation bled away from me, I realized Kenn and I were standing on sand. Soft sand that caused discomfort through the bottoms of my Chuck Taylors.

As we did so often, Kenn and I had been ruminating over pizza and beer about the state of rock 'n' roll. About why gigs never came through town and how we had revolutionized our experience by discovering time travel. Before long, we were loading the album *Battle Born*, by the Killers, into the mixing table that I had attached to Kenn's Guitar Hero console with the intention of crossing into a Killers show.

"Once that demonic mixing table of yours is ready, you can count us in," Kenn said.

"I like calling it 'Louie Louie' better," I responded, before counting out a fierce "One, two, three, four . . . Kick out the jams, mother f—," and as I heard the thundering guitars of MC5 mixing with the Killers, the floor began to move. Slowly I started spinning as my nerves screamed at the bombardment of light and sound. Time travel, or crossing, was something I hadn't gotten used to. There was a sensation of being shot through a garden hose, or being trapped inside a piece of fabric that was disintegrating around you. Never the same, yet not unpredictable. Worse if we were listening to something nuanced or ethereal like the Cocteau Twins or Brian Eno. Some of Stewart Copeland's post-Police work left us staggering as though the mushrooms on our pizza had been spoiled. I certainly found the experience was always uncomfortable and bordering on violent, and now I felt as though I had been hit in the chest with a concrete block. When I tried to move my feet, they resisted, sinking further into the ground as though I were melting. Hot lead flowed through them instead of blood, or so I thought. Worried that our dalliance with time travel had failed desperately, I looked to Kenn.

"Look, dude, we're at the Atlantis Hotel," Kenn enthused while clipping my arm.

I turned around to survey our surroundings; Kenn was indeed right. We were on the massive grounds of the Atlantis, and the Killers appeared to be taking the stage.

"Awesome." Kenn continued, "This must be Sandance. We're in Dubai. Did you know that you can see these man-made palms from space?"

"So what? Kenn, you're rambling."

"So what, what?"

"So what that you can see the palms from orbit."

"Are you kidding me? That's cool. They're manufactured features that you can see from space. That doesn't impress you?"

"I don't know. Maybe, but I thought that you and Vinnie said a few weeks ago that the NSA can read license plates from space, or watch people cross intersections. To me, if the NSA can do those things, they should be able to see a giant artificial island."

Kenn gave up on the discussion shortly after that point, but I didn't care. I was starting to feel better, and my focus was turning from sensations of nausea to the reason we had crossed: to see the Killers.

This crossing had been my idea from the start. I had wanted to see the band once Brandon Flowers returned from his solo "experiment." Looking around, I tried to anticipate what we were in for. I was thinking about the gigs that Kenn and I had attended under the guise of the Little Red Hen theory, where we helped the roadies and watched the soundmen set up. I always found this fascinating, some times it was the best part of the gig.

In David Byrne's book *How Music Works*, the main theme is how musicians craft their art to match the venues that they play. The acoustics, the audiences, the instruments, and the processing capacities are all part of the context that molds the song. Art and politics become the same. You play to your audience.

Byrne even suggests that live performances are often balanced by soundmen to sound like studio sessions. I never understood if this was to placate an audience that was familiar with the recordings or for the band to retain control over their art. Regardless, somewhere someone is always controlling what you're listening to.

A vigorous opening of the Killers' debut single, "Mr. Brightside" banished my contemplative thoughts. Ever since learning that they took their name from the fictional band in the New Order video for "Crystal" I've loved the Killers. The fact that the Killers were also interesting enough to collaborate with Lou Reed and seemed to head in a different direction on most new albums was even better.

Kenn and I made our way through the eclectic throng of sweaty Killers fans. America is supposed to be a melting pot of cultures, unified in the pursuit of liberty and all that, but here the desert was a pressure cooker of diversity. You would expect people to be crowded together for a gig, but even after the departure of the hot sun, which spent the day pouring its energy into the sand, the result remained. More than just the sand, the bodies around us were hot, and moving to the music and all getting hotter, like a visualization of boiling molecules. But heterogeneous molecules moving in such a manner as to make a single body of rock 'n' roll fan.

Looking around, I saw a mix of cultures as diverse as the United Nations. Pale-skinned or sunburned expats ostensibly from Europe or North America, shrouded Arab men with garish watches and fancy-looking leather sandals, and then a collection of Indo-Asian men and women—indiscernible, from my sheltered Oregon perspective. Striking diversity in contrast to the relative uniformity of my American melting pot experience, this was a real mix, joined under one desire, a love of rock 'n' roll. Ironically, the band with the violent name found its way past rhetoric, unifying an otherwise divergent group. It was another example of the influence of rock 'n' roll and the power of the Killers.

Flowers was captivating, alternating between strutting around with his microphone in tow, vigorously playing behind a lightning-bolt keyboard stand, and hopping up onto the black crates assembled on stage—spurring the crowd into a fervor under the hot setting sun. Before long he discarded his leather jacket onto the stage, sweltering in Dubai's heat, providing a short distraction to the audience while he interjected some dialogue, further engaging the Sandance patrons. It was the usual paint-by- numbers intervention that fills the pause for a band, the fermata that allows a band to regroup and unleash another torrent of music, while making the audience feel connected to the performance. For me, this wasn't a pause but a reminder of my own black jeans and heavy shirt, which were draining the life out of me faster than a Winnebago burning gas in the Grand Canyon.

Ninety minutes later, Kenn and I were walking away, looking for Gatorade or at least bottled water, and hoping to return to his basement. Predictably, we didn't notice that we were becoming dehydrated as we discussed the stunning performance; Kenn and I were still laughing over the whimsical rendition of Tommy James's "I Think We're Alone Now." The Killers. Pure showmen.

"Kenn, have you noticed we haven't crossed back?"

"Yeah, Dick, I've noticed that the streets of Dubai are markedly different from my basement. But thanks all the same for pointing out the obvious. What's next? You're going to tell me that we're surrounded by sand? I've got an idea. Let's grab a taxi and some beer."

It wasn't that Kenn's idea was so bad. Kenn's ideas often flirted with the line between reckless and idiotic, but I felt as though our options were limited. Although I always had a choice, a choice to check his recklessness or offer an opinion, it was easier to let someone else take control. Easier to say, "We really didn't have any other options," even though I knew that I did. Again I would pay for my complacency with Kenn as we all pay for complacency, even when we dress it up as a lack of choice.

Outside the hotel gates, we found buses idling along the road, with a long line of Sandance patrons waiting to board, all with concert passes on flashy lanyards.

"Kenn, this isn't us. They'll never let us on the bus."

"Let's go inside and see if we can get a taxi."

Eventually a taxi was arranged, with the reluctant assistance of an indifferent concierge. It was all about how the concert had resulted in road closures isolating this section of Dubai, so he said. It sounded dubious to me, but it allowed Kenn and me to grab a few beers while I cooled my feet in the pool.

"Racist pig," Kenn hissed under his breath as we moved away from the cab into the hot night air of Dubai.

"Kenn, you offended him."

"How?"

"Probably when you asked, 'Dude, where can we score some beer?' We're in a country governed by Islam, where you can't just walk around and buy a can of beer like back home."

"We got beer at the hotel."

"Yeah, but they would have a different license and they cost about twenty bucks each."

"He's still racist."

"Yeah, I'm not feeling you on this," I continued. "Racism is when you're treated differently because of your race, not because you've pissed someone off. Prejudice isn't the same as racism."

"So?"

"So, I'm just saying that I'm not sure we've got the same rights here as we might enjoy in America, but regardless I think you pissed the dude off."

"So you think he's got a right to hate Americans? Or white kids from Oregon? He doesn't even know me."

"Kenn, there's lots of people who know and hate us. I'm not sure that I'd say 'a right to hate,' but people hate and have prejudices. Prejudice actually comes from the act of prejudging, and while it may have undesirable consequences in some cases, it's often expedient and actually linked to our survival as a species."

"So evolution is based on prejudice? Now you're promoting hatred, or defending a bigoted jihadist? I thought you were an artsy college kid. Are you the last non-liberal to have a degree? You really did waste your time getting those degrees."

"No. Not bigotry or hatred. And just because someone doesn't like American kids doesn't make him a jihadist. I'm just saying we have the right to prejudge. Look, it's how we know a situation is dangerous when looking into a dark cave, or why people don't usually venture into dark alleyways without reason. We assess situations based upon our experiences and make conclusions. In fact, you've done that with your Eve theory.

"The Eve theory is sound. Anyway, racism can't be contingent on legal protection. You're confusing the motivation with the context. This isn't "Know Your Rights" by the Clash. I thought you always said that there are certain non-alien rights."

"Inalienable," I corrected. "Certain rights are inalienable. They can't be taken away."

"Well that's bullshit, too. Anything can be taken away, dude. Rights or otherwise."

"OK. I suppose I should have said 'should not' or 'ought not.' Certain rights should be inalienable."

"You should never confuse what ought to be with what is. Pizza ought to be good, but too often it's not; live music should always be awesome, but it sometimes fails; and the CIA ought to come clean about assassinating Tupac."

"Really? We're back to the kid of parents with the Black Panthers thing again with Tupac? I thought we were talking about inalienable rights."

"Like being prejudiced?"

"Kenn, are we going to keep circling the block looking to park this conversation or are we going somewhere?" I asked, following him along a dusty lane, trying to split my attention between "Should prejudice be a protected right" and why the hell were we still in Dubai and where were we going?

"There ought to be an underground punk gig here."

"Really? Ought to be?"

"No, Dick. I'm still looking for beer."

"Fuck off with calling me 'Dick.' So you really think that going to an underground punk gig in Dubai is a good idea and going to help us cross back?"

"How bad could it be? Plus, what else are we doing? A punk gig seems as good a place as any to find our way back. Worst case, we see something we otherwise wouldn't and carry on our search for a way home. Besides, you know how this works: if we're left behind from a crossing, it means that something or someone needs our attention. But I have to tell you, there has to be another beer in the city that wants my love."

Beyond the spill of the city lights, an indigo sky stretched above us, sprinkled with stars brighter than I had ever seen. Dubai. We were in the Middle East looking for beer, a punk gig, talking about racism, and the air held a dry crispness, like a warm sheet that had just come out of a dryer. What a funny existence. Kenn was right. Time travel was a limited experience: we had vague control over the band we'd cross to see, but not where or when. Returning to Kenn's seemed random but always involved passage through a door of some kind; it just didn't always happen on our terms, sometimes even leaving us temporarily trapped in a past.

"So you don't know where we're going? We're just going to wander around until you piss someone off enough for us to get hurt? Maybe we'll end up at one of those rendition compounds operated by the NSA. You've heard Vinnie's theories."

"We're not going to end up in an NSA rendition camp for looking for beer; those are for non-Americans. Americans are interned at Area Fifty-One. Don't you pay any attention to our discussions, or is it just about the coffee at Ka'Fiend for you?"

"The coffee and the music. I tolerate Vinnie because he owns the café and seems to know a lot about music."

"Whatever. Vinnie also mentioned punk shows in the UAE, so show some respect. Appreciate the artistry. Apparently, there's a whole underground movement, mostly in basements away from casual inspection, but if you know what you're looking for you can . . . Hey! Do you hear that? It sounds loud, and it's coming from behind that door. Let's check this place out."

Kenn started moving toward a dilapidated red door. The paint was fading, likely from years of neglect, the searing Arabian sun, and what I could imagine were sandstorms that felt like industrial sand blasters in a metal fabrication shop.

Immediately behind the door, we found a small foyer with a podium-style desk attended by a slender youth who looked calm, yet studious and resolute. Low seating and mirrors extended the sense of the space beyond its narrow physical constraint. It dawned on me while looking at a reflection that the despite the illusion, the foyer operated to physically control traffic, like the smallest hole in a dike, regulating passage into illicit acts beyond the door.

"Hey, dude, we're looking for live music," Kenn said.

"Good evening, gentlemen, I'm Youssef," the slight man said. "You're in the right place. But you must mind our rules."

Youssef spoke articulate English with a soft, discernible accent suggesting that he had been educated in England or on the Eastern Seaboard. He was casually dressed but poised, with impeccable posture.

"Look, we're not here for any trouble; we just want to check out the local scene and listen to some rock 'n' roll."

"Certainly," continued Youssef. "I'm always here to help, that's what we do. Cover charge is five American dollars or twenty UAE dirham. Unlike the gigs that you might have been to before, things in the Emirates are a bit different."

"We've got American cash," I said, handing a twenty across to Youssef.

As he was providing change, he said, "No alcohol is allowed on the premises; we do not have a hotelier's license, this isn't America you can't just buy beer or guns at any shop on any corner. There will not be any inebriated audiences causing trouble. There are no mosh pits, stage diving, or any other activity that might cause harm or injury to our patrons; the expectation is that you will observe these rules and enjoy yourself, without disturbing the peace of the imarah. Your enjoyment shall not impinge upon that of others. If you want to dance, dance. If you want to sing, sing. If you are asked to leave, you leave. If you refuse . . . well, since you boys don't look equipped for time in the desert, you won't refuse. It's important that you understand all of this, as underground clubs are tolerated in Dubai so long as they don't offend social rules. So then it's agreed?"

Kenn said something and I nodded.

Having passed through the foyer, Kenn and I took in the show.

Here we were, a world apart from our lives in Oregon and worlds apart from the Killers gig that we had just seen, but all the same a punk gig where we'd least expect it. Punk rock, in stark contrast to my conjured images of Dubai's conservative restraint. Immaculate order, planning, and affluence, from the artificial palm fronds visible from space, past the massive highways that bisected an ordered urban plan, to the architecturally and aesthetically magnificent skyline. The conditions were unlike those of Southern California, Washington, DC, or throughout the UK that incubated punk rock; I saw no natural connection to punk rock here. Yet there was something that welcomed the seed of punk on the barren, inhospitable sands of the desert, and while this all seemed foreign to me, it also seemed familiar because rock 'n' roll had long been my sanctuary.

Punk in Dubai was a variation on a theme, not a response to the deprivation of affluence, but a response to cultural rigidity. Punk, like life and music, functioned through building and releasing tension.

Life, music, Dubai, and tension all converged at the underground gig. Kenn never did find beer, instead we had effervescent mineral water at the gig and then, once the house lights came on, we said goodnight to Youssef and left the club, only to return to Kenn's basement. Without further adventure, the surprise lingered for days.

"Kenn, had you heard of those guys before?"

"Nah, still can't really find anything about them online. They were good enough, but like many local bands, just. They'll really have to find another gear if they want to make noise outside of basements."

"Yeah, tough to know. A good break here, chance meeting there, and a hell of a lot of gigs in between, and you never know. Imagine what Joy Division sounded like the first time they played together."

"True. Even the Ramones were thought to be a joke when Hilly Kristal first booked them."

Life was trundling along as usual, except for the fact that I was spending time with a girl. I was more or less going to work regularly now—well, probably three or four days most weeks, depending upon the excuses that I managed to fabricate and what my manager, Eunice, was doing, but always running my radio show. Kenn and I would spend some time most days together laying out rock 'n' roll information or reorganizing our collections over and over. We had a couple of crossings, nothing adventurous, but what had now changed was that I was spending most nights with Pyrah. Still, the time didn't seem right to tell Kenn. So I didn't. The right opportunity was sure to come, tomorrow.

"Why don't you just tell him?" she would inquire.

"Because Kenn's complicated," I would reply.

"You're embarrassed by me," she would say with a pout. Even then, I would marvel at her beauty and how she could manipulate me. She was a contrast, a perpetual tension between a demure surface and an aggressive undercurrent. Like watching a slow bend in the river where the water pools and appears motionless.

"No, baby," I would implore, "it's just that it's always something with Kenn, and he wouldn't understand." But perhaps I wasn't ready to admit what Pyrah was coming to mean to me. Secretly I thought that it was easier to have separate worlds and to keep Pyrah and Kenn as far apart as possible. To allow space to blur the details.

"I'm not embarrassed about us, baby. You're a knockout. Way out of my league. How could I be anything but thrilled to be with you?"

"Well, I suppose I am hot and currently out of your league, but you're a work in progress. Why am I never invited along to any of your music nights with Kenn? I don't even get to see you as much as he does."

"It's not like that. It's just healthy to have separate interests. You've got friends and meetings that I don't know anything about."

Pyrah was undeterred. "But you don't ask. I'd take you anywhere, introduce you to anyone. Just ask."

"Sure," I responded. "But I don't even know what to ask or where to start. Look, why don't you join me in the booth when I run my radio show?"

"Really?" Pyrah sounded thrilled. I mean who wouldn't be?

"Of course. I mean, you listen anyway, we met on the air, and I love having you close by. You can leave as early as you want if you're working in the morning." With her smile, the joy that Pyrah felt was immediately obvious.

The radio show provided the Big Bang that brought my worlds together. Most of what I had said to Pyrah was true. Sure, I offered the idea of her joining me in the booth as an appeasement, but it worked.

It was a great idea, successful in assuaging her feelings and bringing us closer; Pyrah also provided input in programming the show. Although I told her it was a way of proving how much she meant to me, and that I really wasn't ashamed of what we had, this really wasn't much of a concession. Just a concession that also allowed us to spend more time together. A win-win.

That night my program started with Kirsty MacColl's "Treachery." Like the pull of a receding wave at my feet, I could feel a catalyst that would once again be changing my world. As the song faded into the next, I saw, in the reflection off the glass panel in front of me, the beginnings of a collision. One image of Pyrah holding up MacColl's album *Tropical Brainstorm* and another of Kenn sauntering into the DJ booth through the door behind me to make one of his random surprise visits. Irony, again the bitch mother of conspiracy.

"Sort of a late slot for a trainee?" Kenn asked, displaying the catalytic antisocial traits responsible for his isolation. It wasn't just a question. I could see Kenn stiffening like he had just seen a venomous spider or bit into tinfoil. No, this wasn't a question at all; this was an anticipated indictment.

Images of rogue waves, worlds colliding, my hand being stuck in a cookie jar, unexpected bombs detonating randomly in a crowded market flashed through my mind. Kenn and Pyrah in the same room, with me on the air. A confined space filled with three surprised parties. Not only were the walls closing in on me, but the air was being sucked out of the room as well.

As I attempted to formulate a plan, the room began to spin, lights were flashing, and Kenn's voice was droning into a blur. One indicator on the console was notifying me of an incoming phone call, another warning that the current song was ending, yet another reminding me to cue the next song, meaning I would have a transition to attend to. I thought, *Right, Kenn will understand.*

Wasn't it just a few weeks ago that we had come back from San Francisco, where he had been smitten with a girl who Tasered him? So I was convinced that he would understand. Because we all want to be loved.

Running a radio show is not terribly complicated. I always remembered my initial instruction, "It's like playing musical chairs. You just need to be paying attention when the music stops." It's a lot like the old kung fu or Quentin Tarantino movies with short bursts of action followed by relative inactivity.

Trying to regain control, I said, giving Kenn a smile and a thumbs-up, "Dude, just a sec." Turning back to the console and picking up the phone: "This is Sid, thanks for calling . . . Yeah, you know, I've got most of the show programmed already tonight, can I play that next week? . . . No? OK, why don't you call earlier another week and I'll make sure that I catch you then, OK? . . . Yeah, thanks. I love the show, too. I'm glad you do. Thanks for listening."

I finished setting up the next track and braced myself, then turned back to Kenn and said, "Hey, Kenn, so this is Pyrah. Pyrah, Kenn. Kenn is my best friend. Pyrah and I have been seeing each other for a while."

"Seeing each other for a while?" Kenn and Pyrah said simultaneously, with shared expressions of incredulity and betrayal. It might have been the only moment that Kenn and Pyrah were ever completely in sync with each other.

"Well, more and more," I vacillated, trying to protect the feelings of my two closest friends and my own feelings of guilt at having actively deceived them. "But, hey, look, you've got so much in common. You're both important to me, you both like rock 'n' roll, and . . . you're both surprised. Maybe after the show we could go for pizza?" Yeah, I was desperate and panicking, but what else could I do? While the idealist part of me hoped to unify my worlds, the realist in me knew better. Kenn was just too much. He was nearly too much for me, so how could someone as lovely and demure as Pyrah even cope with him?

"Fuck this. Fuck you, I'm leaving," Kenn said curtly.

"Wait. We can talk about this," I pleaded, while Pyrah stroked my arm, providing me with support and compassion that I had never before experienced. "Kenn, I'll tell you everything."

So in the pause Kenn granted, I did. I told Kenn everything that Pyrah and I had been doing, at least in general terms, of course. About how we met, her taste in music and how great it was, my feelings. Everything.

I felt loquacious and compelling. This was my opportunity to clear the air and to express the things to Pyrah that I previously lacked the fortitude for. Not everything came out. I was careful not to talk about our crossings or to mention the bass player that Kenn was infatuated with. Especially given that he had known her a few weeks, but had met her over twenty years ago, challenging in the best of circumstances.

Kenn should have understood, but clearly from his expression he didn't. It was as though I were suddenly rich and expected everyone would be happy for me. People might want the same thing, but more often than not, they hate you for possessing what they covet. While this seemed like a simple lesson, it was taught only through the deepest of cuts.

"Is this why we're not—not—" Kenn stammered in his rage, "you know, going to gigs like we used to?"

What could he say? Time traveling? No, I guess not.

"Kenn . . ." I tried to calm him but was beginning to panic myself.

Lights were flashing again, and the soft scratching sound of the finished Beastie Boys album that I had last queued was an insistent reminder that I was now responsible for dead air, but for how long now, I had no idea. Sure, the FCC frowned upon that sort of thing, but sometimes, especially in late-night slots, it would happen and was usually overlooked. "Kenn, we went to a show the other night. I've been over most days this week, dude. Nothing is changing."

I muddled through a couple of transitions and gamely kept music on the air, but it was hardly my best work. There were gaps of dead air, transitions that mixed tracks over each other, and songs brought in not only with the wrong levels but often mid-stride because I forgot to queue them properly. Before too long, I simply surrendered and signed off for the night.

"Everything is changing," Kenn, now reinvigorated, said. "Girls are evil. They conspire against rock 'n' roll. I thought you understood . . . they're agents of the Evil . . ." Kenn trailed off. "This is the worst thing that you could allow to happen."

"But, dude," I insisted, trying frantically to restore order to a universe, where Kenn and Pyrah could be friends and the airwaves were alive with music from my show. "You just have to get to know her. Pyrah is great. We met on the show; she loves the Velvet Underground, so how can that be bad? Besides, love isn't a lifestyle choice; I'm supposed to be on the air."

Pyrah was silently sitting on the stool across from me, allowing Kenn the space and perhaps time that he needed to process this revelation. Watching her, I was smitten. Pyrah bounced her gaze between Kenn and me while half looking at the floor with an awkward smirk. The very paradox of someone invested in a situation but incapable of knowing where to look. She was as isolated as a lighthouse while Kenn was running aground on the shoals of my shallowness. Worse, my heart broke as I saw her now caught in something that she thought I should have addressed weeks before.

I implored Kenn to stop, for Pyrah's sake, and mine, too, I suppose, but I knew it was futile. There was always something with Kenn, and presently I was unable to convince him of anything.

"So, what?" Kenn continued in his petulant fit, motioning with a derisive cocking of his head in Pyrah's direction as he left the booth. "She, or this, or whatever the fuck this is, is just about getting handjobs for the holidays?"

3

Handjobs for the Holidays

Good evening, or morning, depending upon the side of the day you're on. This is a Thanksgiving installment of Transmission, and I'm Sid here on KQSF 91.9 FM.

I hope you're enjoying your holiday, and if not, then retreat with me into some music. Holidays, Thanksgiving and Christmas in particular, are times of enormous stress. Pressures resulting from various expectations of how we should fit into the world. Who we are. What we've achieved. All of our failures and successes subjected to vigorous cross-examination, added to the gratuitous consumption of food and alcohol in close quarters with our most severe jurors.

We all want love and acceptance. We all want to be seen as successful, having some intrinsic value. Unfortunately, the only way to get there is through being judged.

Judgment. Internal or external, the source doesn't matter; it's enough to curdle the feast in your stomach and drive you to drink. It's OK to be driven to drink, just don't drive after.

Family conflict is the hallmark of the holidays.

Rock 'n' roll isn't like that, so enjoy the respite for the next few hours. Up next is "Holiday in Cambodia," by the Dead Kennedys, followed by the Hellacopters' "Holiday Cramps" and Broken Social Scene with "Handjobs for the Holidays."

FCC transcript KQSF 91.9 FM 21.11.18 0151

File as: "Subversive"

"Handjobs for the holidays. So now you've got a girlfriend; is that what this all about?" Kenn was miserable. Angry and inflamed like a festering boil. "You're wasting your fucking time. She's evil and she'll be the end of you." With a flourish, he was gone.

I turned away from Pyrah, and turned off the turntable and put the booth on standby power. There was nothing I could do to salvage the night. I had hoped the opportunity to introduce Kenn and Pyrah was going to be a triumph, but instead they ruined everything.

Inundated by my guilt and exhausted from the subterfuge with Kenn and Pyrah, I realized that my show was ending in dead air, a complete failure. With the burden of these defeats, more than the litany demanded by most days, I opened the mic, began signing the station off for the night, before I realized that I had already powered off most of the systems. Shaking my head and silently cursing myself, I started the recorded message that would play a loop of station identification every fifteen minutes, until the morning jazz guy reanimated the programming spots for the day. I was at the epicenter of mayhem. Not the active sort of mayhem but the silent shock of loss that follows a crisis. Hoping, with my FCC broadcasting requirements in hand, that I could return my focus to being trapped between the opposing tectonic plates represented by Kenn and Pyrah. Kenn was gone, abandoning me again, but Pyrah remained. I knew that I wasn't thinking clearly, but still it seemed like a clear indication that my life had changed and that Pyrah was now there for me, while Kenn wasn't.

"Baby," Pyrah purred, "it's been a long night. I'll call in sick tomorrow and we can spend the day in bed."

"I do love you," I said. "I wish I had told you before under different circumstances."

Pyrah smiled and said "It's alright lover," savoring the 'r' like a hard candy or a long kiss. "It's just important that I know."

Just like that, I let her take my arm and guide me from the booth, out of the station offices, and across campus to where her car was parked. After that, the world spun into a blur. We returned to her place, slept, woke up late, and mechanically called in sick to work and returned to bed. We ate, we drank, and we slept and made love. I was exhausted and distracted, but content. Distracted by Kenn's strange turn and distracted by the attention of Pyrah. Finally, the spinning of the world slowed as Monday evening became Wednesday morning and we returned to a more normal life. Sort of.

My attention was stretching like an elastic band, thinning and becoming increasingly weak, until the gravity around Pyrah replaced my interest in anything else. Things like my Forestry job and radio show. While I had never been particularly engaged with my job, my apathy toward it grew daily, ignoring the messages on my machine requesting medical certificates for my sick days and threats of being fired.

"You're going to fuck up everything," Kenn would say when I'd call, making it sound like he was concerned about my job, but he wasn't really. All Kenn cared about was what my distraction with Pyrah meant for him. "When was the last time you were even on the air? If you don't keep your radio spot, they'll have to replace you."

Again, everything was about Kenn. This was no different from when I was in college and my parents hated the courses that I was taking, that I wasted my time at gigs, or that I hung out with Kenn. Standing before me, I knew that it was Kenn berating me, but I could only hear my parents. Kenn was becoming just another person judging me as being incapable of making my own decisions. Someone else who thought I would be better off taking a different direction with my life. The difference was that I expected better of Kenn. I felt betrayed and isolated. Pyrah would never do this to me. She wouldn't make me choose.

It was again as though Jonathan Richman were living my life and writing songs about me: "You can't talk to the dude." Or maybe "Someone I Used to Know" by Kanye West. The songs were right; but things would never be right until I could talk to Kenn. Kenn was wrong. I wasn't losing touch with music. Nothing was changing. Nothing but him.

"Just talk to him," the infinitely patient Pyrah would suggest, seemingly understanding my disquiet.

"How do you connect with someone you can't talk to? It's like my parents; I relive the same problem every time we speak." It was true. I struggled to talk to my parents, and most people really; sometimes even Kenn. Communicatively, I was secluded. Isolation kept me on the periphery of life, but it also provided me with insulating protection from the torments of life; I found comfort there.

This is why I found comfort in radio. I was used to people not listening, and when I was on the air, I couldn't tell if anyone was there or not. With radio, I didn't need a reaction or confirmation; the experience was a form of personal expression that was mine alone, lacking permanence and judgment. I relished the ephemeral creativity as though I were drawing on steamed glass.

Naturally, I retreated from conflict and any difficulty that I had connecting with people. Radio was a perfect place. I could retreat into it and find sanctuary within. It was easier for me, because I could simply conduct a monologue rather than carry on a conversation. Certainly there wasn't anyone to argue with me, or attack my views. There I was at peace.

Kenn ought to see that Pyrah was important to me—excusing the fact that I hadn't told him about her, but surely he could see now. It wasn't like I had lied to him, at least not directly. It wouldn't kill Kenn to empathize, drawing upon the feeling that he had experienced with the sexy bass player from the martini bar in San Fran.

"Go see him," Pyrah would encourage. "He's your best friend. You guys have been through so much; he'll understand. I'll be here waiting. You'll be great."

So I did. I went to see Kenn bearing peace offerings of pizza and beer, like I would any other night. For all the love and support that Pyrah proffered, she was wrong. It was a discovery that I feared and recognized entering Kenn's, and he started the conversation with the same vigor and caustic manner that he had shown leaving the radio station.

"Kenn, I'm sorry." I searched for the words but realized that I simply thought that an armful of pizza and beer was the path to redemption. "Look, I really like Pyrah, but nothing's going to change. I haven't talked about the crossings with her. And . . ." I trailed off as Kenn interrupted again.

He continued, without offering any quarter, "So, what? You're really going to give everything up that we've worked for and achieved for a fucking handjob?"

Ahhh, right. It was about a handjob. I mean, after all, the handjob was the pinnacle of casual sex. Casual yet intimate, without too much commitment. Nowhere was our realism and understanding of our shortcomings as acute as it was with girls.

Sure, we had other goals for intimate contact, but none as realistic and achievable as a handjob. Actual intercourse was ambitious, and oral sex, well, that was the Holy Grail of sexual relations for Kenn and me. Really, not only did oral sex represent an ultimate achievement, but it was also the stuff of legend. Well beyond the bounds of what Kenn and I could reasonably expect to find ourselves in the grip of, with an unpaid but willing female companion. So it was perhaps natural, Kenn's interpretation of what was happening, and now the source of his condescension toward me—that I was simply chasing a regular source of second-party yanking.

"Look, Kenn," I said firmly. "Normally I would tolerate this and perhaps even indulge your whims, but not this time. Not this time, because, Kenn, you're wrong about me, just like my parents, and sometimes I have to take a stand. You don't really know what's best for me. You don't know what I need or what I'm thinking. You think you do, or you want to protect me, but it's not your responsibility. I make my own decisions and my own choices."

"Fine, do what you want. Just not when it affects me."

"Kenn," I said, my tone and disposition becoming more conciliatory. This wasn't about Pyrah, a handjob, or sex. This was about Kenn. This was about his endless jealousy. Kenn had been changing, and his general asshole nature was now reaching a fevered pitch. This, more than the fact that I was now fraternizing with an imagined enemy, was the root of the problem. More than that, I was finding something that didn't include Kenn. This wasn't about some imaginary threat to rock 'n' roll that Pyrah represented; in fact, after all, she was a fan. I had met her through my radio show.

Sure, I would agree with Kenn that I was a rock 'n' roll hero, and vital to its continued existence, but I wasn't actually part of the music. Besides, we had long established that rock 'n' roll couldn't die. My actions or even neglect wouldn't cause the end of music any more than all the other tests it had faced over the years.

No, this wasn't like the type of threat that Yoko Ono or Nancy Spungen represented to rock 'n' roll. This was about Kenn. This was about who Kenn was, what Kenn needed, and how I fit into that formula for him.

"Kenn, how does this change anything that we do? Anything between us? Everything will stay the same, man. We're friends. Best friends."

Kenn was hurt. I never really understood why, but he was; it was as clear as a beacon at night.

"I trusted you. I trusted you with my discovery and trusted that you'd have my back. That we would do this together. I trusted you with my world."

"Kenn, your world? Are you kidding me?" Sure, Kenn was the Einstein who made the initial discovery of time travel, but I was the Oppenheimer who refined and improved the crossings that we frequently enjoyed. Again, Kenn was caught between projecting his delusions and manufacturing conspiracies.

This wasn't about Pyrah at all. This was about Kenn needing to be better than me, and now finally being forced to concede that this wasn't going to be the case. In my frustration and disappointment with him, I considered telling Kenn that it wasn't about handjobs. That in truth Pyrah had given me surprisingly few handjobs, but instead we had gone so much further. But I certainly wouldn't tell Kenn that. I contemplated baring everything and crushing his smug ego. Kenn deserved it, and it would help him grow up and see me, finally, not as someone with aspirations to being his equal, but as someone surpassing him.

In the face of Kenn's outrage, the realization dawned that not only had Pyrah and I gone further sexually, but intimately as well. The awareness broke like the unexpected relief of cold water quenching an unnoticed thirst, leaving me refreshed, but with an overwhelming sense of disbelief.

In Pyrah, I had discovered something about myself. Something pure that I hadn't anticipated, and now Kenn was forcing me to defend time spent with her.

As I approached the brink, I thought of flaying Kenn's heart and telling him everything. But then my rage and anger departed. Instead of Kenn's sneering petulance that I was currently facing, my mind wandered to the nights that Pyrah and I shared. The sort of nights that Shriekback spoke of on the liner notes for *Big Night Music*: "nights—fragrant with blossom, incandescent with moonlight and dreams, possessed by a cool beauty which evaporates with the dew." Except that the beauty of these nights didn't evaporate with the dew—it flourished into a new day. The dew nurtured my parched yearning and renewed my sense of the world, a world in which the sun felt warmer, the rain fell softer, dogs seemed friendlier, and everything possessed possibility. Nights seemed to pass in the blink of an eye but simultaneously remained suspended, with details blurring into one another and bodies yielding against each other like a ship in its mooring.

As I drew in a contemplative breath, straightening myself and steeling my mind to the conflict at hand, something stirred, checking my will. I didn't really want to hurt Kenn; I wanted him to discover this too. I wanted him to enjoy a Shriekback existence as I was. Really, everyone should. But it was more than that. I also didn't want to share Pyrah.

"Look at her. She's way out of your league. Can't you see that? So where does that leave you? She's evil. She's part of the government or the forces set on destroying music. This isn't about you, it's about rock 'n' roll."

"Kenn, are you saying this is still all about the government? It seems awfully hard to believe that the government is watching us. There's no reason."

"Why do they need a purpose? No one asks why the tides ebb and flow. Fuck, we don't even question how time travel works, why sometimes we get stuck on the other side or even why we can only enter gigs. But we do know that the government is listening to your show. Recording it, making notes and categorizing it, assembling improbably immense hoards of data, and yet no one questions that. We don't even question why we only change the history of music and nothing else."

"Would you want to engage other parts of history, Kenn?"

"Sure, no, I mean—that's not the point, but of course. It doesn't matter, though, because we can't get there from here? If we could, I'd put an end to the clandestine surveillance of citizens by our government. It's just wrong."

"Kenn, this is just a figment of your imagination."

"Evidence is suppressed; it's the course of action you should be watching. FCC has filing requirements for all broadcasting sources. You're a fool to think that your radio show isn't being monitored, everything from your set lists to your interventions. I'd choose your words wisely. The only reason this harpy is with you is to destroy rock 'n' roll. It's all related."

"The FCC is looking for inciting hatred or sedition, not trying to find me a girlfriend."

"Keep drinking the Kool-Aid and big brother will make it all right."

Although Kenn did have a point about the mercurial nature of time travel and the FCC monitoring radio broadcasts, once again he went too far. "You don't really believe that the Evil has staked out my radio show and baited me with Pyrah, do you?"

"No," Kenn said, seemingly concurring. "Of course not. That would be ridiculous. It's far easier to believe that some random girl called into your show to become the love of your life. Does she ride a unicorn as well? Have you seen her music collection?"

Details of Pyrah now became visions flashing though my mind as Kenn was admonishing me. Visions of full nights that were no longer about Kenn and me together, poring through vinyl at his house or reading postings about bands, discussing tours. Time that we spent together listening to rock 'n' roll, drinking beer, while planning our crossings and being part of the very fabric of the music that enlivened us.

Instead, these nights were about Pyrah. Rock 'n' roll was still a part my life, just a different part.

Time spent rounding out Pyrah's musical experiences. While she was teaching me so much about sex, personal intimacy, and just being with a woman, I was surprised that she had virtually no music in her apartment. How could this be? I remember asking her, "How could it come to pass that you found me through my radio show, but you don't have your own stable of favorites?"

"Baby," Pyrah had purred, "you play all my favorites. All I have to do is listen to your show."

My heart would leap like it would hearing a new song when she spoke or stroked me. My ecstasy was indiscriminate; she could hold my hand, touch my cheek, graze my arm; anything would send my pulse racing. Watching her body move, sitting in the radio station booth or making us dinner, was as captivating as if time ceased moving incrementally in seconds, instead lurching forward a quarter hour at a time. Sometimes hours.

With Pyrah, my appetite knew no bounds as I delighted over her naked body. Playing these details over and again, savoring them and giving them life. Recalling the black rose tattoo on her wrist and the Latin inscription low on her hip. How everything about her was as vivid as the music that I loved. Pyrah made life beautiful.

Life became more than good enough for me. Even though I was now skipping as many show as I was hosting, I continued to program them. I started keeping my radio shows in iPod playlists for her and busied myself becoming a different kind of hero. A hero who saves the girl; I was saving Pyrah from a life without music. The playlists kept coming, inspired by my muse. Soon I was previewing my show for Pyrah before it aired, if they aired at all. With most of the programming completed, I merely had to manage some of the PSAs and interventions, or announce the time, or the station call letters as required by the FCC and my station manager. Even if my show became less impulsive, it was still good. By the time I surrendered my radio spot, the shows I was programming were still outstanding.

Even now, contemplating my response to Kenn, knowing that I had to say something, I was conflicted. But in my mind, I could hear "Mrs. Rosenthal" playing on a stereo somewhere, maybe even at Pyrah's. It didn't really matter, because everything was becoming about her and me.

But that's how it always was: rock 'n' roll explaining my past, reflecting my experiences, without providing direction or counsel. How could I tell my friend that this wasn't what he thought, that it was something real? Emotional evolution, as real as pizza, beer, or rock 'n' roll.

"Kenn," I said, "think about all the love songs. All the music that has been and will continue to be written about love and women. How can this be wrong? Why shouldn't we explore this? Why fight it?"

"Two words, Dick: *Eve theory*. Eve even sounds like evil." Sure, he had well documented conspiracy theories about girls, and in particular girls and their impact on rock 'n' roll, but certainly he had to look beyond the stereotypes held by his conspiracy theory. Certainly the girls who propelled rock 'n' roll and the bass player that Tasered him counted for something. Worse than Kenn's theories was the fact that until now we had managed to do very little to dispel the notion that women really didn't dig us.

While there was a reasonable explanation for Pyrah's affections toward me, history was against proving that my current torrid relationship with her was anything other than a wild aberration from the norm. But wild aberrations instigate change. Unfortunately, Kenn would not be assuaged and continued his fanatic siege.

Now I had found Pyrah, and she was always happy to have me at her place and always had a fridge full of food and wine. Pyrah would listen to the music that I programmed for us. Defer to my preferences, which I knew, from Billy Bragg's song "Something Happened," was the definition of love. It was that simple, and for me something had happened.

This was terra incognita; intimacy was unfettered and seemingly constant. I continued to be in a perpetual state of arousal and intoxication around Pyrah. I had gone from wondering if we were going to make love while we were together, to not noticing when we did or didn't. I was flushed with infatuation—not an obsession that caused yearning, but rather one that satiated my desires. For the first time I felt a contentedness and calm in my life that wasn't about music, everything fell away, except the importance of being with Pyrah.

"Time with her is time away from rock 'n' roll," Kenn reiterated. "Time is a finite resource, even with . . . even with what we know . . . what we do . . . There is only so much time we have, and now you want to dissipate it on frills and perfume? Astounding."

"No, Kenn. It's not like that at all. Sure, time may be limited, but human capacity isn't. Love isn't. In fact, the more you give the more you receive. We need to give this a chance. You, too. My affection for Pyrah isn't coming at the cost of other things. It was as though I was capable of more now than I used to be." It was true that I felt capable of being engaged in more things, although I suppose that I didn't really engage in them anymore. In peril of losing both my job and radio show, I was doing less and less everyday, but at least the potential was there.

I still loved rock 'n' roll; it was a love inextricably linked to Kenn and our crossings. I continued my research, and I was engaged in being a hero. It was even possible that I was becoming better. Connecting with the love songs more than I had before. Listening more actively, visualizing how the lyrics conveyed my experience. But I was also learning, learning that the experience wasn't just about intimacy, and certainly not the intimacy that I had expected, having been a fan of the

Cramps. I simply wasn't interested in "What's Inside a Girl" or asking Pyrah "Can Your Pussy Do the Dog?" These songs and so many, many more had once been the benchmark for my hopes for sexual exploration, but now they were no more. Well, not entirely at least, as some of the provocative questions had been answered while others were still to be explored, but it wasn't the only thing that I was curious about.

Now it seemed that the Cramps, as campy and overtly sexual as they were, painted a broader picture. Rather than merely a vehicle for wanton lust and sexual gratification, the Cramps, in my mind, painted a picture of exploration through intimacy and respect. A place where sexual gratification was a product of trust and sharing similar interests and not just a drug and alcohol-fueled appetite for depravity, although Pyrah and I tried that occasionally as well. This was certainly more than a source of handjobs for me. Pyrah had shone a light upon me, dispelling shadows of ignorance and guiding me to a place with a palpable levity that led to intimacy. Into an environment that produced a sensation like being submerged in effervescent water. A place where I felt empowered and energized but also now recently awakened and aware.

I was now aware that emotional intimacy complemented and enriched physical intimacy. Sure, I was listening to the Cramps still, but also at the same time, love and intimacy were understood in the words of Darren Hanlon, Katie Herzig, Love and Rockets, Sting, Lou Reed, the American Music Club, the Sneetches, Modest Mouse, Radiohead, and so many others. A realization struck me like the opening chord to a Ramones song; this really was love. More than simply falling in love, though, I was beginning to understand that love was just like rock 'n' roll. Love came in many forms and was a different experience for different people. I couldn't wait to share this epiphany with Pyrah. Drinking wine, maybe we could get some takeout pasta with the garlic bread she loved from Il Pico, and we could listen to music and talk about love.

If I had time, after I found myself clear of Kenn, I could even build a set list and program a similarly themed radio show for my spot next week. This would even explain the two-week absence that I had from being on air or the last three shows that I had done that were cut short. Pyrah would love this discussion. Something that she and I could share and make our own. It would be thrilling to share this with her, because this wasn't really something that I would be able to express to Kenn. He wouldn't understand, would he? He would see this as evidence of a plot by Pyrah to undermine my relationship with him and to destroy me. Of course this is what Kenn would think.

"You don't know anything about her."

"I know that she has the Golden Rule tattooed on her hip," I replied, feeling smug, sharing something intimate without divulging too much.

"That's a Brian Wright song; you don't know the difference between reality and fantasy."

"Brian Wright? You mean 'Over and Again' by Neil Finn?"

"No. I mean the Brian Wright song; from the Bluebird album. It's shocking that you'd even confuse Neil Finn for Neil Young and a Neil Young song for Brian Wright—what's next, you'll mix up Kanye West with Gotye?" Kenn said despondently.

I thought about crushing Kenn, sweeping upon him with the power of a tsunami. It would have been easy. I could have retorted, "What? You'd rather have me be like you and toss off after a gig to a fantasy about a girl that almost spoke to us? Or maybe continue to fuck the occasional girl who was drunk or ambivalent enough to let either of us have a go? You know the girl, the one who's looking around the room, distracted by her term paper, or considering whether she even cares enough to retrieve her discarded panties when it's finally over?" These experiences were familiar to Kenn and me both. It was a powerful truth that we knew. But sometimes friends need something stronger than the truth; they need understanding and compassion. Subconsciously, I knew that if I hammered Kenn with the truth, I wouldn't be a friend, I would only be cruel.

I knew that Kenn wouldn't accept Pyrah. That was why I had hid my feelings for Pyrah like an addiction. Something that I couldn't admit or own up to, but at the same time knew to be true. Something that was left in plain sight for anyone with a modicum of attention to see, but in my lack of lucidity I perceived to be hidden. I might as well have track marks on my arms, or rotting teeth. Even though I told people, "Yeah, I'm OK, it's cool," I was hooked.

"Fuck, Dick. Did the cat eat your brain?" Kenn spat, returning me from my contemplation to insult both Pyrah and me again. "Are you fucking talking to me or what?"

I always did hate rhetoric, and I hated "Dick" as my moniker even more. Clearly, my reflections had created a long pause in the conversation, which only served to further aggravate Kenn and make the silent contemplation of Pyrah more uncomfortable. Surely I could talk to Kenn. Surely there was a way to connect with him and I didn't need to scuttle our friendship, as suggested by Richman's lyrics.

"Kenn," I said, "let's talk about this later. Give it a chance, put it out of your mind, I'll be back in a day or so. We can have some pizza and cross. Just let it go for now, OK? We'll talk about it later."

"Why? So, you can continue to get some tail until she's tired of you and then we can be friends again? There's just something wrong with her; she's evil."

"Look, Kenn," I pleaded, trying to hold his gaze and imagine Pyrah watching me with pride and wonder. "You don't even know Pyrah, and you haven't spent any time with her. Besides, I really love her."

"Are you fucking kidding me?" Kenn erupted, laughing with a caustic scorn. "You're an idiot. What do you know about love?"

4

What Do You Know About Love?

I love music. I love these sorts of introspective narratives that college and community radio afford me, especially during late-night spots.

Up next is the Socrates of romance, Mr. Lloyd Cole. Lloyd is an expert because he's wise in his lack of wisdom. I know it's early, but can you tell me if Lloyd Cole is actually engaging in dialogue or if this is merely rhetoric? This is KQPL 90.1 FM. It is 3:27 in the morning, and my last question was rhetorical. I don't want you calling me.

FCC transcript KQPL 90.1 FM 09.18.1994 0327

Operator comments redacted.

Keyword: Socrates

"Kenn, what do *you* know about love, you fuckin' guy?" I replied, matching Kenn's contempt and raising it with a venom reserved for best friends or mortal enemies. He had done this before. It was one thing for him to exert dominion over our knowledge of rock 'n' roll, like attempting to entangle Billy Bragg into our private arguments, but Pyrah was mine. Kenn's competitiveness and petulance had gone on long enough.

For the first time since Kenn and I had become friends, I had a relationship that I didn't need to share with him. Was this the cause of the problems for Kenn and me? Why couldn't Kenn just be happy for me?

Maybe New Order was on to something when they wrote "Confusion."

Life didn't have easy answers, and the more time I spent in contemplation, the more confusing things became. Both Kenn and Pyrah cared about me, but seemingly in different ways. Actually, New Order had it right—not in "Confusion," but rather in "Bizarre Love Triangle," a song that tells of confusion and stress from being pulled in different directions. This wasn't a love triangle but merely a childish state of wanting something beyond reach.

Maybe my confusion was the result of neither Pyrah nor Kenn knowing what I was feeling. Neither Kenn nor Pyrah knew that I didn't want to leave either of them behind in order to pursue experiences with the other. I wasn't the image of Janus, the two-faced Roman god who could only look in opposite directions: I was a friend of both, capable of caring for both of them at the same time. *Maybe*, I thought, *Pyrah should join us on our crossings*. The world could always use another hero, so why not Pyrah? I could build a playlist of music, use the themes to talk Kenn through it, and then he would understand. My feelings would be self-evident. Natural. A part of the larger rock 'n' roll reflection of the human experience. Listening to the music and my explanation, not only would Kenn accept this, he would embrace what I had found. Our world would once again enlarge, rising on a John Lennon vibe, rather than contracting like some narrow-minded xenophobe's.

"Kenn, why don't we . . ." I began as I looked across at him, his sullen, petulant expression matching the soft failing in his shoulders bowing under the weight of our conflict. I thought about our shared history and a past that had formed us as individuals and shaped us into friends. All the various circumstances that guided us along our current course had made us heroes and, until now, inseparable. It was our common song, the reason that teams have theme songs and nations have anthems. Music drew us together into a unified force.

But now Kenn wore the jealously of a jilted lover.

"Come on, Kenn, surely it doesn't really have to be like this—that we can only be friends at the expense of everything else—does it?

My time with Pyrah is without compromise. We're still crossing and spinning disks in your basement. She's supporting all of this. You should give her a chance."

"Yeah, sounds like a great idea," Kenn said with a despondent sigh. "I just need to be more like her. Because she's so great. She's supporting you? Are you kidding? She's fucking changing you; that's what girls do, and they do it in the name of Evil, to destroy rock 'n' roll. You're blind."

While Kenn was chasing me, brandishing his contempt like a torch, Pyrah was offering me a safe harbor in her arms.

"Kenn, just give her a chance. I trust her."

"Trust her?" Kenn looked shocked, incredulous in fact. "Trust her? She's a fucking Harpy, you dumbass."

When Kenn introduced me to rock 'n' roll, we found solace in our lives and even sanctuary together from bullies, from the pressures that our parents put us under; life made sense and became safe. It seemed only natural later, when Kenn discovered crossing, that he shared this discovery with me. Together we had refined time travel and together increased the depth of our knowledge immensely, to the point of traveling through time to intervene when history needed our help. But didn't we also deserve, and in fact need, to have our own experiences? Didn't everyone deserve to experience love?

What did I know about love?

What did he know about love?

It was clear that Kenn and I saw the world through the lens of the rock 'n' roll photographer and lived largely on experiences enhanced by amplifiers. In the dark recesses of our souls, where honesty found refuge. While we thought we knew what life was like, ultimately we lived through the expression of the experiences of others. Our emotions articulated by their words.

Of all the passions that rock 'n' roll has extolled throughout its colored history, love has rung out the most frequently. Billy Bragg sorting the priorities of love and lust in "Something Happened," and Katie Herzig conceding that she didn't want to know anything sweeter than a simple kind of love. The ultimate bliss found in pools of ignorance with her song "Sweeter Than This." And of course, the simplicity of falling in love with someone because of how they've asked a question, as expressed in "Charlotte Street" by Lloyd Cole.

But here I was, falling in love. For the first time feeling something, something for someone else. Something other than the kinship that I shared with Kenn. I suppose I always felt that Kenn was a brother, and maybe that's how I loved him. Certainly, we'd say, "I love you, man," but again in a brotherly manner. My relationship with my family was devoid of any true connection. Though I suppose I must have loved them, as you do family, even if only through an expected obligation rather than a truly independent choice.

Personifying a Jazz Butcher song, I had a bad case of falling in love. I had heard about love, but I never really figured that passion would stop at my door and seek residence. Actually, if love were to stop at my door at all, I expected that it would have been in the guise of a door-to-door life insurance salesperson with a disingenuous claim. Pariah, not Pyrah. Exactly what Kenn was saying: This wasn't about me, but about Pyrah's inherent feminine trait of being hell-bent on destroying rock 'n' roll.

"Kenn, think about this. Think about the music and what we've learned and experienced. This is more than just hanging out with Vinnie at Ka'Fiend. We've traveled through time, saving rock 'n' roll by helping Billy Bragg, Lemmy, Mike Ness, Robbie Smith, and Meat Loaf back on track when they needed it. None of this could have happened without us."

"Yeah, and you're ruining this. You're just like anyone or anything else: you take what you want and then discard the mess. You'll be the ruin of rock 'n' roll."

"Kenn, it's not like that. Think about all the amazing things we've seen and done. MC5 and the Velvet Underground. We've seen Andy Warhol at a gig. But none of this would have happened if we didn't first give it all a chance to occur. If we closed our minds to these experiences, where would we be? You've got to believe in the amazing before it can happen."

"Love? Are you still on about that? You're in heat, you fuckin' loser. What do you know about love?"

What was with this guy? "Kenn, I'm in an existence that is teetering back and forth between you and Pyrah. Come on, you consider yourself a scientist; help me. Help with the exploration."

"Find your own fucking balance," Kenn said with disinterest.

I felt like "One Man's Hell," by Sad Lovers & Giants. Drawn between two forces, where the merely changing perspective of an experience defined heaven or hell on earth. Looking at Pyrah, I saw heaven. Listening to Kenn berate me, I felt as though I were in hell.

I laid siege upon Kenn with arguments as structured and nuanced as Lloyd Cole lyrics. In fact, I gave example after example of songs that expressed my feelings: "Forest Fire," "Undressed," "Perfect Skin," "Ice Cream Girl," "Sweetheart," and "Baby."

"Sure. Good one, Dick," Kenn said sardonically. "But you've also forgotten 'Impossible Girl' and 'Are You Ready to Be Heartbroken?' And that's just for Lloyd Cole. Every argument has two sides. It's just difficult to see it with a throbbing erection diverting all the blood away from your eyes. Good luck, I'll see you around when you come to your senses. Until then, get the fuck out of my place." With that, Kenn turned to his computer screen and started scanning articles on the *Spin* website. Over his shoulder he said, "Maybe you're right, Dick. Maybe it's all about Lloyd Cole. Think track four from *Don't Get Weird on Me, Babe*. Lock up on your way out, dumbass."

And with that, once again I was unbidden. Slinking out of Kenn's now as a beaten and abandoned dog, I felt a cool chill of wind run down the back of my neck. As I was wallowing in the renewed rejection from Kenn, I heard the frequency sweep that indicated the start or end of programmed music on a cassette. It had been years since I had listened to recorded music on cassettes, but I had set the audio file as the ring tone to alert me to new text messages. I fished out my phone, expecting, or at least hoping, to discover Kenn had reconsidered and was welcoming me back.

It was Pyrah. "How r u doing?" she texted.

"All ovr now—kicked 2 curb," I replied.

"Come 2 me lvr."

My mood was instantly transformed. She was my girl with the perfect skin who lived four flights up, and once again, Lloyd Cole was speaking to me.

Obviously, the time that I would have been spending with Kenn was being taken up with Pyrah. Surprisingly, at least to me, I was OK with that. Kenn had made his decision, I had made mine, and Pyrah had made hers. By my calculations, two out of three decisions were in my favor, so that was a pretty good result, even if it represented the cheesy Meat Loaf song "Two Out of Three Ain't Bad." Still, even the facade of success didn't stop me thinking about Kenn and the directions in which our lives were heading.

But all the same, here I was, and in spite of what Kenn wanted, I was falling in love. A love that was real and had me reeling. I must have known *something* about love; after all, love was all around me, in music and in life. The music that I knew told stories about lovers, of loss and redemption, of discovery, of the pleasure and the pain, all about love in all of its many forms.

I tried to explain it to Pyrah one night. "I can't believe that Kenn can't see this. Just like the music that expresses love, love comes in many flavors. Everything from the Cramps' unbridled (or sometimes even bridled), gratuitously self-indulgent acts of sexual gratification to the simple innocence of Katie Herzig lyrics. There's something for everyone. He thinks there's a conspiracy, that you're just spying on me because you're too hot for me."

"Well, a conspiracy is just a theory, although I am too hot for you, until you finish your transformation. But don't you think people can get lucky from time to time? And speaking of lucky," Pyrah purred. "Why don't you put on something else to listen to, something softer, and maybe I will, too, and then, you know, we'll see where it goes. I'll get more wine."

It was like Pyrah could read my mind and knew how to take my mind off the distance between Kenn and me. I took all of this simply as a sign that I was really in love. I thought that I knew what love really meant and how to respond when it finally came my way. I thought that by simply having been exposed to the songs of love, I knew what it was all about. I mean, why not? After all, it was working. I had a girlfriend who made me feel like she was the only thing that mattered, creating a great sense of ease, as though my soul were being unburdened while I was with her. Priorities became refocused with the blur of love yielding to a sharp image of Pyrah.

For me, love was a kaleidoscope of experiences. Love was like crossing to a gig through Louie Louie. One moment I had a fever, then chills, then a sense of exhilaration. I felt dizzy, tired, invigorated, restless, contented, discontented, ill at ease, rested, and fresh . . . in fact my life had turned into a Lloyd Cole song. Probably each and every Lloyd Cole song. As more and more of my days were spent with Pyrah, I found that I was spending less money, less time, and less attention on rock 'n' roll. Sure, we made love. We made love often and indiscriminately; not always like the wild stuff in the movies, breaking dishes and furniture, but that wasn't really how physical our lovemaking was. Our passions grew incrementally, slowly building momentum, "like a forest fire," Lloyd Cole would sing.

Our lovemaking was a metaphor for everything I was experiencing, slowly expanding to all aspects of my life. Walking with hands joined, sharing a dessert, dressing, running out for morning coffee and warm, freshly baked muffins, all seemingly routine acts that bordered the new nation of our physical intercourse.

Instead of being aware of how the coffee tasted, the sweet lightness of the steamed milk contrasting against the bitter, dark espresso, or the light lemon scent in the freshly baked muffins, still warm enough to transform butter into glistening rivulets dripping onto the paper parchment that the clerk handed to us, all I could describe was Pyrah. Conversations faded around me like the background noise of a sound track, with her voice ringing clearly through it all.

Her hair would fall against her shoulders, miraculously giving the light substance. Or her loose ponytail would be held in place by my baseball cap, borrowed as we ran out for a quick morning coffee. To me, Pyrah was like watching the time lapse of a season. In the glint of her eyes, it was as if I were watching a sunrise wake up fields of flowers, cleansing the night's dew from their tender petals with a loving warmth and miraculous glow. Everything about Pyrah was marvelous.

Rather than returning to my radio show, my evenings would be spent with Pyrah, either physically or in my preoccupation. Noon would cast warm light upon the world, chasing the last of morning's chill from my skin and banishing shadows; we would spend time holding hands or walking arm in arm. Gentle afternoon breezes would stir summer air as we gazed into each other's eyes, and absently and unhurriedly we would rub our legs together beneath a bistro table, enjoying the perception that the summer sun would last forever, like our love, and teenaged bravado. A belief held even as the shadows regained their courage to welcome the tide of evening. Preparations for autumnal evenings would require warmer dress and the gathering of provisions for the winter of the night, in which we would seek the warmth and sanctuary of each other's barren landscape.

Of course, I loved exploring Pyrah's body. As we listened to rock 'n' roll, I would feel her pulse race to the driving guitar. I would feel her skin and her muscles as taut as that of a drumhead. In our exploring of each other, I would hear our breathing and words spoken loudly and so close to each other that they were amplified in our ears.

I'd replay the conversations with Kenn over and again with Pyrah. Recalling how shocked Kenn looked, coming through the door to the radio booth, as though I had thrown cold water on him while he was in a hot shower. Remembering how, after a long silence at the end of his rant, he'd simply turned to leave the booth.

"I should have told you that I was in love."

"Babe," she cooed, reclaiming my distraction and sliding her hand up my leg, "maybe now that you've given up hanging out with Kenn and gigs, we can go somewhere and can try over and again until we get it right, or until we're exhausted." Her touch moved from my leg up to my arm as she was talking, leaning into me while lowering her voice in an attempt to draw me closer to her. An attempt that was immediately successful, and without a second's hesitation I accepted her alluring invitation to retire to somewhere else. But as much as I was drawn to Pyrah and her promise of intimacy, my mind wandered back to my conflict with Kenn.

"Tell me you love me again. Say it like you've been practicing. Like all you need is me, and not music or Kenn."

Maybe I was the character in Lou Reed's "Coney Island Baby," overwhelmed by the glory of love. Awash with emotions: confused, engaged, tormented, enthralled, optimistic, and engulfed in the glory of love. I could think of little else. Like a functioning timepiece: intricate and complicated, but if understood, straightforward. Even accounting for the differences of people's peculiar tastes only makes sense once you understand their inner workings. Music. Kenn. Pyrah. Love.

Ultimately I knew that Kenn was wrong; I knew what love was. I just needed to find a way to convince him.

All the time with Pyrah had a rock 'n' roll element. As we watched movies or sat in a café sipping chilled wine and sharing a warm salad, music was always setting the ambience, but loud enough to be heard and to form a basis of conversation. It was like being with Kenn, but without the challenge or the argument every step of the way. Well, and with sex.

Pyrah's hanging on my every word was intoxicating. And she seemed content to do so; she never wanted to shop, or discuss fashion, or watch TV. In fact the movies that we watched together were almost always my choice, or if she did suggest something it always had a strong rock 'n' roll basis: movies like *Singles, Hard Core Logo, Sid and Nancy*, or *The Commitments*. It was perfect. Well, perfect for me. Couldn't this be love?

Rather than scouring the Internet for stories of bands and tours, we'd grab a coffee and take long walks. Shirking the stark minimalism of Vinnie's Ka'Fiend, I now sought out something quainter with shared plates, comfortable sofas, scented soaps, and diligent cleaning staff.

Rather than spending money on music, I would take Pyrah for dinner or purchase her a small gift. I was smitten, and while not ready to give up on rock 'n' roll completely, I was certainly distracted. But I didn't mind. Rock 'n' roll had been there so long, it would always be there.

And hey, hadn't I already done enough for the cause? Wasn't this love?

Sure, I understood what love was. I had read about it. I had heard countless songs and seen story lines in movies about love. What more to it was there? Just like a surgeon in medical school, I had studied the texts. I was versed in what love was. Wasn't that enough?

I knew I occupied a place of cowards. A place where refuge was found in lies and procrastination. A destination where I simply refused to completely confide in Pyrah about music and time travel.

It seemed better to keep things like that separate and perhaps less complicated. I could always tell her later. Maybe after she understood rock 'n' roll better. There would always be time to tell her later. We were in love; there was always tomorrow. Tomorrow Kenn would come around and maybe all three of us could cross to gigs together.

Until tomorrow came, I was content to keep things simple. Certainly, Kenn would never let her cross with us, so maybe it was just easier to keep the two worlds separate. Tomorrow I might find a way that she and Kenn could become friends. Tomorrow. Although there would always be a tomorrow for Pyrah and me, there was no telling what tomorrow would bring.

And, really, why did I have to tell her at all? I mean, it wasn't like I was being dishonest. All I was doing was traveling back into the past, catching some gigs, and from time to time tampering with the past to correct the future. And really, very little time ever passed in the present. As far as Pyrah would know, it would simply be the same as my not being able to answer the phone when she called, but then calling back immediately after. What was wrong with that? Where was the harm?

In fact crossing wasn't affecting my life with Pyrah at all, so did she really need to know about it? My parents didn't know every detail about each other's day, nor everything that their jobs involved. I didn't tell Kenn everything that happened during a day. Why should I tell Pyrah? Justification or fact? The answer didn't matter, because I wasn't going to tell her anyway. It had been weeks, maybe more, since my last radio show. Strangely, it had been nearly as long since I had seen Kenn and I didn't seem to be missing the show or him.

I was right keeping Kenn and Pyrah apart; it was best for everyone. Or at least for me. Even if I was certain of the result, I didn't completely understand the consequences. I had to be shown. Consequences are simple; they exist or they don't. There's no reason for exploration; they are by their very nature the *result* of something else. They are a reaction to an action, and therefore, without the initial action there would be no *reaction*. What makes consequences tricky is anticipating them, something I've never been completely successful doing.

Lying on the couch, I was content to do not much of anything one morning—well at least nothing that involved leaving my apartment. It was a Saturday, and neither of us had any commitments for work or anything else. The night before, we had gone for dinner and had some drinks, then a late dessert, and had made love immediately when we arrived home. For a change we ended up at my place, rather than Pyrah's.

"Please, honey," Pyrah had implored, "I think the hot water tank is fucked at my place and the super won't do anything about it. I'd love a hot bath in the morning with you—well, maybe two if you can keep up.

We've never been to your place, and since you said that you love me now . . . maybe it's time for me to finally see it. Besides, I want to see your music collection. I imagine it to be so . . . so expansive." It was the way she elongated the s sound in *expansive* that made her request sound like a promise. Consequently, I didn't need much convincing; or at least not with the enticement of a long, hot bath and an assortment of my music. So just like that, it was decided that we would return to my place.

Falling through the door, we set upon discovering each other with the urgency of reunited lovers who had suffered a long separation. Like perhaps weeks over a vast distance, where the time zones frustrated communication but couldn't interfere with the fact that they had thought of each other from the first moment upon waking until the time that sleep finally overtook them. But this was not us. No, we had only just been at dinner, together across a table from each other, holding hands, rubbing our ankles against each other's calves and talking about my radio show hiatus.

Turning on the light interrupted our passions. Pyrah was speechless. I wasn't surprised in the least. Not that I'd had many girls back to my place, but the reaction was always the same. It's like they thought my place would be cool, but never really knew how awesome it could be. What wasn't to love?

Sure, the place was kind of a small one-bedroom apartment, and some of the appliances like the oven and dishwasher weren't reliable, but everything else was all rock 'n' roll. Sure, I suppose that because the dishwasher didn't work there was probably a stack of dirty dishes in the sink. And probably a few on the counter as well, and maybe even a pot or two on the stove still. But most of the clothes that were on the floor and furniture had been washed, some even since I had last worn them. People never noticed these things; they weren't the obvious focus that one's eye was drawn to, because I had learned a thing or two about lighting.

Placed strategically in front of the futon couch, illuminated by the yellow cone of the lone floor light I owned, was the black majesty of the heart of the apartment. Clean, sleek stereo components all meticulously researched and purchased with a singular purpose of providing life-supporting nutrients to both the world at large and me.

One's eye couldn't help but be drawn to the compact yet sturdy shelving unit that was as important as any alcove in the most pious abbey. Rather than candles or frescoes, a Yamaha YP-D8 turntable sat neatly on a shelf above a Sony STR-DN1020 amp and receiver and a Harman Kardon HD 990 CD player. A place for everything: the meticulously clean lint brush for the vinyl, cassette deck cleaner (not that it had been used in a long, long time; cassettes really were a poor medium), and a lens cleaner for the CD. All of the wires were gathered neatly behind the components, leading like veins and arteries to four Blaupunkt speakers spaced exactingly around the apartment for optimal performance and audio fidelity.

As Pyrah was looking around, surveying the majesty of my apartment, she was slack-jawed. "So much—"

"I know, it's amazing."

Alongside the stereo was a long desk with my iMac, also with wired output through the amp, and then a collection of magazines, books, articles, and music to be categorized, played, read, or simply put away.

"What's in these little boxes, honey?"

"Cartridges, extra needles for the turntable. Cool, hey?"

"Wow."

Trying to assist her with processing the grandeur, I held her hand firmly against my chest and said, "Look, there are a lot of important things going on here. You really can't tell anyone that you've been back to my place," I said, obviously adding to the allure and already mind-blowing coolness of my home. "It's kind of a big deal."

"Don't worry," she replied with measured reservation that was full of awe. "I won't tell a soul."

She said, "I won't tell a soul," which in my book was close enough to *Don't Tell a Soul*, the classic album by the Replacements, which hosted their only Billboard Top 100 track, "I'll Be You." It was a sign.

A sign that Pyrah wasn't part of the problem or the conspiracy, as Kenn maintained, but part of the scene. She embraced and loved rock 'n' roll and I knew that I could love her.

When I woke during the night, I could feel Pyrah moving against me. Something more than just the deep breath of sleep, but yet not fully conscious. Lit with the pale blue light of night beyond the walls of my apartment, we were a tangle of limbs, starting and stopping and mixing. Hers, mine, ours. Quietly I stroked her hair and she turned and kissed me. I could taste the stale, coppery taste of sleep on her tongue, and we began making love again.

Looking back on that moment, it was the first time I noticed an absence in my apartment. Music. There was no music playing. It was the first time that we didn't make love to music chosen for the mood and the first time I didn't have a song playing through my mind or have something softly in the background.

We turned music on and made love in the morning, but without the urgency of the night before. With the soft, lazy pace that says "time stops when you hold me with your eyes." We had a bath and made love again and then had another bath. I had gone out for coffee and fresh bread for us, returning to join Pyrah naked on the couch, and while I suppose we talked, I don't recall what it was about. Probably music. Well, almost certainly about music.

Rising from the couch where she had been curled up with me, seemingly intent on some objective, Pyrah was now distracted and distant. I was distracted but present. Distracted by the naked figure walking across my apartment, having shared my bed with me the night before. Transfixed, I watched as she walked away from the couch and turned off the music again with her left hand, as she had something else in her right. Her phone? Why had she turned the music off? It seemed so strange. It was a good morning montage of bands like the Cocteau Twins, the Beautiful South, Adele, Gotye, and Everything but the Girl. I would realize later that it was ironic that Tracey Thorn was sweetly singing "This Love (Not for Sale)" when she turned it off. There seemed no reason to do that. Not in my home anyway.

"Pyrah," I asked, "you'll stay with me, won't you? I love you. I want nothing else but you." For the first time since I had discovered rock 'n' roll, I considered a life without the music. Completely absorbed by Pyrah, my life was becoming tethered to her. My world had shifted and she had become the sun that I orbited around, the moon affecting my tides.

"Of course," she said, distracted. "Everything is as it should be." She had her back to me and was holding her left hand over her shoulder signalling with her index finger. Starting to collect her clothes from the floor with one hand, she began stubbornly pulling them on, while continuing to hold the phone to her ear, she seemed to be nodding.

I now noticed that she was talking on her cell phone. *One minute, she must mean*, I thought; everything made sense again. Being distant and distracted. Turning off the music. Getting dressed. Of course, she was on the phone, perhaps with her mother. Funny I didn't even know if her mother lived nearby or not. Perhaps a colleague from work at . . . again I didn't have those details about her, or maybe her cousin was in town. I couldn't hear what she was saying, but she was nodding and seemed deep in contemplation, now holding the palm of her right hand out toward me. But I was sure that she replied to my query. "Sure. Of course. Anything you want."

Anything I wanted? I wanted her. What I wanted was for her to tell me that she loved me, too, and that she would always stay. I wanted her to tell me that I was the music that gave her life meaning. That she couldn't think of anything else. I wanted to feel like Lennon and Yoko staying at the Plaza Hotel in New York City. I wanted Pyrah to love music as much as I did, to become obsessed and really understand it. To want nothing more in her life but me, me and rock 'n' roll. I wanted her to be a girl version of Kenn.

Finally she looked back toward me and said, with a marked sense of annoyance, "Look, I've got to go out." Gone was the sweet, demure manner that offset her sexual appetite and playfulness. She seemed distant. Pyrah was still talking on the phone as she walked to the door of my apartment. "Wait for me," she continued, sort of waving, and then she winked before firmly closing the door.

I savored the words she left me with. She said, "Wait for me."
She said, "I'll be right back."
She said, "Of course."
She said, "Trust me."
She never said, "I love you." She didn't even turn the stereo back on.

I had been falling in love. I knew that. I understood that I loved Pyrah and that I was vulnerable. The falling associated with love was exhilarating because I knew she was there to catch me. If she weren't there, I would just fall. Feeling her absence, I started counting the moments, prepared to go on counting until the finite became infinite. But that wouldn't happen; we were in love; there was always tomorrow. But as the minutes of her absence spun into hours, the hours folded out into days, and the days expanded into weeks, all the time I continued falling. Falling. Falling. Falling.

Along my decent, I remember thinking that maybe Kenn was right, that I didn't know what love was like. Whatever it was that I knew now, I knew that falling was like this.

5

Falling Is Like This

This is KQRL 89.9 FM Redlands, and you're with Sid. It's 1:45 a.m., I suspect that some of you are up studying for finals. If that's the case, good luck.

Do you believe in luck? Do you believe in hard work? Or God? Or talismans? Belief is a funny thing; some things simply won't work without belief, like a self-fulfilling prophecy. Others, like gravity or mortality, happen independently of your views. I never believed I would fall in love, lose a friend, or become a hero, but I did. Belief is like gravity, and gravity causes me to stay grounded or to fall. And like Ani DiFranco is going to demonstrate next, "Falling Is Like This."

FCC transcript KQRL 89.9 FM 08.27.2014 0145

Operator comments: license checks cleared

Keyword: Watch list

Falling is like this. Sensations of exhilaration and fear. But I didn't notice. Like with drips filling a bathtub, the fractions that make a whole were imperceptible.

There was always the promise of a tomorrow, because of love found, so my world was frozen in a moment while I was caught up in the action of it all. Focusing on details that I was incapable of understanding.

The exhilarating sensation of the world rushing past didn't register with me. If you were simply going to fall forever, through each promised tomorrow, you wouldn't be afraid; you wouldn't even feel the slightest thrill.

Love like this would last forever.

I was riding a thermal, unaware that my feet were off the ground until the sun disappeared behind a cloud, the thermal cooled with an icy wind.

When I expected that the soft cushion of love was there to embrace me in Pyrah's arms, falling was exhilarating. Now that she was gone, there was nothing to ease my plummet; I felt hopeless and racked with fear. The idea of my fall being broken was less reassuring and sounded more like an inevitable fatal, jarring termination of a free fall that I couldn't control or understand.

Falling is an action, not a consequence. An action *with* a consequence. The reaction to falling is that you have to stop, which is another action, an action that has the likely consequence of shattering the exhilaration of falling and replacing it with the reality of a harsh, unyielding pain. I suppose that following others is also the consequence *of* an action.

She said, "Wait for me."

She said, "I'll be right back."

She said, "Of course."

She said, "Trust me."

I did all of these things. I was doing what she asked. Wasn't that enough?

She never said, "I love you."

I had told her, "I love you"; she never replied. But couldn't I assume? I thought it was unspoken. Of course she loved me—why else would she spend so much time with me? All the intimate moments, not just the sex; the interludes between our intimacy. It was always about time. Time spent together meant time not spent elsewhere, so if Pyrah had chosen to be with me, not just for the sex, certainly not for my money or fame, then it had to be love. Didn't it?

She had turned off the music. Why? Because she was on her phone, but it had to be more than that. She had kept the music off when she left. Pyrah left me in silence, with nothing but loneliness. No music, no friends, no radio show, no Pyrah, no love. And no music.

Where was Ani DiFranco? She knew that falling was like this. It wasn't like an addiction that you could stop sometime, or when you wanted. No, falling was knowing that you would stop and that the stopping would happen with or without your controlling it. The only thing controlling my fall was Pyrah; she would catch me.

At some point during the first day of Pyrah's absence, the quiet blurred into disquiet. Like chasing color gradients, change was imperceptible. Ultimately I noticed the change, I just didn't know when. Details so insignificant slid past until they became noticeable. And significant. There is a point when purple becomes indigo and then blue and then black and then you've missed it all. Where did you start? Red? Pink? Lavender? What was the question? The only way to capture the moment was to return through time.

It was a moment that I hadn't been watching because I anticipated it would never happen. Pyrah was my sunset, as spectacular and beautiful as always, but then in her absence I realized that I had taken such splendor for granted. Now, without a sunset, there would be no sunrise and only the cold loneliness of darkness.

Because her departure was just temporary, I got up and thought about the rest of the day that lay before me like a newly offered promise. Full of optimism. I was a Katie Herzig song, playing all of her albums in wait. I waited for the certain imminent return of Pyrah. *This is good,* I thought. *I can plan our day. I'll get organized; it'll be a surprise.*

Working through my plans, I started to move the stacks of dishes from the sink to the dishwasher, surprised that it did work! *Maybe she's taking longer because she's stopping for coffee and bagels,* I sighed while changing CDs. But still no Pyrah. After the dishwasher finished filling, I showered and shaved.

It's cool, I resolved. *When she gets back, we'll go for brunch somewhere. It'll be a treat.* But when the phone never rang, we never spoke, so I emptied the dishwasher and started on the laundry while I thought about lunch.

Brunch plans faded into dinner, which became a late drink, and then takeout and a movie. Looking around, I discovered that I had cleaned nearly my entire place. Clean dishes were put away, laundry was folded and collected from errant locations. I had opened the blinds and windows, letting in fresh, sweet air, richly perfumed with the fragrance of flowers whose names I didn't know.

In a satisfied tone, I proclaimed, "All of this achieved in the time that Pyrah has been out. Won't she be impressed!"

It would be a moment that we could count together, as we embarked further on our time together. Now more than ever, I was looking forward to all our coming shared moments.

But the moments alone soon eclipsed my numeracy skills. Plans replaced plans, Katie Herzig became Darren Hanlon, who yielded to the Killers, who became Rancid, Operation Ivy, and Nirvana, or maybe it was the Pixies or Pearl Jam? I suppose it could have been anything. Soon my emotions faded from a freewheeling morning into an outright free fall, clipping past checkpoints marked by the Smiths, Sisters of Mercy, Nine Inch Nails, David Bowie, Bauhaus, and then finally Lou Reed, Lloyd Cole, and Leonard Cohen. Leaving me to ponder mysteries such as "Why did depression's given name start with an L?" Maybe I should trade Reed, Cole, and Cohen for lofepramine, lisdexamfetamine, or lubazodone. Antidepressants, experimental or approved, did they really matter? Was there anything that could pierce the fog of my malaise?

Where, or even why, had Pyrah left me? Had I fallen into a pit of sorrowful song? Songs that once gave my life meaning but now echoed through me as if I were an abandoned church, leaving me cold and bereft of faith. How could all of this music describe my feelings, only to betray my hope and optimism with crushing sorrow? Was this what the human condition was really exposed to? Pain. Pain of loss caused by departure and disappointment. Confusion. Despair. Incomprehension. Suffering. Isolation. These words appeared before me as menu items on the stained Curry Citchen takeout flier that was in the back of a cutlery drawer, soiled with yesterday's stains. These words offered me limited choices—choices of things that I didn't really understand but had some slight idea of what they were. Rogan josh. Depression. Dark and simmering. Samosa. Confusion. A mixture of indistinguishable ingredients, each incapable of description, simmering together. Each emotion a new meal that I would eat alone.

My confusion had once been born out of conflicting loyalties to Pyrah and Kenn, but now that had been replaced by isolation from them. Fucking Kenn and his fucking conspiracies. There was always something with Kenn, and now he—he and Pyrah—had conspired to bring about my pain and loneliness.

It wasn't that my apartment had become a place devoid of meaning; the opposite was true. After one single night of having Pyrah in my home, she had cast a pall over it all. Everything was a reminder of her occupation there, amplifying my acute pain. Strands of her hair curling in a cursive stroke on the bathroom floor, leaving the word *despair* or forming the infinity symbol. Perfect. Despair and infinity together condemning my future.

Pyrah's aroma lingered on the bedding and couch. I thought breathing it in would dispatch my malaise, but rather it felt like a torture sent to cause me anguish, as resolute and incessant as a raven's cry in the night. The stains where we tracked mud in through the door from cutting through the park in the night's rush to retreat to my bed. Stains that were once a badge of honor, of how liberated in love we were, now told me that Pyrah had left an indelible mark upon my soul. Where I was once content, I became wistful, but even that emotion was yielding to something more powerful. The reminder, once playful and arousing, now awoke repressed memories of muddy footprints that had shattered another.

When I was finally so overcome thinking about Pyrah that I dropped a coffee cup, the ceramic shattered into pieces like my heart and remained littered across the floor with my concerns. I stared at the broken shards that were bleeding their hot blood onto my floor. As I half reached for a paper towel, I said, "Fuck it," my voice mockingly echoing thought the empty apartment. I walked away with the footprint of a single coffee-soaked sock following me.

Of course I tried to call her. What was the trouble? I had no idea. She would answer the phone with "Hi?" or "What do you want?"

What did I want? I wanted the music back in my life. "Ah, hi. Hi, Pyrah," my voice unsteady and wavering. "Hey, it's me . . . I just wanted to, you know, well, to maybe see if you were OK . . . ?" I'd trail off impotently, leaving myself brimming with self-loathing and increasing my exceptionally elevated frustration.

"Of course," Pyrah would respond ambivalently.

Oh, right, "of course." Of course, *she* was OK. She was probably just fine. In stronger moments when I called, I'd ask, "OK, good, great to hear, so, well, are you coming back? Maybe we can meet for dinner?"

"Oh, I don't know" or "Are you still waiting?" she would say, in a manner that seemed distracted or indifferent. Or she would comment, "Yeah, I'm really not going to be hungry then." Or sometimes she would simply ask, "Why?"

Why what? Why was I waiting or why was I asking? Of course I was still waiting. I was waiting because I was in love. We were in love. I was waiting because my life had turned its focus to her and her alone. I would write Pyrah letters and send her e-mails. Short text messages. Her responses started with ambivalence and escalated into mocking and scorn. As the days or weeks passed, my optimism flagged and desperation took over my hopes like marauders preying upon villagers. Anything that I had once held as a wish was trampled upon the ground, besmirched in blood and dirt. You know, the sort of moment when you're looking at abject ruin and then you say, "Well, I suppose it can't get any worse," and then the rains burst the levees.

Yet I still waited for Pyrah. What else was there for me to do? Well, there was falling. Sure, falling was scary, but it wasn't so bad and could certainly be worse. When you're falling there comes a point where you suddenly realize that not falling is worse, because that means you've stopped and stopping hurts.

The ghost of Kenn spoke to me through Lloyd Cole's lyrics, "Get out while you're still whole. Before you're addicted."

An empty bottle exploded against the wall. "Fuck you, Kenn, you're just jealous. It's not like an addiction." An addiction you can stop, you just have to want to. I would stop when I was ready.

When falling is scary, your fear or desperation accelerates with your descent. Even your fear achieves a terminal velocity. It must. Kenn could probably explain it, but like everything else, Kenn was beyond my reach now. There is a concept of terminal velocity that is known to be associated with free fall. I certainly felt like this was going to be terminal. Did falling in love have a terminal velocity, too? What about a terminal velocity for heartbreak? Kenn would know. Maybe.

I didn't know anything about science. What did I know about love?

"How did this happen?" I asked the gape-mouthed mute takeout containers that were gathering around me.

"Pyrah was supposed to have been the impetus casting a warming light, illuminating my ignorance and leading me out of the shadows into revelations wondrous and new," I told the indifferent containers.

"Kenn was supposed to be my friend," the wall echoed back.

"And then they ruined everything," I sighed.

Pyrah had indeed led me into a new world, but in doing so had cast me into the forest of despair, a darker and more foreboding place than any I could have imagined, only to abandon me without a guide. With Pyrah in my life, there was lightness and a future. Like the optimism and reflection of a Poe song. But now with her departure, she left the hollow loneliness and despair of a Poe poem.

Hope was now in outpatient treatment.

Things measured by their relative temperature suggest an experience: *the water is too cold for swimming, dinner is warm enough to eat*; hope and despondency are relative, too. For me, music measured hope and desperation. My world was vacant and dark, and while the music still spoke, rather than speaking to me, it spoke of me, in mocking tones.

Music now spoke to others, whispering salaciously, spreading rumors of my isolation and anguish. Like the empty church in the Sad Lovers & Giants song "The Best Film He Ever Made," or Social Distortion's "Cold Feelings." Reflecting experiences of an absolute blindness so pervasive, it was a source of pain, ironically, a living reference to Joy Division's "Isolation."

I was forsaken. Forsaken by Pyrah. Forsaken by love. Forsaken by Kenn. Forsaken by rock 'n' roll. All I had left was myself, and I was pathetic.

During the time that I was still eating, I was listening to Darren Hanlon and Rancid, but I had ceased to eat by the time I exhumed the Smiths from my collection. It was simply too much effort to shop, cook, and then eat, and for what? Certainly not pleasure. It wasn't like eating was going to bring Pyrah back or make me feel any better, was it?

Sometime during my fall, I surveyed the world around me. I saw what Pyrah had left me with and what I'd once had. Everything that was previously within my reach didn't matter. Trying to consider if I could reach things at all, I soon became exhausted with the exercise. Bored and contemptuous of my own existence, I surrendered to my self-loathing.

Someone sang, "No one really knows the ones they love." Isn't that what Kenn meant? *What did I know about love?* Didn't I know Pyrah? Maybe not, but maybe I only knew her like I knew Kenn, or myself for that matter. Maybe I only knew her in love, and when that ended, only to be replaced by loathing, I didn't know her at all. Just like I didn't know Kenn. Or myself.

I heard Modest Mouse playing, lyrics about God forsaking everyone, I was a victim, but also a joke. Maybe that wasn't the same song, but it didn't matter. Modest Mouse was immodestly mocking me just like everything else. Maybe that was why Pyrah had turned off the music.

Resigned to my isolation and now regarding my future with futility, I sought solace in music. And whiskey. And bourbon. Or vodka. Anything with numbing potential.

As I remained bereft, awaiting the tide to return to carry me to safety,

I reflected upon the time that Pyrah and I had spent together, suddenly unsure how long it had been. We had met before Lou Reed and Metallica released *Lulu,* but had it been before or after Katie Herzig's *The Waking Sleep*? Had our relationship been months? Weeks? Over a year? The length that a One Direction hit holds the attention of a starstruck tween? It really didn't matter. There had been a promise, at least implied, of a tomorrow. This wasn't something that I had expected to end. But it had. And with the ending of my time with Pyrah came other endings as well.

But as time marched on, time became irrelevant to me and made less and less sense. Time, something that Kenn and I once manipulated for our own needs, satisfying our whims and purposes, now dripped upon my forehead like an infamous water torture. Time itself dripped on me, echoing with voices from my unanswered answering machine. Or maybe imagined.

Somewhere beyond my periphery, there was a metronome or the tapping of bony fingers on a ledge or perhaps the windowpane, counting out my existence. Marking my time. Saying, *"Give up."*

Tip. Tap. Tip. Tap. Tip. Tap. We have noticed that you haven't been attending work and have no choice but to assume that you have quit your employment.

I had lost my employment, as mercurial as it was. My voice mail had told me. I had given up my radio spot and it had been taken over by someone else. There was a text message saying as much. I hadn't spoken to Kenn in weeks. Or months? The duration of a Ramones song? It couldn't have been months. But maybe it had been. I had lost the grasp that I once had on time, a grasp that I had relaxed through indifference and complacency. I could hear a sink or shower faucet.

Drip. Drop. Drip. Dude, this is the program manager at the station. What happened? Dead air? Not cool. We've reallocated your spot to a sports review show. Call me.

Drop. Drip. Drop. Can you count the drops? We will start over if you lose count.

Drip. Drop. Drip. Can you count the drops? It's OK, start whenever you want, we can wait.

There was no music being played at all now, and the dust of my apathy was cloaking my audio equipment. I had little idea what day it was; the food in my fridge had gone from bad to worse, so I continued to order takeout when I got hungry. But only when my body was racked with cramps did I consider seeking food. When that little sustenance arrived, I ate it sparingly. Even now, with that food spoiling around me, I barely noticed. Without Pyrah I had lost interest in everything. She had taken my soul. She had turned off the music to my world.

My days passed by with the irritation of a healing scab. Dry, itchy, scratching, always a nuisance, but then when touched it fell away, leaving the wound open to start the healing process again. Wasn't there some song about one of the Beach Boys wallowing in depression and self-loathing? I was sure that my existence was like that, but I couldn't be bothered remembering the band or the song, or even what the Beach Boys' names were. Why did it matter? My heart was a hole.

Itch. Niggle. Itch. How about more whiskey? That will help, won't it?

Niggle. Itch. Niggle. If anyone really cared about you, wouldn't they be here?

Itch. Niggle. Itch. Come on, put some music on. It will make it better. I dare you to move; it won't stop me from itching you.

I was scratching all the time. Trying to attack, to destroy, and to interrupt the irritation that I felt consuming me from within.

Scratch. Scritch. Scratch. Doesn't this itch? Aren't you irritated that she's gone?

Scritch. Scratch. Scritch. Aren't you hungry yet?

Scratch. Scritch. Scratch. Isn't this the sound a record makes at the end? This is the end. Your end. Give up.

I felt the hot examination of an unseen dark presence, passing judgment or waiting. Waiting for something.

Demonic nuisances besieged me with the unspeakable tenacity of the tide. Steady, unyielding, and covering with its inky, mercurial blanket. Demons were lurking everywhere, crouching in my shadows. What was the good in being isolated if you weren't actually free from torment? There was no odorous rot of spoiling food, just the soft, sweet fragrance of her perfume lingering in the air, as an ultimate cruelty.

I just needed to call her. To talk to Pyrah, just a little bit, then I'd be OK. Maybe she would come by, or we could get my radio show back. I just had to call her. I'd be OK. The station's program manager had said to call him. I could still make this work.

It was then that I realized, remembering how I was sitting naked with her in my bedroom, and then later on the couch, then watching her slowly dress and leave; hungry but without desire for anything but her, what Pyrah really was. An anagram. *Pyrah* was *Harpy*. The oldest trick in the book. Kenn was right; girls were the ruination of rock 'n' roll. Fuck. Kenn had known. He'd even called her a Harpy.

Divorced from logic, even to this day, I feel a yearning for Pyrah's caress. A wave of enlightenment washed over me, understanding why sailors dive to certain death, seduced by sirens of the sea. Just like one who had been in contact with malaria, ever vulnerable to reinfection, my yearning for Pyrah and my weakness for her would always reclaim me with a fever, and still there was a presence assuring me it would be better to surrender to release.

But now, perfectly obdurate; somehow sustained on a diet of decaying pizza, tepid curry, and cheap whiskey in dirty glasses, dressed in the same clothes that I had put on . . . put on when? I had no idea. It simply didn't matter; there would always be a tomorrow. Talking to the resolute food containers or slipping into fitful sleep, seeking refuge from the anguish of my waking memory of Pyrah, the Harpy. Welcoming asylum from the agonizing consciousness of the world around me that sleep promised. A sleep that provided escape, only to allow me to be tormented by dreams of her. Of Pyrah. These torments came with the punishment of a new tomorrow, a tomorrow in perpetual supply.

Dreams I had of Pyrah and me coming through the door together. Dreams in which we would find ourselves making love wherever we fell. Nightmares of Pyrah walking out the door, never to return. Nightmares of my conflict with Kenn. Nightmares of being alone and isolated.

Dreams of Kenn rendering my door to splinters with a thundering crash as he breached my apartment to save me. Nightmares of him standing beside me, doubled over retching, forcing the contents of his stomach onto my floor. Voiding what he had internalized on me.

In this apparition, Kenn's eyes were bloodshot-red like those of some hideous undead abomination. In my dream, I was safe only because something in my apartment repelled him (maybe Pyrah) and he was immobilized, fighting the desire to continue emptying the contents of his stomach. His mouth couldn't form words but his eyes were trying to tell me a story that I couldn't comprehend.

A splash of cold water swept me from my drunken nightmares with an unyielding, merciless slap. "Fuck," I groaned, the room gradually coming into focus, although it was still spinning and oscillating as if the floor were tilting on a ball bearing. Finally, the tidewaters returned to save me, but now perhaps I was drowning. "Fuck," I groaned again, at a loss for anything else to say.

"Fuck—your—self," Kenn managed between retches. "What the fuck has been happening here, asshole?" he asked, still retching. "This place is fucked up."

"What do you mean, 'Fuck yourself'?" I replied, gripped in thick confusion. "I didn't call you."

"No, not 'Fuck yourself,' but 'Fuck your self.'" Kenn tried to navigate the fog that had been laid over my safe harbor, placing emphasis on words that I couldn't discern.

"Whaaat?" I managed, weakly trying to sit up, rubbing my eyes and temples, attempting to grasp what Kenn was trying to express.

"Two words, not one word. 'Fuck your self,' not 'Fuck yourself,'" Kenn said, attempting an explanation before stopping and changing direction. "I told you Lloyd Cole was right: you should get out while you're still breathing. Come on, let's get you whole again."

"Fuck yourself, your self," I countered, still confused but angry, too, for being awoken, now wet and being told to fuck myself by Kenn, who could only be here to gloat. "That's three words, asshole."

"Fuck. No, I meant . . . fuck," he continued. "Never mind. What the fuck am I having this conversation for, anyway? You need help. I didn't come for a fucking grammar lesson or to play let's count words."

"I'm fine. Just go. Please, just leave me. Fuck Lloyd Cole. Your self," I implored weakly with my tongue truant to my instruction. I didn't need Kenn here. I didn't want to hear that he was right and I that I was wrong. That the Harpy had proved Kenn's conspiracy theories and that I was just a fool. I had lost enough without having to face this.

Looking around my place, and then past Kenn: "Fuck, did you break my door?" It was the first time I had seen sunlight in days. Well, actually weeks. Maybe longer. The sun burned my eyes and the fresh air laid foul all that I had left to rot in my wallowing despair.

"OK, asshole, this is how it's going to be . . . Fuck." Kenn had walked away, and I could hear him vomiting in the kitchen sink. When he came back he said, "We've got one chance here to get you on your feet. Things are really fucked up, and we've got to get on this now."

"Fucked up? You don't say. My door was kicked in by a nightmare and is now hanging in splinters on a single hinge for real." That was only the start; my personal hygiene was so bad that I couldn't tell that my home was rotting and that food was transforming into science projects. I had been living on alcohol and takeout food, in various states of decay, for longer than I knew. My life was frayed, my heart ossified, and I didn't even care.

"I'm fine," I said, knowing that I really wasn't. "Just leave me alone and I'll come around. She's gone and you were right. Happy? It's not like I'm going to ever see her again," I pleaded, like a junkie. "It's OK, I've got this under control, just one more . . ." But even as the words were passing my lips, I thought, *Well maybe, just once, just for a second, maybe I could talk to her on the telephone*. With the words came a yearning like a sore muscle wanting to be kneaded. Or a blister to be cooled, or an infected sore that you can't leave alone.

"Sure," Kenn seemed to say in agreement. "We've been here before, you're right. You were right back then, too."

Really? I thought. This was going to be easy.

"Sure, dude, I'm sure you'll be just fine, or maybe it won't even matter," he continued. "But this is bigger than us. Let's look at your records."

"Not now, I'm tired," I said, thinking that I was going to get him to finally leave me alone. "Maybe after I shower I'll come by your place and we can try the 'Fuck yourself, your self' conversation again. I think that's important for us, to resolve things. We can start there." *That's right, just one more hit, then I'll kick. I can get there on my own. I'm still in control.*

"Right now, buddy," he insisted, ignoring how absolutely correct I was about the incomplete conversation. "What was the last album you bought?"

"Fuck, what is this, Twenty Questions, Kenn? I don't know. I don't care," I said, growing surly and impatient. I was undernourished. I had been drinking now for weeks; my mouth felt swollen and as though something had died in it, perhaps my tongue or a small cat, or even a large fish, and worst of all I had a broken heart. There was no Pyrah, Harpy or otherwise.

"Humor me," Kenn continued, still insistent. "Just put something on from the last six months."

"Right, because I feel like telling jokes. Besides, you know where . . ." Fucking intervention, that's what Kenn was doing. He was fucking interventioning me; fucking asshole, and *interventioning* wasn't even a real fucking word.

"Now," Kenn interrupted, "get the fuck up and put something on the turntable that you've defiled with this covering of dust and soiled food cartons."

Kenn's voice possessed a brusqueness that I didn't recognize.

Maybe he was just being an asshole again like he had been with Billy Bragg or when he first met Pyrah. Lording over me that he was right and that I was stupid. If it weren't for me, he'd still be limited to seeing shitty MC5 gigs. He needed me more than I needed him. Isn't that why he was here now? I hadn't gone looking for him. In fact I didn't even really need him. I needed her. *She would answer the phone this time.*

"Why don't you," I spat back at him, feeling beleaguered and persecuted. I took a cheap shot, hoping he would leave. I needed to do something. "Maybe grab a CD that you'd like. You remember CDs, don't you?"

"Of course I remember CDs," he said, his eyes narrowing in rage for a moment and then releasing. "I'll never forget, but this isn't about that time, or me, or really even you. So indulge me. Pick for me—it doesn't even have to be new. How about *Prairie Home Invasion*, 'Are You Drinkin' with Me, Jesus?' That might be appropriate for the occasion. Maybe you'd rather listen to the Vandals, you know, so you can remember how to tell people your girlfriend is dead," he added.

What? I thought he was cutting to the quick, but now he was too quick; Kenn's reaction was wrong. My head was pounding and I was still drunk and feeling the effects of my descent into poor nourishment. All of the rot and depravity had remained undetected, although part of a frozen atmosphere that perfected my isolation. Now with the door kicked in, the sun and fresh air awakened my senses to the squalor I inhabited. Why did he have to bring all this shit back with him? Asshole.

It was always something with Kenn, but now I just couldn't cope with it anymore. I couldn't cope with any of it. I couldn't cope with my apartment, the smell, my headache, the nausea I felt, how loud Kenn was, whatever new crisis or conspiracy he had developed, discovered, or imagined, or face the fact that Pyrah had left. "Will you leave if I find you that fucking CD?"

"Of course," he said.

I winced, but Kenn wouldn't know why. "*Of course*," she had said. To me it was just another lie. Another stain left on my life. It wouldn't matter. I would be alone and drunk again soon. Of course I would.

But maybe I would call her. I could tell her that I had been away, too, and pretend that nothing had, or hadn't, happened. Nothing had been happening; maybe a crossing would help me find a time that things were right with Pyrah, just for a while.

Maybe I could find a way to be alone, before her. Or with her and Kenn. I could use Louie Louie to set things right, to make something happen. I could restore her "of course" to mean what it was supposed to mean. "Of course" means that something will happen. "Of course" means there is a tomorrow. A promise. "Of course" isn't just a way to dismiss someone, is it? Of course, the phrase could mean anything.

Feeling crippled and defeated, I hobbled over to my CD collection and in my stunned state tried to find something to play. I fumbled through my seemingly sparse collection and found nothing. Nothing? How? I looked up at the ceiling, as though the answer were written in the stars and glimpsed the image of water cascading over a waterfall. As the feeling of water rushed over me, I could sense its crushing weight buckling my knees, causing me to fall backward into darkness. I knew what was happening, I knew what this was; falling is like this.

As Kenn lifted my eyelids deliberately, his face flickered into focus, spinning slowly around me with the ceiling light in the background. I struggled to make sense of it, to regain focus and control over myself. My head was pounding, but without rhythm, and my nausea was becoming overwhelming.

"Dude, it's OK," Kenn said softly. "You blacked out. Maybe you had a head rush or something. Could be the shock, or poor nutrition maybe. Most of your music is gone, you haven't eaten for days, and it looks like you've been drinking vanilla extract," he said kicking away a bottle at his feet. "There is a lot that is wrong here, and discovering that you don't have any recent music isn't helping."

Even the most basic of things I was struggling to comprehend.

Nothing made sense. Why couldn't I find my music? There was nothing. No Killers. No Offspring. No Nine Inch Nails. No Katie Herzig, or Darren Hanlon, Green Day, Gotye, Lloyd Cole, or Modest Mouse. Half of my Bowie collection was missing. There were Smiths albums but no Morrissey, although that might not have been too bad. What happened to Johnny Marr? My feelings of betrayal started to overtake my hangover. From first glance it appeared that there was nothing in my collection that had been produced in the last twenty-five years.

"She stole my shit, too?" I asked, in shock and confusion. The stereo equipment was still there, just not the music—at least nothing new. "This is fucked up. She left the eighties? Why just the music? The stereo was worth so much more and just as easy to fence." It didn't make sense. When Pyrah had left she didn't even take her clothes or a small bag, and other than the various delivery guys, no one had even been to the door. *She's just borrowing the music because she misses me. She'll come back. She'll bring all my music back and we'll be happy.*

Then the realization dawned, and everything was better. "That means she's been back here. She's been back since she left." Enthusiasm was starting to fire my blood and calling endorphins to action.

"Pyrah's gone. She's not coming back and you know that, dude. You just have to face it. I'm sorry," Kenn said. "Your music, no, it's not stolen. Things are worse than that, buddy," he added with a dawning compassion, showing me that even my vinyl had been decimated and that virtually nothing that I had purchased digitally even existed. "This is bigger than Pyrah, at least I think it is. My collection is wiped out, too. Someone has killed rock 'n' roll."

OK, Kenn, this is helping, I thought sarcastically. "Killed rock 'n' roll?" I managed, sitting up slowly. "That makes less sense than the 'Fuck you, you fuck,' or whatever the fuck you were trying to say. What are you talking about? And you're here to help me? I think you need the help . . ." *Pyrah was coming back.*

"Get a shower. I'll clean up," Kenn ordered firmly, but still with a sort of kindness as he reached down to help me to my feet. "We'll grab something to eat on the way back to my place. C'mon, buddy. We gotta get out of this place."

6

We Gotta Get Out of This Place

We've all had experiences that we've wished to escape but couldn't. Places or conversations that we were trapped in. Conrad, Dante, Kafka, and Umberto Eco all come to mind. Are these metaphors or a physical reality that the authors found themselves in?

Road trips are like certain conversations; they've become the new limbo. A place for lost souls to languish. A party that only plays ABBA or J. Geils. Muzak in an elevator. Circumstances where you need a safe word and a wingman to extricate you. This is KRXF 92.9 FM at 4:53 a.m. Don't worry, there's escape from my narrative. We gotta get out of this place, and here to help is Jello Biafra with D.O.A., covering the Animals.

FCC transcript KRXF 92.9 FM 04.11.1983 0413

Operator comments redacted

Keywords: Kafka, Vinnie, Target 3872

"We gotta get out of this place," Kenn said, referring equally to my apartment and a world without music. Both disasters of human neglect and despair. Barrages of questions were hemorrhaging in my head as though I had become a frustrated adolescent's piñata. Questions with wills of their own: Rock 'n' roll, the very thing that had provided me sanctuary, escape, and meaning to my life. Now it was gone. How could that be? What had happened?

A fog that was clouding my thoughts and tainting my emotions found no escape, expanding gas in a jar.

Had rock 'n' roll died during my drunk and catatonic state? Rock 'n' roll couldn't die. Rock 'n' roll survived on the very essence of humanity and freedom. A form of art. A fire that burned eternal. Burning hotter when threatened, fanned by adversity. Something that transcended a single action, band, or person; no more could rock 'n' roll be killed than could the moon be plucked from the night sky. Sure, the moon would wax and wane, but like the moon, rock 'n' roll would always exist, exerting an invisible force.

"Kenn," I groaned, wincing in pain, "I don't understand. What's happened?" Incapable of following the basic logic, finally I simply surrendered to Kenn for an explanation.

"Go clean up," Kenn replied. "You smell as bad as your place. I'll explain after you've showered. Don't shave. You'll cut the shit out of your face with that mangy growth. We'll head down to Max's."

Trudging off to the shower, I was stunned to see it was occupied.

"Kenn! There is a crazy-looking hobo in here."

There he was, standing between the sink, and me just staring at me. He was stubbornly mimicking my every movement, looking through me but still casting judgment. Even when I said, "Excuse me," he just ignored me like vagrants do, yet he maintained eye contact.

Patchy, matted facial hair, stains on his clothes and skin, bloodshot eyes, with a disposition that appeared both surly and pathetic; one could only imagine what he might smell like. The sort of degenerate that you see the police collecting off bus stop benches—you know, where the cops are wearing rubber gloves, carefully covering Dirty Hairy in a blanket as they whisk him away. I had always thought that they were trying to comfort their ward, but the blanket was probably for their own safety.

"Look, Dirty Hairy, I need to shower. You need to leave." He stared at me, and despite my being startled, soon my confusion yielded and he and I shrugged our shoulders in resignation.

Kenn's instructions were exactly what this vagrant needed: a shower and a visit to Max's barbershop. Maybe a coffee. Certainly something to eat.

Calling to Kenn as I pensively stepped from the shower: "Hey, did you send that homeless guy away?"

"Huh? Are you high? What are you talking about?"

"The dude that was standing in the bathroom when I got in the shower?" I said as Kenn started walking away.

"Dry off. Let's get you feeling better."

During my shower, Kenn had busied himself trying to clean my apartment. To me it seemed like it would be an easy job, because I *had* cleaned the place the morning that everything began to unwind with— the Harpy. *Pyrah*. I could no longer bear to even speak her name.

The reality for Kenn was so much different; everything in the apartment was garbage and decay, so he threw out most of what was left, the things that *she* had left, the clothing that I had resigned myself to over the period of my convalescence and subsequently ruined with my own filth and poor hygiene. Anything else that was rotting or hazardous to the environment found a new home in two large black garbage bags that Kenn doubled. We—and I really mean Kenn, on my behalf—started rebuilding.

After Kenn had managed to cleanse my place of the most grotesque squalor, and I had emerged from the shower having de-defiled myself and had made an abortive attempt at shaving my face, Kenn brought me food.

"I've called a service to clean the rest of your place. Pro . . . Dude," Kenn said with gentle exasperation, "I told you to leave the shave. What the fuck are you trying to do?"

"I don't know," I replied, gesturing with trembling hands. "I just thought I'd . . . is it that bad?"

"You're going to cut your fucking throat open. Your hands are shaking like a hobo with low-grade alcohol poisoning." Handing me a bottle of green Gatorade and plain white bread that he had lightly toasted, he said, "It's fine. Max will sort it out. Here, this will help your stomach and dehydration. As for what happened? I don't really know. After you . . . well, after your . . . Just have some Gatorade and toast. If you can keep this down, I'll get you more with peanut butter."

Why did Kenn stop? Did he mean after my radio show or after our fight?

Kenn looked away, then back to me and started over, seemingly skipping large tracts of dialogue as though they belonged to an unimportant backstory. "After . . . well, after a while," he sighed, "I started crossing again on my own, because . . . well, just 'cuz, and at any rate, one time I came back and my collection had been ravaged, just like yours. It was trippy. I was totally freaking out. There was no visible explanation, and since I couldn't reach you I checked out the library and the radio stations, the Internet, and it all just stopped. As though a gate shut, after which no more music was produced. There were still a few reviews, but it just sort of tapers off as though rock 'n' roll were choked off by a dam or something."

"Kenn," I asked between sips of Gatorade, "how long has it been since I've crossed with you?"

"It's like Vinnie has been saying: the NSA is using the FCC to keep tabs on music and then selling us out to the Evil. That's why they monitor your transmissions. They're keeping a file on you and your show, on all the DJs, actually. There's Evil at work here," Kenn continued, ignoring my question. "Maybe all the music has been collected and sequestered in the Vatican's Amber Room, and they've issued a decree for the modern-day Knights Templar to hunt down all rock 'n' roll. I'm working on the details, but there is some indication something like this has happened."

Kenn articulated his papal theory. Even after we discovered an alternate explanation, Kenn held fast to the papal theory, claiming that it simply hadn't been fully implemented yet. If nothing else, it seemed to explain how certain bands like the Sundays, Died Pretty, and the Sneetches had evaporated into oblivion. Plus, Kenn didn't have any other conspiracy theories that involved the Vatican, a cardinal sin for conspiracy theorists.

Finishing the Gatorade and wiping my mouth with my sleeve, I asked again, "Kenn, how long has it been since I've crossed with you?"

Looking away with shame and awkwardness, he said, "Look, it doesn't really matter. What's important now is the situation at hand. I need to tell you this straight. There's no other way, but you need to know. While you were . . . away . . . rock 'n' roll died."

"What?" I asked in sobering shock, looking down as the Gatorade splashed up against my leg, diverting my focus to an empty hand that had released the nearly finished drink bottle of its own accord. "Rock 'n' roll is dead?"

"Dead," Kenn confirmed. "No new music, no live shows; everything stopped in its tracks. As dead as a bar on Election Day." Kenn lacked the sardonic manner or wry smile that he always had when he was setting me up for something or spinning one of his fantasies. "Go ahead, try to sing something."

Just like that, a chill ran through the room as though an ethereal specter had materialized from some repressed fear. Rock 'n' roll was dead. Killed. Forgotten. Not as some journalistic embellishment or quip about a specific musician. Not like the death of John Lennon, Jimi Hendrix, Kurt Cobain, or Sid Vicious or the breakup of the Smiths, R.E.M., or Oasis, which were situations where others would sling the guitar strap over their shoulder and carry on. Really dead. Dead and forgotten like a second cousin that you never really knew you had. A final death and forgotten memory like the name of the goldfish you buried in the garden when you were young.

The chill weakened my tenuous grip and checked my legs, which had become steadier through the restorative effects of my shower and the sustenance provided by Kenn. Even the stings of my facial cuts from shaving brought a superficial pain that allowed me to slowly focus through the fogginess in my mind. I was getting better, but not strong enough to bear information as heavy as this. "Kenn, you know I can't sing."

"It doesn't matter," Kenn continued, shaking his head. "We have to use everything that we know. Or what we knew. Everything that we can remember in order to recreate rock 'n' roll. If we can do that, we can discover where the break was, and then we can cross and restore history to how it should be. Just like our other interventions."

"Doesn't anyone else notice or care?"

"I don't know. All I've been able to discover is that there are some articles that talk about rock 'n' roll being irrelevant and then it just fades into oblivion. I can only remember bits, but something tells me there's more to my record collection than I can find."

"OK," I replied meekly. My equilibrium was still in flux and swinging wildly from feeling as though I was in control of my body to feeling like a door beneath my feet was about to open. I could hear Kenn and was starting to understand him, but I couldn't comprehend the breadth of the situation. "Right. I'm with you. Sure," I said. "So we just have to cross again?"

"Well, yeah," replied a less than completely confident-sounding Kenn. "Once we figure out where we've got to go and what to do once we're there."

Right, that would be easy. Of course, we'll just cross back and reset history. You know, just like resetting a tripped circuit-breaker. We had done it before, a bunch of times actually, so why not again? We've all reset fuses without being electricians; Kenn and I had crossed to correct history without being historians. Same, same.

Actually the only difference was that rather than crossing into the wrong history, our current history was wrong. Our present was absent. As if this weren't enough, much of our past was also gone, leaving only our memories, if such a thing could be trusted at all. So Kenn and I carried the faded memories of a love lost and sought a means of reanimation, setting off like a musical Dr. Frankenstein to a pet cemetery seeking another chance. Again, using time travel to make things right, to say the right things and to take the proper actions. I guess that was a significant difference. Like Dr. Frankenstein, Kenn and I didn't have even the hint of a clue of what we were facing. But Kenn was a scientist; I held trust in that, when looking for a place to happen or shadows in the rain.

Rock 'n' roll had died, but inexplicably Kenn still had a functional Guitar Hero device without any recent music. While it seemed paradoxical that our games like Guitar Hero and stereo components continued to exist despite the loss of rock 'n' roll, we didn't complain. I suppose it was just like weapons of mass destruction or nutrition data on donut boxes, things created and supplied without any meaningful use.

Although our cataloging methodologies changed from time to time, we always adhered to a strict diligence when it came to our music collections. It was this organization and our dedication that had propelled us from being the slackers that people once considered us to the heroes that we became. Again, it was another example of how repetition leads to excellence. Repetition was how we saved rock 'n' roll.

All of our research and passion for rock 'n' roll had prepared us for this moment. A moment when Kenn and I would triumph to take our roles as rock 'n' roll heroes to another level. Sure, Kenn and I had put Lemmy, Mike Ness, Billy Bragg, and so many others back on the right course of history. Sometimes the tasks that Kenn and I were set upon were significant, and others were relatively minor, like dousing the flames of jealously and repairing the disharmony that was caused when the Reid brothers, of the Proclaimers, broke into a Gallagher brothers–type brouhaha during their rendition of "My Girl." As it turned out, they were both harmonizing about the same girl, an awkward discovery. That was easy, but this time we faced something with more gravitas than jealous brothers attracted to the same girl.

Kenn focused his attention on building a methodology to resolve the crisis. A structure to frame our efforts around, but also one to keep me on track. While I would like to say, and probably even did say at the time, that I had snapped into action, putting all thoughts and torments of *her* behind me, that wasn't the case. Kenn was firm but exhibited an unexpected compassion while I waited for an admonishment that never came. Any vestiges of the Kenn that I had remembered with Billy Bragg or confronting me about *her* were now nowhere to be found.

"Kenn, you were right all along. I shouldn't—

"Of course I was right," Kenn would respond. 'It's obvious. There's no new music. It's a fact; there isn't even any discussion of music." Kenn would grant me unanticipated concessions on, well, *her*, for which I was grateful and confused.

I suppose Kenn knew well enough about consequences that couldn't be changed. I suppose we all did, but there is a difference between logic and emotion as vast as any ocean. Proving the point, there I was standing at a gig in my mind with the house lights on, waiting for an encore that would never come. *That girl* had left the building, but I still chanted to encourage a return. But there would be no encore, no repeat performance. All that remained was a crumpled ticket stub in my hand.

Suddenly the quiet overtook us, the type of silence that follows a wild digression or personal interlude. Perhaps it was just the silence that accompanies an awkward confession, like when a child admits to sticking his tongue to a frozen pole or a friend you're sharing a sandwich with confides in you that he's contracted an STD.

As much as I'm inclined to glamorize saving rock 'n' roll, to delight in the details of history that color the facts of the past, especially the history that we created, I know it's simply not true. The reality is that Kenn became the hero and I followed him because I had nowhere else to go.

Whatever unknown reason caused music to disappear, it would be as simple as putting a cassette back in the deck and pressing play, and everything would return to normal, at least once we knew what we were looking for.

I was glad for the preservation of our electronics and the limited scope that our music collections retained. With it we were able to continue our crossings and seek a reordering of the universe, one gig at a time.

But it all became a ritual for us, helping us to cross through time and space, enabling us to enter a gig by the band we happened to be listening to. If we wanted to go to a specific gig at a specific time, well, that was significantly harder. Time is like that. To recreate a moment, to reenter a conversation or an instant, was as complicated as landing a space shuttle without fuel. But that was what we needed to do, if wanted to find the right spot in time. Society needed us.

"A certain amount of venting of frustration and angst is healthy. Rock 'n' roll provides a safe forum to release pent-up emotion. People look at the emotion of music and think it's dangerous, without thinking about what would happen if that energy were released in a different form," Kenn explained.

"Like the same reason a caged tiger requires daily exercise?"

"Exercise and, well, tranquilizers. Just like inmates, soldiers, and other government employees are controlled with medications in the food and water supplies. People think that it's just exercise that keeps the tiger under control, but they're wrong. It's mostly mind-control drugs. The CIA administers drugs prescribed by the NSA. The same thing happens with people who are within easy reach of the Man. That's why you shouldn't eat from the cafeteria at Forestry."

"Don't worry. Eunice is always there; that's reason enough." I shuddered at the thought of my corpulent supervisor cramming some sugary food into her face. "But I take exception to being compared to an inmate."

"It's the drugs that make her who she is. The government has the same access to you for psychotropic drug trials; in their eyes you're all the same. Just rats to test drugged food on," Kenn concluded. "It's in the bottled water, too. It's the Montecore theory."

"Montecore?"

"Yeah, the cat that went off its meds and ate those Germans in Vegas."

Kenn might have been right about Eunice, but government mind control conspiracy or not, there were other problems with Eunice—problems that for me, disappeared with my Forestry job. Kenn was partially correct, not about the drugs but about the release valve. Without such a safety release, society was on stage with Siegfried and Roy waiting for a medicated tiger to be misunderstood. Now, the death of rock 'n' roll made society more susceptible to a crazed tiger rampage, which is why Kenn and I needed to find and resurrect it.

But how do you find something absent? Something erased or removed from view? What happens if your family leaves? What happens if a parent dies? Or you lose a prized possession? You search for it. And if you can't find it physically you manifest it. In your heart. In your memories. But you can't search for a family if you're left in a basket at the orphanage door, or if a parent dies before you're born. Night yields at dawn and your prior existence is erased like a troubled dream.

As the severity of our situation expanded before us, Kenn and I made notes of everything we could remember that was missing: recordings, traces of bands, newspaper and magazine articles, blogs, and even the bars that once hosted rock concerts that were closed without leaving any trace of their former being. As the inventory of absence increased, Kenn said, "Fuck, this really changes the DEFCON status."

Only half listening, I replied, "A deaf conference, or is this an Ebonics thing?"

"Come on, Dick, keep up," Kenn said indignantly. "DEFCON, the military term, not convention for the deaf."

"Ahhh," I said, still somewhat distractedly poring through what was left of Kenn's music collection, searching for information that would help our cause. "What exactly does DEFCON measure, like how much worse is DEFCON 2 than 3?"

"It's sort of a science thing," Kenn replied. "Like the Richter scale, DEFCON is sort of logarithmic, but rather than measuring the distance of tectonic movements, DEFCON measures how far feces will spread if a certain situation should occur. It's short for 'Defecate On.' DEFCON

1 is where it will be virtually impossible to find a single thing that isn't covered in excrement. Thus 'Defecation on One and All' is what the status reflects. By comparison, DEFCON 10 means that you can find at least ten things that aren't covered in shit."

I wasn't sure that Kenn had this one right, but I didn't have the fortitude for another discussion of his dubious science pedigree, and what was more, looking around, the excrement was starting to flow. So I sort of agreed and continued to take stock of what remained in our world. "Ahhh, OK. Makes sense, I suppose, dude." There wasn't much left for Kenn and me to examine, or to rebuild after the death of rock 'n' roll, but we knew that there had to be something. We just had to find the feathers among ashes to build our phoenix. But from where?

"DEFCON status is a reflection of how bad things get when the shit hits the fan," Kenn concluded for clarity's sake.

In my bones, it felt as though we were close to a solution.

Rock 'n' roll is about breaking norms. About rebellion. Not just musicians. Rock 'n' roll also attracts those people who press the boundaries. Rock 'n' roll forms a bond between artist and audience like the symbiosis of the Stockholm syndrome, and did so even before the Hives appeared on the scene. However, the Hives belonged to a missing future.

What was left of our modern collections were various forms of rap and hip-hop that we liked: Ice-T, Public Enemy, Gil Scott-Heron, and Boogie Down Productions, and acts that were raw and later would cross the floor to rock 'n' roll or tour with bands such as R.E.M., U2, or the Sisters of Mercy. Rap bands that Kenn and I enjoyed because of their energy, clever compositions, and of course their unrelenting social stands. Before the Great Disappearance of Rock 'n' Roll, these artists would provide a brief interlude to our musical experiences, but now they provided our anthems.

"I can't believe that I'm excited to see my rap albums left intact."

"Yeah, I guess the meekly talented actually do inherit the earth. What was once peripheral and a curiosity is now the sole source of contemporary music. But it's probably just a matter of time before the Moral Majority extends its charge against all music."

"Yeah, rap was once the early target? The Righteous Right targeted punk and rap in the same breath, claiming that music was an evil and immoral influence, causing everything from male-pattern baldness and juvenile delinquency to class war."

"Uh-huh, right down to images of America laying in smoking ruin with black people in power and whites running scared through the streets. An apocalypse. But I guess they found a different path. Rap has been spared, at least for now."

It seemed, from what little media coverage remained about music, that the Evil was at a high DEFCON status as well. If rap fell, like rock 'n' roll had, then what would be next? Jazz? Spoken-word poetry? And then what? Written poetry? Essays and short stories? Movies and radio broadcasts? Would the five-second delay for live television be extended to radio interviews, political speeches, and assembly in public?

Would the destruction of spontaneity follow the downfall of the arts, favoring a regime based upon state control? While one could imagine an argument supporting a practical reality of everything having a five-second time lag, giving the brain time to consider what the mouth might be saying, state control over the individual should never be that absolute. Kenn and I had seen the desolate streets of London when Prime Minister Bragg's alternative history swept through the world like a dark cloud ushering in Armageddon. An Armageddon producing a chilling effect and turning the masses into sporting spectators who weren't allowed even to express their preference for one team or another. Voters without expression? Humanity without ideas or a dissenting thought?

Eventually, our preparations became tedious. Preparations always are. While perfection maybe born out of repetition, so is boredom. Kenn and I crossed, going to gig after gig, and the repetition became the hallmark for what was at stake. Boring gigs with the same mediocre local bands lacking inspiration and talent. It wasn't always a chore; sometimes we were lucky. We saw the Flaming Lips as an opening act at The Bowery in Oklahoma City, before they ever released an album. In our new reality, they didn't exist in our collection at all, so they would be just another local band consigned to some basement bar if Kenn and I failed to retrieve rock 'n' roll.

We crossed hundreds, if not thousands, of times in order to refine our plan. Chasing rumors of live music or breakups, stories about bands that never were or that could have been bigger than they turned out to be, our efforts were exhaustive.

One time we even crossed to see the Replacements, only to find that the gig had deteriorated to such a degree that the bar manager was as drunk as Westerberg. A couple of local clowns who barely knew how to hold a guitar had taken it upon themselves to mix with the remaining members of the band and were engaging in what would have been the eighties equivalent of karaoke. I had never wished as hard for more lenient gun control legislation. We all deserved to die, and dying violently and stopping our prolonged agony would have been a truly merciful act.

While Kenn and I were wondering what to do, we ordered beer, you know, to strategize.

"Two," Kenn called out to the bartender, then looked at me. "I can't believe that this is actually a waste of time. Crossing for this?"

The rakishly thin bartender with short-cropped hair returned with two freshly poured beers. "I'm Joey. You guys want to pay now or open a tab? If so, I'll just need an impression of your credit card. Although I must say"—he cast an uneasy eye toward his bar manager, who appeared unable to decide if he wanted to play video games or balance himself against the wall—"this isn't going to last long, at this rate."

"What do you mean?" I asked, clearing my first draw on my beer, having tipped it toward Kenn as a sort of inchoate "cheers."

"Look, I'll be honest with you," Joey said. "We book bands to fill the place so we can sell beer. Nothing new with that. But when bands start falling over or getting messy, like these idiots"—he spread his arms toward the stage—"no one drinks as much, and it's really a waste of my time. I'll probably call the cops from the pay phone outside in about thirty minutes."

"Why?" I asked, shocked.

"Because, it'll give you time to finish a couple beers."

"No, I mean about the cops."

"Oh, because, they'll come and break this up, throw everyone out, and I can go home. It's simple economics. I own this place, and my manager is barely able to stand, much less assert control over this shit show. I can't afford to stay open, pay wages, and have people break shit if they aren't buying drinks." Turning to the guy beside us, our conversation over, Joey asked, "What can I get you?"

"Beer. OJ, too. Separate drinks."

The voice belonged to Chris Mars, the drummer of the Replacements.

"Joey, since we may not be here all that long," Kenn said with a wink, "put it on my tab for him."

"Cheers," Chris said to us, without much enthusiasm. "What a fucking *Gong Show*. Night after night, the shit hits the fan and we don't even duck anymore. Did you guys travel for this, or was paying at the door as bad as your night's been?"

Not knowing what to say, I managed, "Meh, it's part of the scene. Part of the fun. This is my buddy, Kenn. He and I have seen a fair number of gigs; you never know what you're gonna get, but true, this sort of shit gets tired."

"Doesn't matter if you travel or if it's local. You OK?" Kenn asked.

"Fuck, I don't know," Chris confessed. "This was supposed to be fun, and now there's all the pressure. Pressure to be something. To say something meaningful, pressure from outside and inside the band. Now there's all this tension between what Paul wants and what we think we want. I don't know. It's like being with my parents all over again. Or school, or some other shit."

In the pause, Kenn and I looked at each other and then toward the stage, where things continued to fall apart.

"What else are you going to do?" Kenn asked, as diplomatically as ever. "I mean this is rock 'n' roll; is there anything better?"

What was it about Kenn that made everything he said always sound condescending, even when he wanted to pay a compliment? Was he so divorced from reality that he just didn't have a clue?

"If I wanted responsibility I'd go to law school or be a fucking librarian. This is everything that I want to do," Chris said, finishing his beer, turning to his orange juice. It was then that I noticed he was glowing slightly. There was a hologram of an older version, probably a vision of him years after the Replacements disbanded and went their different ways. Chris Mars needed our help.

"Look, dude," I said, "you'll be fine. You'll sort it all out, and in one form or another you'll be guided by your passions. It may not be with the 'Mats, but as long as you follow your passions you'll be fine. Embrace them. Maybe you just need a break, maybe in a different future you'll take a hiatus and pick it up in a few years."

"Yeah, maybe you could compose music, or paint," Kenn added.

Yeah, that's just how thoughtful Kenn could be. Take a guy who was preoccupied and seemingly on the cusp of ruination and suggest that he take up painting.

"Again with the painting, Kenn? What? Just because it worked in Canada for that other drummer?"

"It's also a form of psychotherapy," sighed Chris. "Painting."

"So it works on a bunch of levels."

"Kenn, not really helping."

"Meh," Kenn responded with a shrug.

With a perplexed look, Chris Mars left his half-finished orange juice, and walked away from us, looking nervously over his shoulder. As Joey brought us another round, I noticed that the aura and hologram had disappeared from Chris. Maybe I didn't notice, maybe I just decided. After all, if rock 'n' roll was going to die anyway, Chris might as well find another form of art to pursue, at least while art was still alive.

As strange as it might be, the Replacements did break up, prematurely and without much commotion. I suppose that wasn't strange at all and almost a certainty, even without the benefit of hindsight. But what of Chris Mars? Drummers don't often survive the dissolution of bands particularly well. In Chris's case, he did become a composer and a painter. Kenn and I went to a couple of his showings, but Kenn never did receive any thanks for setting him on his alternate path; in fact Chris acted as though he'd never seen us before.

Fortunately, the Replacements, in the reality that we knew, would reform later for a few years, but without Mars.

Shortly after we finished our round of beers, and as Joey was slipping out to call the police, Kenn and I found ourselves transported back to his home. It was all part of the research and rigorousness that we endured to find where and how rock 'n' roll died.

As tedious as it might have been, Kenn and I couldn't complain to anyone about it. I mean first of all we were living in a time that was devoid of rock 'n' roll, and nobody seemed to have noticed its absence for nearly thirty years. There was also the fact that the bulk of our research involved time travel, which is usually a difficult subject to broach with people. And then even if you could a) find someone who was interested in the rock 'n' roll of the seventies and eighties, and b) convince them you traveled through time, your complaint would sound ridiculous:

"Yeah, it's such a hardship. Kenn and I crossing all the time to see rock shows. No, it doesn't cost us a dime and takes only a few seconds out of our day. Yeah, it's sort of limited, you know; how many times can you see R.E.M.?"

Yeah, a tough sell indeed. To me it was as sympathetic as listening to a porn star complaining about his day:

"Look, it's tedious. We did this shoot that was supposed to be a foursome, but then one of the girls didn't show up so we shot it as a threesome. That took forever, about a billion takes, and they couldn't get the AC to work, so it was really cold, then too hot. Then the third girl finally showed up, so we all had a snack and chatted, then we showered, yeah together, and tried again, for the foursome I mean, not the shower or the snack, but the sandwiches were good. They're from that new deli—you know, the one across town? Yeah, well right. But then the first two girls from the threesome couldn't play nice with each other, so we had to do more takes and then the lighting was wrong and by that time the hot lights and lubricant had irritated my skin. You know, some days, I just wish I had finished law school . . . Worse is that when I get home all my girlfriend wants is to have sex, which is fair I suppose, but really I'd just like to find a good book, maybe a glass of wine . . ."

Not really the type of scenario that tugs at the heartstrings because of our perceptions that the gig itself isn't so bad. At least it's certainly not as bad a job as working in a salt mine or cleaning up a violent-crime scene.

Renewed in focus and kept on task by Kenn, I considered how the days progressed with the steadiness of Kenn's first car. Speeding along at times, barely managing sweeping corners on the highways, and at other times lurching and laboring as the transmission slipped and caught. At the time the car was a joke; well, it was always a joke, but at one time it was a specific joke that was somehow funny. Something that he had bought without his parents' blessing and probably in direct opposition to their wishes, but it was his own money, and they lacked the interest and resolve to really intervene. As horrendous as the car was, it led us to another great discovery, a discovery that was also part of the joke, when I bought him the Galaxie 500 album *Today*.

"Hey, Kenn," I said, "Galaxie 500 is missing. We should be making notes of what we're remembering; that might help us find where we're going."

"Yeah," Kenn agreed, grabbing a notebook. "But I'm also noticing that I can't remember things. I seem to remember parts of songs, or a *feeling* that a certain song or band or something might have been there, but then I can't remember all of it. You know, like somehow I think that R.E.M. had more albums than what I seem to be able to find now."

"Hmm," I considered. "Well maybe we should try to think of other associations. That's how I came up with Galaxie 500."

I remembered the band only because of the connection I had with it and Kenn. The rest of the story went as follows: Never one to judge a record by its sleeve or a band by its name, Kenn inquired with his typical expressive manner, "What's this? I drive a shit box with the same name."

"Yeah, I know," I replied mischievously. "How bad can it be? Or at least what are the odds that two things that share the same name are both shitty?" Unlike the automobile, the band was great. Unfortunately, Galaxie 500, the band, didn't last as long as Kenn's car, but both became a source of entertainment for us. While I don't know much about cars, you can't go wrong buying anything from the band Galaxie 500. It was a band that the world would be worse off without, even for the relatively short—too short—time that they existed.

Discovering when music died should have been easy. All we had to do was sort our collections by release date and we were there. Well, halfway there, also the opening line of "This Car Climbed Mt. Washington," by Damon & Naomi, the pairing that was left after the acrimonious split of Galaxie 500.

"There was also Luna that split out of Galaxie Five," I said.

I was remembering! The linking of associations as a key mnemonic. Somewhere within the two of us was an ember of the flame of rock 'n' roll.

Once again the headquarters for our adventures was Kenn's place. Almost immediately, we relocated my remaining music to his place. It made sense; Louie Louie was there, and it sidestepped the residual memories of *her*. It suited us very well.

Industriously scouring the release dates of the albums and the various articles and information that we had gathered over the years, we discovered that no new music had been released since 1984. While it seemed that an Orwellian element existed, we discounted a government conspiracy of such proportion as would be required to make such a sweeping change, mostly because what we had seen was just a gradual fade-out rather than a vicious clamp-down. Vinnie would have a different view, but he couldn't be found, and his coffee shop didn't exist, so we remained on our own.

What Kenn and I couldn't find was the intervening event. We faced the seemingly impossible task of having to find something that wasn't there. It was as though the final sounds of rock 'n' roll had just faded out like the end of a record, and no one seemed to notice the soft static of the needle scratching incessantly on the album's paper label. By July 1985 there were virtually no new signs of rock 'n' roll remaining in society, nothing but what had come before. Nothing to illuminate what had occurred so that we could correct what was wrong. Knowing our minds were the last remaining archives of volumes of musical information, we faced the challenge of unlocking the fortress of our memories. Although we knew that other music had existed for us before, now it no longer did. Rock 'n' roll had died.

Kenn and I started working backward from the albums that we could find. David Bowie's *Tonight* existed, but nothing after. (Later we noted that *Never Let Me Down* was the first one missing.) Kenn and I had *The Top*, by the Cure, but that was all.

"OK, Kenn," I said. "Here's an album by the Dead Kennedys, but wasn't there more? Something with some controversy about the cover art? I just can't remember the name."

"Yeah, that's right," Kenn mused while tapping a pencil on a pad of paper. "Something about photographic rights, or maybe obscenity. Frankly. Frank and Ernest."

"Frankenstein?" I asked hopefully.

"Nice," Kenn said, starting studiously to make notes. "*Frankenchrist.* Banned art by H. R. Giger, leading to litigation that killed the band and led to the alienation of Jello Biafra from his bandmates and many fans. Good. This is a start."

"Here's the Red Hot Chili Peppers' self-named album," I continued.

"It's still in our collection, but not the other one that we listened to in high school. Was it *Freaky Styley*?"

"That's right." Kenn continued. "OK, dates, producer, and L.A.—what else? Keep going, buddy."

And so the list went on. Sure, this wasn't so bad. And collectively our music represented a vast amount of rock 'n' roll, but still, nothing new? For Kenn and me, this was a disaster. The end of days.

As the days went on, we busied ourselves looking for the missing piece of music that would unlock the puzzle. We continued to avoid matters relating to *that girl*, and Kenn and I returned to being Kenn and I with both the tension and the acceptance that braid themselves into most friendships. There was still the lingering change that I had witnessed, something of an edge that showed itself in an occasional tone or intonation, perhaps a gesture or reaction, but always a tension.

But even in the shadow of latent tension, I was hardly in a position to judge. Kenn had offered me acceptance and I owed him the same. I owed Kenn a debt of gratitude for extricating me from my self-loathing, and while I was still haunted by the thoughts of her, we also had the crisis of a world without rock 'n' roll.

Here was a world without song. Without the soulless advertising jingles, without the energy of the staccato fire of drums heard in the white noise of construction equipment or unmaintained automobiles.

People without inspiration, dissent, or an expressive outlet.

Dance limited to disco, or waltzes, or polkas.

Sporting stadiums devoid of music to whip the crowd into a frenzy.

Art that was homogeneous, incapable of deviation or alternative forms.

Television lacking music, music stations, or anything considered current in terms of pop culture.

No humming in elevators or whistling along the streets.

Children skipping in silence.

As I returned from my isolation, Kenn and I found a world marching toward ruination. The prospect of a disassociated and robotic world without an outlet for dissent, as described by the bands of the late seventies and early eighties, focused my mind upon my fear that without dissent the world was headed for the abyss.

Armageddon. Yes, Armageddon was upon us.

"It was sort of cool buying Chris Mars a beer," I said. "Have we checked the Replacements yet?"

"No, but they seem destined for their own failure. Chris looked depressed; you could hardly blame him, with gigs like that."

"Yeah, remember what he said when he was walking away? He said that when the band started it was a vehicle for what they wanted, but after they developed a following the shit hit the fan. That was the expression he used. *The shit hit the fan.* Obviously he's talking about alcoholism and added pressures, but didn't they also release an album called *The Shit Hits the Fan*? Or maybe a single?"

"The single was off the Circle Jerks' 1983 *Golden Shower of Hits* album," Kenn said, making notes of things coming back to him. "Sort of a double entendre—or a few, I suppose. I think Chris was talking more about the DEFCON type of thing. The album *The Shit Hits the Fans* was actually a bootleg cassette that was released."

I looked through the R section of our collection. "You're a fucking genius!" I exclaimed. "That's it!" Our copy was missing.

"Of course I'm a genius," Kenn agreed. "I told you it's about DEFCON, but it's not so complicated that it would make me a genius; it just seems that way to you because it's science."

"No, not about DEFCON," I said. "Your last comment, dude. The last album we're missing is *The Shit Hits the Fans*, by the Replacements. Kenn, the live bootleg is missing. What if that's what's caused the death of rock 'n' roll? If we can recover that album, we can revive rock 'n' roll! Remember you used to bootleg cassettes of live shows that way, too."

"Look!" I exclaimed, "*Let It Be* is the last Replacements album in your collection!"

After *Let It Be* was released, the Replacements toured to promote their albums, see the world, shirk responsibility, meet girls, and drink free beer. Paradise perhaps not, but it was in the same time zone.

"Kenn," I said in astonishment, "we were so close. The night we met Chris Mars, that could have or should have been all we needed."

"Meh, what are you going to do? We'll cross again and they'll actually play this time. It couldn't have been that night we met Chris because the gig had exploded into a reenactment of *Lord of the Flies*. I'll get some beer," Kenn said, disappearing.

Notes and jots of partial ideas rushed from us like torrents and then dried like summer creeks. Half ideas, imperfect memories, random thoughts, fractured puzzle pieces, but all cobbled together, were starting to build mass like a child's frozen snowball. Gradually our memories created and recreated what had been lost. Within an hour Kenn's whiteboard held the following:

Title:

The Shit Hits the Fans

Released:

January 25, 1985, by Twin/Tone Records

Description:

Live recording of the Replacements at The Bowery, Oklahoma
City, November 11, 1984, on a Maxell XL II-S audiocassette that
was confiscated by Bill MacLeslie from an unknown, uncredited fan
covertly recording the performance with a personal recording device.

Misc:

Cover art by band member Chris Mars (percussion) on the
J-Card cassette cover.

<10,000 (legitimate) copies.

These details represented only the factual portion of the story. Like dates in history. The implications and context become the muscle and skin that complete the body, allowing it to move. It was these details, intangibles that Kenn and I would drape on the frame provided by the facts, that would provide us the complete picture that we needed to complete our mission. In terms of actual details and witness accounts of this event, the assassinations of JFK and Tupac were more straightforward, but again, Kenn and I would have to be resourceful in our examination of rock 'n' roll history. Ultimately it was not the tangible details, but those that were not, that Kenn and I would have to focus on. Returning to the whiteboard:

Intangibles:

Source of urban legend and a rock 'n' roll myth:

      1. The influence of the band

      2. The relatively modest circulation of the recording

      3. Everyone secretly yearned to be *that* guy

"I totally want to be that guy. The guy that not only gets caught surreptitiously recording a great show, but it's later discovered that the tape is of such great quality that the band adopts it as a live album."

Of course, multitudes of people falsely claimed the recording as their own, igniting competing counterclaims and rebuttals, all adding to the mystique and overall coolness of the entire thing, all of this merely enlarging the urban legend.

But provenance was never resolved, at least beyond knowing that MacLeslie had relieved the tape from the perpetrator, a perpetrator who held a threshold between villain and hero, defined by the thickness of a Maxell XL II-S tape.

It was only after retracing our steps and finding that *Let It Be* and not *Tim*, by the Replacements, was in our possession that the epiphany was confirmed. Kenn and I had been looking in the wrong place. As compelling as the evidence appeared, to be sure we still had to go to The Bowery in Oklahoma City.

Why did the loss of a single live album halt rock 'n' roll? Sometimes it doesn't matter why something occurred, just that it did.

And so it began. Kenn and I pieced together everything that we once knew and could now remember about the Replacements and The Bowery. While the band was easy enough for us to work up, Kenn and I immediately had struggles with the venue.

How do you find out about a legendary bar that existed in the past but occupied such a slight sliver of time that it was difficult to access it, even with a time machine? Well, you go to other gigs and ask people. So, once again, Kenn and I found ourselves in unfamiliar territory. In a time without Facebook, Twitter, or Tinder, we found a social outlet. We were *talking* to people at gigs. Talking to the bands afterward, journalists who followed the scene from the road, the roadies, the drifting fans, sometimes bartenders. Anyone.

Rock gigs were a social interaction before live streaming and social media. Kenn and I would usually just go to listen to the music; talking to people seemed like a lot of work. But now we needed to talk. We needed to learn as much as we could, and there was nothing left but the oral tradition of rock 'n' roll, listening to stories from those who had traveled the roads before us.

Searching for our break, we saw bands like Romeo Void, Translator, Wall of Voodoo, the Call, the Gun Club, the Violent Femmes, as well as R.E.M. at The Bowery, but that was just the start of our research. The Bowery was open for only a few short years, and in our new reality, the club was open for more than half of those years after rock 'n' roll had died. So there was no media coverage for us to review and few albums that could get us back inside. Unlike CBGB, propped up by the massive population of New York City, The Bowery lacked the same stature and accordingly was more arcane. Still, The Bowery hosted bands, and that was all we needed.

I still remember the feeling of going into The Bowery for the first time. Even after Kenn and I had crossed a few times into the bar already, it was the act of actually entering that was so profound for me. It was a cool night, probably late fall, as the evening was still light, but the shadows were long and pointing northward. This was auspicious, as we were hoping to get to early November to see as much of The Bowery as we could before the 'Mats gig, but still the cold air shocked us.

Every time we stopped too long we could feel the crisp air, which left us with a quick chill through our light shirts and jeans. Consequently, North Walker Avenue was quiet and virtually empty. Kenn and I walked along the wide street toward a two-story redbrick building called Plaza Court.

"Hey, Kenn, look at that," I said, pointing toward the center of the city.

"What? I don't have time for the sights. It's cold. Let's get the fuck into the show," he replied, shivering in his long-sleeved cotton shirt. We had crossed to see the band X and continue our reconnaissance, and while we were dressed for a raucous night of live music, the autumn chill was cutting us to the bone, so it was understandable that Kenn wasn't in the mood for sightseeing. We were paying this price now so that later we would succeed and be eating pizza at Kenn's with our music collections restored.

Time isn't waiting," Kenn said anxiously. "So unless you've got something I'll never see again, let's go inside and get a beer."

"That's what I'm saying. Look, dude. It's the Murrah Federal Building. Still there," I said, unmoved by Kenn's mood. Kenn stopped shivering and silently turned to see the top of the structure, a mere outline of a building that would later become a memorial site. Another building seen from a nightclub where Kenn and I had been, but subsequently destroyed. Another example of destruction caused without any connection to rock 'n' roll or the evil that it was supposed to espouse.

After a moment of somber reflection, I nudged Kenn and said, "Let's go see this band." With that we left the cool, clear air and turned toward a basement door from which the distinct sound of rock 'n' roll was emanating. The coolness started to abate until it was completely overcome by the dense smoke as we entered the bowels of the building, where the air became dank and fetid, ripe with odors of human contact, sweat, and spilled beer. A subterranean jungle with a primitive beat; not a heart of darkness, but the womb of rock 'n' roll. My head spun, not only from want of fresh air, but from being part of a place where rock 'n' roll was sacred. It was like somebody put something in my drink.

7

Somebody Put Something in My Drink

Why do we do what we do to people? Why do we hurt, humiliate, and harass? Do we really need to control others to feel better or important? Is a personal view of gender, sexuality, race, religion, or nationality more important than letting people be free? Isn't true freedom the ability to be happy without fear of persecution or torment? Can we be free if others are not?

This is why I love rock 'n' roll, because it's freedom.

The Ramones are poking fun at society, not justifying actions. Rape. Murder. Domination. Theft. Lying. Perjury. These are all actions born out of entitlement. Take a stand. No one is entitled to dominate others. This is Sid Itious signing off with a first track off Animal Boy, by the Ramones.

FCC transcript KRXF 92.9 FM 03.21.1982 0453

Operator comments redacted

File under: Sympathizer

"Somebody—puuuttt sumthin' in my drink—." Kenn was walking toward me belting out the Ramones classic, buoyed and boisterous, obviously confident in our pending success, and rightfully so. "Here you go, dude," he said, handing me a beer, as was the practice after we crossed.

"You might want to lay off the singing, especially songs that might not have been recorded yet, at least until we can confirm what time we're in," I said, taking the opened beer from Kenn. It may seem like a bad idea to take an open drink from someone singing a song about spiking drinks, but I figured I knew Kenn well enough. In fact, I'd often suspected him of using roofies, or at least procuring them, but I also assumed that he self-dosed to combat insomnia or to prevent recurring nightmares. Given his family history, he might have even found a sympathetic doctor to prescribe flunitrazepam. At any rate, Kenn needed my full attention and wouldn't likely be slipping anything into anyone's drink.

Drinks in hand, we surveyed our surroundings.

We were back in The Bowery with the Replacements, playing "Can't Hardly Wait," working their way through their set and the numerous bottles of beer that adorned the stage. There was a discarded newspaper on the floor, besmeared with something indescribable, human in origin and vile in result, which bore a headline relating to various Veterans Day services that would be held with Mayor Andy Coats in attendance at the 45th Infantry Division Museum. The year was 1984 and we were in Oklahoma City. OKC, as the locals we overheard called it.

I confirmed the date at the bar by requesting a receipt for our beers, sort of a loser move, but you know I had to be sure.

"Wha'? Are you kidding?" the bartender sneered. "Is this for your accountant or parole officer or something?"

Plaintively raising my hands, I said, "Yeah, I know, I know. It's a sort of dickhead thing to ask, but my buddy over there is obsessive-compulsive and needs the receipt for his Replacements scrapbook. Joey's not in tonight? He was here last time we were through."

"Fuck, Joey," someone from the far end of the bar interjected. "Get him the fucking receipt for his boyfriend already, and keep the beer flowing."

"I'm Joey," the bartender said, getting my receipt. "I just started; you must be thinking of someone else."

"Yeah, maybe," I said looking at the receipt and scrutinizing my memory to recall the details of all the Joeys that I had met in my life.

"Thanks. Yeah, maybe it was another gig. Sorry, sometimes I'm not so good with names, and it's always loud."

With that, the bartender shrugged. We were still in a basement rock bar; I'm sure he had heard and seen stranger tales. My petty indulgence was easy enough to accommodate. The receipt confirmed the day that the bootleg tape had disappeared from The Bowery. The date that first blood was drawn against rock 'n' roll.

This was ground zero. The audio equivalent of the Smithsonian exhibit with the saber-toothed tigers attacking the mastodon immobilized in the tar pit, a scene resulting in mutual extinctions.

But unlike a Smithsonian exhibit, Kenn and I could save the species. We were ready, and with the benefit of foresight could position ourselves in such a way as to intervene and keep rock 'n' roll safe. Why jump in front of a speeding bus that was going to run over a baby carriage, if you could stop and chat with the mother a block away, delaying her and the carriage until the danger had passed?

So, with beer in hand and a steely confidence, Kenn and I surveyed the scene. Everything was good, better than good. After all, this was rock 'n' roll. So Kenn, channeling his best Perry Farrell impersonation of the "Rock 'n' Roll/Sympathy for the Devil" cover, sang, "And it was allll riiiigght."

"Right venue. Right band. Right day," he continued. "Let's restore the universe to its rightful state."

"Pretty good, hey, Kenn?" I said, clinking my beer bottle against his.

"Man, this is going to be so easy," he agreed, grinning with self-delight. "All we have to do is find the kid who's bootlegging the tape and threaten to tell his mom that he was out late with naughty boys. While he's standing there pissing himself, we just demand the surrender of the tape and turn it over to the soundman. Could this get any easier?"

I wanted an easy win. It was just a time when I needed success without resistance, something to inflate my confidence and smooth the wrinkles of self-loathing that continued to linger. As much as I needed a win, I should have known that just like the interventions with Billy

Bragg and Lemmy, this was going to be difficult. I was fatigued by life's demands and daily concessions. Tired of the struggle, I just wanted to be a hero and listen to the music that had disappeared. Disappeared with *her*.

The first complication discovered was the actual kid making the bootleg. In my mind's eye, I had imagined the perpetrator down to the last greasy pimple. He was a skinny, awkward sort with a fake ID, a bunch of cash for beer (mostly fresh twenties), an expensive portable recorder, and new-smelling sneakers. This was the sort of kid whose skin condition was nothing compared with the other complexions that he would have when we confronted him. He would be begging us, actually begging us, to keep him out of trouble. This would be a moment that I always relished, an instant where the perpetrator becomes the victim and victims heroes. In a flood of stage lights and adoration from the Replacements, Kenn and I would be the ones who would turn the tables, rescue rock 'n' roll, and be immortalized as heroes.

As we walked around the bar, our suspect was easily discovered. Unfortunately my expectations were wrong; he was really more of a moose and likely twice the combined weight of Kenn and me. On his own there wasn't anything suspicious about him, except that he was glowing. He possessed the same shifting, shimmering hologram that we had seen during other crossings when an intervention was required. Folded beside him was a black leather jacket decorated with various iconic badges—the Clash, the Exploited, Misfits, and whatever else. But the one that was most distinctive was the sinister pair of stylized musical notes, a pair of triple note beams, but laid over each other to look like a pair of capital-letter M's that we had seen before. This was the goliath we had seen in a small storeroom where we had crossed another time. Right. The same human monstrosity that Kenn and I saw at the Talking Heads gig during a crossing before I had met *her*. I thought something was odd about the group when we accidently met them before, but this time there was no mistaking the hologram flickering on him.

Despite the sweltering temperature and subterranean humidity of

The Bowery, a chill caused me to shudder. I realized two things: first, that McCloy and his monster child were at the Talking Heads gig with *her*! Pyrah had been the woman with them. Our suspicions of the Evil being involved were correct. The meaning of the conversation that we had overheard during a previous crossing became clear. "But, Mr. McCloy, why don't we just try to steal their music and then make it bad?" this bald monster had said.

They were contemplating stealing and defiling music in order to kill rock 'n' roll. Collectively they had been conspiring to destroy rock 'n' roll even then. How long had this been going on? Had Kenn really been right? Had we been targeted and followed? Who was McCloy? What was Pyrah's connection to this?

I also realized that we didn't know where or when the Talking Heads gig that we had seen had taken place. Was it before or after our present predicament? Whatever the answers, it was now clear that the complexity of the death of 'n' roll was beyond our anticipation.

"Game up," Kenn snapped at me. "You OK? This is the time and this is the place, and he's the mark. Let's get this done and get the fuck out of here."

"But Kenn," I started to warn him.

"But nothing. This is what we've been working for."

Spurred into action by Kenn, I shook off my reverie and, becoming confident, inventoried the bar. It appeared that Mooseman was alone; my poise became absolute and my resolve was a hard as quartz.

We knew the set list. We knew the bar, which after all was the tough part.

If watching Tom Clancy/Jack Ryan movies had taught us anything, it was that sophisticated extraction ops required a perfect knowledge of the setting, the surroundings, and the target. It was the same principle that most teleportation plots operated on as well. This project was too big to fail. The consequences were too severe, leaving little margin for error. We had to secure the bootleg tape that would become *The Shit Hits the Fans* to restore the history we knew. Our preparations provided us with the advantage of surprise; it was impossible for us to fail. To fail would allow rock 'n' roll to remain as the discarded beer bottles after a house party. A place transformed from a good time to a chore to clean up. Looking around the bar, seeing nothing but reprobates, it was easy to imagine an epic mess.

The Replacements really did break the mold. In fact most nights they broke the mold, and then urinated and vomited on the pieces, just in case anyone even *considered* putting them back together. I think that if I had been at the show without having seen the future I might have felt differently about the Replacements. Not only would the gig have disappointed me, but I might have disavowed any interest in the band at all.

Was there anything about this particular show that was really remarkable? No, it was just like the Replacements themselves. Messy. They personified the "Bastards of Young" that they sang about. The band was like a bunch of kids I knew growing up, surrounded by affluence but raised by indifferent parents in an ambivalent society. Children neglected, reared by televisions and school lunch programs, while simultaneously yoked with expectations by parents and society that were both unreasonable and unsuitable. The same angst and frustration, a sense of being unheard, or heard but not understood, was the burden that shadowed the Replacements and later followed bands like Nirvana and Pearl Jam. It was this same desolation in the face of success, the inchoate achievement and unwanted fame that destroyed these bands from within.

But bands like the Replacements, Pearl Jam, and Nirvana managed to succeed, at least to a degree, in spite of themselves. What struck me as wrong was that while *The Shit Hits the Fans* was the breaking point for rock 'n' roll, the gig itself was barely mediocre. The band basically ran roughly through a series of cover versions that appeared to range from impromptu to just plain chaotic, and as cluttered as the performance was, the band was becoming messier with each passing drink. The bootleg cassette represented a high-quality recording of a low-quality gig.

It was immediately obvious that neither Paul Westerberg nor anyone else was going to be able to help us recover the tape. The Stinson brothers, while not as far gone as Westerberg, were well on their way, and let's face it, they had their hands full enough with playing a gig and looking after Paul. That left Chris Mars, who seemed indifferent or preoccupied, perhaps contemplating Kenn's suggestion of pursuing a career in art. In fact, I doubted that without the understanding of what the Replacements would eventually mean to rock 'n' roll, the bands that they would inspire, I would have been impressed with the show at all. Had this been any other gig, I would have probably left as soon as the covers started getting messy. But this was a Replacements gig, and this was how their gigs were and in fact who they were.

As the Replacements started in on a cover of Bachman-Turner Overdrive's "Takin' Care of Business," I remembered that was our cue. We wandered over to the sound table and handed the sound guy a Pabst and gave him a nod that said, "This is really something else, hey, dude?" in the universal rock 'n' roll language. It wasn't really that great a gig, but what are you going to say to the sound guy? "The boys really seem fucked up tonight, hey?" *Something else* left a wide range of interpretations possible.

"This would make an awesome live album, don'tcha think?" Kenn suggested to the soundman we knew to be Bill MacLeslie.

"Ain't going to happen, boys. Westerberg isn't into live recordings, and what he says goes," replied the soundman, accepting the beer with a gracious nod.

"Yeah, well, my man, the Moose over by the rail says differently. You can see the recorder poking out from under his jacket," I replied, nudging the first domino into motion.

The soundman looked around and said, "Black jacket beside the Agent Orange gig posters and leaning on the wall near the DJ booth?"

"The same," I confirmed with a slight nod and touching my finger to my nose.

"OK, thanks for the tip. I'll be right back, and then I'll get you guys on the list for tomorrow's show," he assured us. The guest list for the Replacements at The Bowery: we had arrived. No duplicity, we'd be bona fide guests. Another story in our collection of tales that no one was going to believe.

MacLeslie walked around the bar nonchalantly, seemingly checking the sound, making notes or nodding his approval. He stood at the rail beside the DJ booth and nodded toward the folded jacked and then said to our glowing Mooseman something that looked like "Good show, huh? Got a light?"

"Ahhh . . . sure," replied an indifferent monster. Reaching toward his jacket for a lighter, he asked, "I suppose you want me to provide the smoke for you as well?"

Moosey grabbed his jacket and the recorder, leaped to his feet, and crashed his shoulder into the unsuspecting MacLeslie.

We tried to call Joey the bartender and bouncers for help, but it was no use with the noise in the bar, so we started after him ourselves, hoping that the bouncers would follow the commotion. The Moose moved with unpredictable speed. Seriously, he had to be 300 pounds and over six foot four, but he moved like he was on casters and powered by rockets. Fleeing from MacLeslie with the recorder and his jacket, he ran toward the exit stairs. Kenn and I rushed toward him from the bar while the bouncers started to give chase as well. In the rush, the evil Moose stumbled and a cassette came loose, falling to the ground. Unfazed and composed, he kept his escape as his primary objective.

I stooped to pick up the cassette when Kenn pushed me forward. "It's a decoy," he yelled. "The master is Maxell, and he's just buyin' time." Kenn was right. I'd failed to notice the detail now obvious as I looked at the TDK cassette I was holding. Cursing myself for not remembering that *The Shit Hits the Fans* was originally recorded on a different brand, I continued to run and discarded the tape. I chastised myself while trying to take stairs two and three at a time, but only managing to stumble and impede my progress.

The commotion from the soundman and the bouncers behind us

stopped, probably as they fell for the diversion that I had unwittingly perpetuated, MacLeslie seemingly confident that they had not only recovered the illicit tape but discouraged the fugitive Moose from trying this again in the future. They were likely right about the future, but not in the same way that they thought. Again I had managed to frustrate our efforts. Kenn and I knew that this could be one of the final gigs and that things were just going to start getting worse.

The evil Moose exploded up the stairs and through the door into the cool November night. Walker Street was deserted, giving our target the space across the flat ground to gather enough speed to achieve orbit. We were steadily losing ground, but the Moose monster was still glowing, beating a hasty trail down the street and turning toward Saint Anthony's Hospital. As the distance between us grew, so did my feelings of despair.

Kenn and I pursued him across the street, toward the parking lot by the hospital. It was then that my fears were realized and we lost sight of the monster. Our frantic search was fruitless; he could have entered an alley, jumped into a cab, or mixed into the crowd moving outside the hospital doors. Kenn and I didn't know OKC at all and felt the stress of having to make a choice quickly, without even knowing what the options were, so we headed back toward the street, where we hoped to gain a clear view of the area.

Everything that we'd thought during the course of our planning was now falling apart. It had all started with such promise, inflating us with confidence and filling us with swagger and poise. What should have been a straightforward trip found a fork in the road and took us onto a path that was replete with hazards. At no time did Kenn and I ever consider that the intervention would leave the nightclub or would end in a chase. We had simply assumed we would intimidate the perpetrator and become conquering heroes returning with riches from a new world.

As our muscles screamed for oxygen, panic was beginning to firmly take hold of us. Then rain started to fall, increasing our difficulty seeing and believing that we were going to be able to recover the bootleg cassette. I cringed. We would be trapped in 1984, and in Oklahoma City, of all fucking places.

We didn't even have jackets; we were just a couple of amateurs. We weren't Jack Ryan; we weren't even Simon Birch.

Clouds had crowded the sky and the autumn rain was getting colder. Falling lightly on my exposed skin like bristles of a brush, leaving a greasy film penetrating everything, the rain started increasing. I cursed how seasons and fortunes were quickly changed. More than getting wet and cold, desperation was soaking through us faster than the cold rain and leaving us just miserable.

At that moment, as surreal as it seemed, sounds of an accelerating engine and spinning tires caused us to turn. A large van struggled to retain control around a traffic circle, its back end slipping on the slick road surface. We stared dumbstruck as the van's engine roared and continued its fishtailing acceleration before coming to a sliding stop in front of us, still swaying from its rapid deceleration. The Econoline van was painted in flat black paint, or with some type of primer, and the cardboard-covered windows appeared to have been scribbled out with a black marker.

"Fuck, what now?" Kenn muttered.

The side door of the van exploded open as the van sat lurching in front of us, revealing a five-foot, nine-inch human gargoyle. This animated mass of muscle, tattoos, frustration, and palpable simmering rage could only be one person: Henry Rollins. Rollins was yelling at us, "Get in the van." Naturally we just stood there like we were cast in clay.

Trying to stay out of the rain, Rollins was bracing himself on the doorframe, he grabbed us by the necks of our soaked shirts and hauled our disbelieving bodies into the van. As the door slid shut, we heard the accelerator engage again and we fell backwards, feeling the van shoot off through the gloom. Our composure returned. As we thawed in the humid interior of the van, a sense of reprieve steadied my nerves—as much as they could, that is, being with Rollins, racing through the streets and the night.

The van. A rock 'n' roll icon. This was the first mode of transportation for any band, legitimate, established, wannabe, or starting out. The rock van was the Marshall amp of transportation and just as essential.

"What the fuck are you guys doing?" Rollins asked. "There are people looking for you." Then, seemingly distracted: "Don't you fucks even have jackets?"

"We checked them in the coatroom," I answered.

"Maybe. I don't think so," Kenn whispered, visibly awed by Rollins.

"Right, you dicks," an unimpressed Rollins said, looking back and forth between us. "There's no coat check in the club." And then turning to me: "Is your friend stupid, or high or something?"

"No," I replied, trying to come to Kenn's aid. "No, it's complicated; he's a scientist. They're all a little odd, but he might also have taken some roofies; he has a condition."

Kenn was indifferent to my comment. Rollins furrowed his brow and just shrugged his massive, muscular shoulders while he shook his head, as though my explanation had offered him no new information.

Rollins would provide safety. Of course he would help us save rock 'n' roll because he was all about taking a stand and kicking ass. Rollins was a rock 'n' roll icon. The very person we could trust to try to help us recover the bootleg cassette. Rollins was the best thing that could have happened to us; for a plan that had gone so wrong, again fortunes were changing.

So with a sigh and my first relaxed breath since the chase had started, we began to explain things to Henry, in a measured manner at first.

Kenn made it somewhat difficult on account of being completely starstruck; he vacillated between telling Rollins about our crossings and asking him about being a rock god. It was like watching a kitten chasing a spot of light down a hallway, only to become distracted by a butterfly, then a ball of yarn, and then the butterfly again, only to forget what he was originally chasing. Even I was confused as Kenn spun his yarn: "Well you know, after I discovered time travel, I knew that we had a duty to the greater good and then so we recruited . . ."

As Kenn carried on I wondered, *Why does he always have to exaggerate?* I mean, really, exaggerating time travel, as though that weren't enough, but invariably Kenn would interject a distracted question of his own, like, "Hey, when Danzig played with you and Black Flag, how cool was that?"

"Yeah, yeah, really cool. Really cool. Danzig is great. But getting back to this cassette thing . . ." Rollins tried earnestly to keep Kenn on topic. The van continued to tear through the streets in the rain, sliding round corners, and then rocking as the driver regained control. Rollins ended up leaving us from time to time in order to make some inaudible comment to the driver or an unseen passenger.

As it became clear that Rollins was neither entertained by, nor believing Kenn, I attempted to take over. "Hey, you know," I started, "it was just that we saw this guy making a tape at the Replacements show, and you know, that just ain't right, is it? C'mon, what would you do?" I tried to keep the story as level as possible.

"And that time you got your hand infected in Australia," Kenn interjected, recounting the story of Rollins punching a belligerent member of the audience in the mouth who had less than exemplary dental hygiene. "Did you really almost lose fingers?"

"Yeah, I've still got the scars. See?" Showing his hand, trying to conceal his frustration and keep the conversation heading where he wanted it to go. Then shaking his head and turning to me, "How many roofies do you think he took? Should we get him to a doctor?"

"Probably only a couple." I shrugged. "I think he's got a dependency. He'll be fine."

Rollins stared at me and then continued, "Right, so you guys risked a beating to run after a guy nearly three times your size over a bootleg tape, for a band you're not even in? Fuck that. You two don't even look that stupid."

Rollins was managing the two conversations well but seemingly not buying what I was telling him. "C'mon. There has to be more," he encouraged us.

"Did you ever meet Rob Younger of the Radio Birdman, when you were in Australia?" inquired Kenn.

"No, yes, no—fucking Christ, Kenn," the boiling embodiment of muscle, tattoo, and frustration implored. "Can we just get back to what the fuck is going on? What's going on here, tonight in Oklahoma?"

"Well, the Radio Birdman are actually a *part* of the story and how we got here," I attempted as Kenn jumped in, unsure if I was trying to help him or throw him under the bus for his verbal dysentery and distracting hero worship.

"It's just that I know you're a fan of MC5; Younger joined up with Dennis Thompson to form New Race."

"Kenn," Rollins said with a heavy sigh, "you know that I hate a lot, right? And that generally I'm considered to have anger issues, right? Could you please, please, just fucking please get to the point?"

Kenn started to say that Younger was a legend but trailed off and then fell into telling Rollins what he wanted to hear. I suppose there was a moment during which we were telling Rollins the entire story, about the time travel, the device, the bootleg tape, and whatever else managed to pass our lips, that I thought, *I wonder if we're saying too much.* Being with Rollins was itself intoxicating, and I was also a little embarrassed for Kenn being so enamored with Rollins, so in summoning kindness, I was probably of looser tongue than prudence would suggest.

After we had finished telling Rollins about everything from our first crossing, our subsequent adventures, and of course why we had crossed to save *The Shit Hits the Fans*, Henry sat back and contemplated what he had heard. "Beer?" Rollins offered up a pint-size bottle of some type of beer, which we heartily accepted. He took a shallow sip and passed it to us as he turned to lean over the driver's shoulder. Kenn took a long pull, gave me a smile, and handed me the beer. I took a long drink, too. It had been a hard and disappointing night so far, and the beer was just what I needed.

"So you're saying the future of music, of all artistic creation, depends upon a Replacements album made from a recording made tonight?"

"Totally," Kenn and I said with the synchronization of twins.

Kenn and I smiled, nodded, and gave each other a mental high five. Here we were, in a rock van, drinking beer with Rollins and racing through dark, rain-slicked streets to save rock 'n' roll, or at least the Replacements. This was monumental. How was it possible that Rollins had come flying around the corner just when we needed him? It was like the rock gods knew and had sent us a savior. Actually, it was like we'd been visited by a rock god himself on winged feet.

In our revelry of congratulating ourselves, I never thought twice about seeing Henry spit a mouthful of liquid out the window into the rain.

It's the details that govern our lives, particularly the details we overlook.

An action causing a reaction or the contradiction of opposites? Our savior becoming our reaper taking us not to safety but through Armageddon to Judgment.

"I'm glad I found you guys. You're right. As unbelievable as this appears, this is a big deal."

"Hey, Kenn . . . I'm not feeling . . . are you—" My sentence cut off like the bootleg cassette that I had made at the All show in Portland when the tape ended prematurely.

Outside I sensed a flash of lightning as it illuminated my closing eyelids, and somewhere farther off I heard the peal of thunder. I was warm and felt like I was pitching on gentle waves; another thunder crash and then the sensation of lightning crashing; just before the cover of oblivion I saw Kenn's father leaning over us and I heard his distorted voice reminding us of our bad decisions. I had no idea that when I next opened my eyes, Kenn and I would be confronted by a Rollins that we had never expected. Not a punk legend. Not Kenn's hero, but our jailer.

PART 2

ATMOSPHERE

Atmosphere:

A noun used to describe the air surrounding a planet;

A noun used to describe a tone, mood or feeling of a place or situation;

A unit of pressure used to measure the force of air on an object; and

A Joy Division song released on the 1980 single with
    "She's Lost Control."

8

Jailer

Am I a cynic? This is Sid on KROR 89.9 FM Monday morning at 12:43, February second. This world is becoming increasingly polarized. It's not about class or race or gender; it's about power. About control. You are either subjected to control or you wield it. The world is just a large Stanford prison experiment. We're imprisoned by our circumstance, our perceptions, or our time. Asa is onto something in her song "Jailer"— that incarcerating people makes us all prisoners. Maybe. But in my mind, you're either a prisoner or a jailer.

FCC transcript KROR 89.9 FM 02.02.2015 0043

Operator search: "Rollins" or "jail"*

Jailer? Really? Rollins? I thought that Rollins stood up against the Man; that was his trademark. He was exploited. Persecuted. Misunderstood, but still managed to be a hero. The music was important, but that was just the beginning with Rollins. He stood for something bigger. Being interned by Rollins and knowing that he might be in league with the Evil was a violent affront to all that I thought I knew. The realization of my world changing again hit me like a backhand across the cheekbone with sufficient force to knock me to the ground.

I could imagine the recoil of the force spreading through my face and causing my neck to stiffen as the other side of my face came to rest on a cold concrete floor. My eyes flickered, and I realized I was tied to a chair and had actually been knocked to the floor. A fiery sensation filled my face as the blood rushed to where Rollins had struck. As the stinging in my face spread out like the warmth of a rising sun, it dawned upon me just how much trouble Kenn and I were in.

Unfortunately, it wasn't just realization striking me, but Rollins as well, this time kicking me in the ribs. Clattering onto my back from the force of his foot, I could see abrasions on the back of his muscular hand that connected him to the violence he was inflicting upon me. These marks on his hands told a story louder than any words, marks that indicated Rollins had been busy for quite some time. Perhaps trying to be convincing. I was no longer relieved to have regained consciousness; the bliss of ignorance was being dispelled by the awareness of the pain coursing through my body.

Righting my chair for me, Rollins started talking while turning me to face Kenn. Even with blurry vision, I could see Kenn was bleeding somewhere around his mouth and was sporting welts on his face and upper arms that were starting to swell and turn an angry red. I had to assume I looked as grotesque to Kenn as he did to me.

I could vaguely hear Rollins talking, the same way you can hear someone yelling underwater, with the complete disconnection between movement and sound preventing any understanding. My ears were ringing in such a manner that they were creating a throbbing sensation that encompassed a band between my temples and the base of my skull. As difficult as hearing was, seeing was only slightly easier, so I concentrated on examining Kenn. Maybe Kenn had a card up his sleeve that I didn't know about. He always had a plan. Billy Bragg, Jerry Dammers; all the near misses we'd had, Kenn had always extricated us. But what now? How many doorways had we passed through? And yet we remained with Rollins.

With an overwhelming sense of dread, I noticed the expression of shock on Kenn's face. He was staring at Rollins, and then I noticed it, too. Rollins was shimmering and there was a telltale hologram flickering across his body. We had lost control of our plan; more interventions were required in 1984 than expected.

Rollins's words started forming more clearly in my mind, almost visually as the haze obstructing my vision began lifting. I took inventory of the room. Plain concrete floors and walls, a metal door that appeared heavy with a locking mechanism crossing it, as well as a small, opaque window. Kenn appeared to be bound to a wooden chair, like the type a schoolteacher would have, with yellow nylon rope. I could feel a coarse fabric gnawing at my wrists and my ass was numb and tension ran through my body.

Immediately adjacent to the door, a small table had a steel pitcher with paper cups and notebooks. Naked incandescent bulbs struggled to light the area that Kenn and I were seated in, but the light was quickly absorbed by the dark expanse of the room. Other sources of light illuminated a reel-to-reel recording machine and other equipment against the wall to my left. Beyond that, foreboding darkness.

Looking up from the floor, the room had seemed vast, almost endless, a combination of the darkness consuming the light and also a manifestation. Simply a projection of the enormity of our peril and the futility that I felt, coupled with a trick of light and sound that confused me. The turmoil of my captivity and physical abuse distracted me like the longing for a habit one is trying to break. As Rollins fiddled with something on the table, he said, "So you guys like music, do you? Well then, listen to this." He flipped a switch on the reel-to-reel recorder and set the wheels spinning. Noise filled the room.

Every fiber of my body ached as I looked at Kenn, and I felt bombarded with desperation at the realization that we had failed. Consequences indeed. We had tried to be heroes and now we were prisoners. As Rollins stepped back from the table, noise resounded in my ears. Noise, not music. Noise. Not simply a sound that I didn't like but noise that was the result of multiple sound sources—voices, different types of music played over one another, conversations, industrial sounds, anything that could have been recorded and then layered on top of anything else. It made no sense that Rollins was playing this, but perhaps this was some kind of torture.

Certainly Kenn and I spent hours playing Name That Tune to see who could identify a song fastest with the fewest hints. Another game that we challenged each other to over nights of pizza and beer.

But here I couldn't hear the music at all. In my mind, I could hear "Hurt," both the Nine Inch Nails and Johnny Cash versions. I could hear them playing as a roundabout, like "Row, Row, Row Your Boat." It was a sensation that was quite disagreeable.

With the noise abating, Rollins said, "Look, in a moment, I'm going to introduce you to my friend. Someone with questions for you. Specific questions." Rollins continued, "You're going to provide answers to his questions, specific answers, and then we'll be done here." It was nice that Rollins wasn't hitting us anymore, and I started feeling hopeful that Kenn and I were going to be able to survive this ordeal and cross home so that we could regroup and make another attempt to return the cassette.

My focus was oscillating through fields of view, reeling like a camera set on autofocus but unable to lock on a point to fix on. The details of the room appeared to slide across one another, accentuating my anxiety and sense of vertigo. Unable to hold my head off my chest only seemed to heighten the sense of confusion and desperation.

My attention returned to the door as the barking of its slamming shut provided a point of focus. The weight colliding with its metal frame filled the concrete room with a reverberating echo, making it seem that the room extended behind me and beyond the reach of the light, into the darkness of unseen walls. Then the sound of heavy footfalls on the bare concrete floor drew my attention to a large drain. Struggling to lift my head, I could see a pair of shiny black shoes, set in contrast to the dull gray concrete floor. And they, like Rollins, seemed to shimmer and glow. More that needed change.

"Lon, these punks should be ready to cooperate now," Rollins said. "But if not, I can help with that."

Lon? The name was familiar but I couldn't place why. I then noticed that the feet were connected to a dark suit that cloaked McCloy. Not McCloy from our childhood schoolyard horrors but the Tor Johnson–looking creature we had stumbled across before at the Talking Heads show. The Moose from The Bowery was his henchman; we were close to the bootleg again.

"Thanks, Henry. I'm sure that won't be necessary. You've been a great service to the cause, a real warrior. Helping to restore morality to music," McCloy started. Then he turned toward Kenn and me. "So, Henry tells me that you boys are interested in a certain cassette that one of my associates has." Rollins, was pacing around the room with the malice of an angry tiger. Each time he clenched his fists, I could see the muscles in his arms ripple as though water were running along them. "Maybe you boys would be kind enough to tell me why?"

Had Rollins not told McCloy about the importance of the cassette? Were we being tested? Maybe this was part of the interrogation to see if the stories matched up. "'Cause we're fans?" I replied.

"Don't tell him," Kenn breathed with a sigh. "Don't fucking tell these assholes anything."

"Oh, come on," McCloy said in a tone of mock insult. "That's not very nice. After the long drive that you've had with Hank. All the medication that we've given you to keep you both alive, the food, water, and not to mention our hospitality. Such language, your precious rock 'n' roll has dulled your vocabulary."

Long drive? I thought. That meant we weren't in Oklahoma anymore. "Where are we?" I asked with a raspy voice and more than a note of panic.

"Well, you're here." McCloy was now smiling and stretching his arms around him. "That's the only place you can be. No, you're not in Oklahoma City anymore, but that's not really important. You're at my country home, and this is your accommodation as guests. You're safe, in a manner. Perhaps not as comfortable as you'd prefer, but life can always be worse. Not to worry. Why don't you just tell us what you know about the cassette and why you tried to stop my colleague from bringing it to me."

Kenn was glaring at me, but what else could I do? So, I started answering, making things up as I went along. I lied. "It's illegal to make bootlegs. The cassette belongs to the band. We were just trying to do the right thing."

"The right thing?" McCloy sneered. "The right thing would be what we are going to do with it. We'll show the world what it is: a disingenuous attempt to rip off other unoriginal noise by a bunch of unruly, inebriated adolescents. This is an example of why rock 'n' roll is dangerous. It is crass and immoral. Worse than all of that, rock 'n' roll is boring."

"You're mistaken. The Adolescents are a different band. They broke up a couple years back. Don't worry, they'll be back." Kenn was still glaring when his head wasn't too heavy for him to prevent it from slumping forward. "Unlike you, traitor."

"What?" McCloy raised his voice, turning toward Kenn. "What did you call me?"

Kenn said nothing, his head sinking back onto his chest. He was somewhere else and unable to hear McCloy. Someplace where he could think of Rollins and the betrayal that he felt. Betrayal that caused greater suffering than the beatings we had been enduring.

Rollins grabbed and started to shake Kenn by the shoulders. "Hey, you fucking dick, Lon asked you a question."

"Traitor," Kenn said dejectedly. "Not Lon. You. You're a fucking traitor, Garfield. A fraud. A stooge. Pathetic. I'm embarrassed I ever listened to your music."

Rollins knocked Kenn to the floor again. Watching Rollins's menace fill the room was like watching a boiling pot with a tight lid. Kenn knew that calling Rollins by his given surname would be enough heat to blow the lid off the pot. Kenn's confirmation was delivered quickly as Rollins struck him again. I could see Kenn on the concrete floor, blood pouring from his face toward the drain. Before escaping to the oblivion I longed for, the blood circled the drain and lingered like a messy Rorschach blot. *Thawing beef* was the first thing I thought of. As Rollins jerked Kenn off the floor, McCloy, who was very clearly in charge, stopped him short.

"Henry!" McCloy's voice rang out as a warning. "I've been clear that I don't want to see that sort of thing here. Besides, what does he know about what we're really doing? He's useless to us."

Rollins stepped back from Kenn but held fast to his malevolent demeanor and tucked it away for later. He may have been put back on a leash, but Kenn and I were still in the same yard and nowhere near safe. McCloy, who again made it clear that his control in this room was absolute, interrupted my spiraling thoughts of violence and the harm we were facing.

"What we are going to do with the cassette is kill rock 'n' roll," McCloy stated with an inflated pride. Strutting now with a puffed chest, like a rooster in the morning, McCloy fixed his gaze beyond the walls of the room that held us.

Two thoughts competed for my attention like lingerie models running in opposite directions: *kill rock 'n' roll—that's impossible*, and *there is no way this guy is really going to start an evil monologue, is there?* I was wrong on both counts, and the naked models escaped from my view, with me barely catching a glimpse of either.

Regrettably, I knew McCloy could succeed. He *had* killed rock 'n' roll; it was dead in the future that we had traveled from. He had brought about Armageddon and left us wallowing here in judgment.

"Rock 'n' roll is evil. Rock 'n' roll is evil because it not only depicts but glorifies base acts. It's not music, it's an abomination. So-called musicians try to incite our youth by glorifying violence against police, worshiping Satan, the degradation of women, rape, illicit drug use, and alcohol abuse. Rock 'n' roll is just a waste of time, and live music is the worst form. The Replacements show back in Oklahoma City demonstrates this unequivocally. Brash, unstructured, boisterously drunk, and barely coherent in parts, this show is going to be an example of how rock 'n' roll is simply a self-indulgent outlet for the insolent. A distraction to our youth, an example of how devoid of value it really is, and when we're done with the cassette, people are going to be bored with rock 'n' roll and see it as a hoax."

I could imagine McCloy's words drifting in the air like charred pages from burning books. Smelling the acrid remains of art, standing over the corpse of freedom surveying the ruination he brought. Moving as if unshackled from my body, I could inspect the room with my mind's eye, but the fragments of McCloy's words rising on the thermal drafts were lingering in the air, creating the surreal effect of seeing the destruction of something while foreseeing its demise. Simultaneously his plan seemed outlandish and sensible. We had seen the trickle of articles that foretold the death of rock 'n' roll, and the theme that they carried was the result of what McCloy had achieved: rock 'n' roll would become irrelevant.

Somehow the value of art had been linked to its relevance, and worse, how someone with an agenda interpreted relevance. Once the assessment of what was musically relevant allowed the censorship and banning of rock 'n' roll, then punk rock would be outlawed, then hip-hop and rap. All gradually at first, and then as the confidence of the Morality in Music grew, their efforts would sweep like a raptor from an aerie and tear apart other forms of art that failed to satisfy the scrutiny of Lon and his brethren. Contemporary dance, jazz, certain sculptures, and even theories, all would be banished, devoured, and spat out like pellets from an owl.

"You resent rock 'n' roll because of what it represents," I managed to say, trying to see if Kenn was still conscious.

"No," McCloy replied, delighting that he had finally engaged someone. "I hate it because it's evil."

"Music is just expression. Evil is something that people create through actions and choices. Music can't be evil without evil people," I said, trying to mount a defense, trying to take a stand and be brave, but I felt that I was putting in a pedestrian effort. My courage, resolve, and acuity had scattered as witnesses always do once a bully has taken control.

"Rock 'n' roll music corrupts and makes people evil. I won't stand by and watch rock 'n' roll be the ruination of our youth. Not when I can take a stand and make the world a better and safer place where morality thrives," McCloy continued.

Morality? Kenn and I were being confined and beaten and McCloy was really talking about *morality*? "You're justifying your position so that it seems larger than simply a preference," I told him. "You want control; you're a parasite."

"Henry, these boys need some rest," McCloy said, ignoring my comment. "Make sure that they don't go anywhere." Then McCloy, laughing as if his own joke were the funniest thing he had heard, said, "I'll send a doctor down to make sure they've got everything they need. Say in about half an hour? Will that give you enough time to . . . well, to be persuasive?"

Rollins grunted some confirmation and McCloy closed the door behind him. I focused on the door. Kenn and I needed to get to the door—well, through the door. The door was our salvation and escape. It was through the door that we would be able to cross back home, like we had so often done. Home to safety and away from Rollins, but the door was like all of our immediate options. Closed. So I closed my eyes, hoping for a better outcome. I might not have been able to avoid the inevitable, but I didn't have to fight to remain conscious.

When my eyes reopened, Rollins was standing above me seething with rage and danger. I could see that he was saying something, but my ears were pounding with the sound of blood seeking escape, and the room was blurring again. I was losing any sense of depth or perspective, but I could see that Kenn was still tied to a chair. His head nodded down—perhaps he was unconscious—with his chin resting on his chest. He had to still be alive. Surely if he had been killed he wouldn't still be here, would he?

I was trying to remember what the obvious signs of life were when I was unexpectedly struck by an unseen force that sent me to the floor.

Cursing my distraction, I knew the beating came from Rollins; if nothing else, that should have been predictable by now.

As I gasped to breathe air that wouldn't obey, pain ripping through my body, the room began spinning again. Charges began running across nerve synapses and veins like a roller coaster, and I felt a familiar constriction in my chest and my temples felt a mounting pressure and searing heat. Between weak coughs, I managed a sigh. I was going to be OK. I knew that Kenn and I were getting ready to cross back, just as we had done so many times before. In blissful anticipation, I closed my eyes, just as I used to close my eyes with, with *her*.

Oh God, P—, *her* name still caused pain, compounding the pain and anxiety of my captivity. How *her* memory still scorched my heart. Parched with such a heat that the nerves should have been cauterized, but they were still tender and raw. Was she the start of all this? No, this was about the Evil and their attack on rock 'n' roll. The grief that was consuming me reminded me that what *she* took was a part of my soul.

I had faith that the heightening of pain meant we were finally crossing back.

Home. We'd be safe. I could use a beer and a shower. Maybe more beer and some pizza.

I opened my eyes, trying to regain focus, inhaling the waft of stale odors I've always associated with Kenn's place. Letting out a sigh of relief, I started to lift my head up, only to see Rollins approaching Kenn with a menacing stride from behind. Rollins struck Kenn between his shoulder blades with a stomping kick that propelled Kenn and his chair sprawling forward onto the cold, dirty concrete. Fuck. We hadn't crossed. The odor wasn't Kenn's basement but our dungeon. My ribs hurt and I was fighting for breath, not from crossing but because of Rollins kicking me on the floor. From where I was lying, in what must have been drying blood and urine, through partially closed eyes I could see Kenn, and it didn't appear that he was faring too well, either.

My eyes flickered open again, only for me to see Rollins returning in my direction to lift both the chair and me off the floor. With a glare, he dropped the chair, and it and I both rattled on the floor, tottering and spinning but, strangely, coming to rest on all four legs.

The room was dark, with two small lights in the center hanging from wires. I knew that this was going to be a long night. Kenn was still conscious. I could hear him groaning and stirring in his restraints. Futility started gnawing me again with the realization that I had nothing to trade Rollins for our own abused and worthless skins. Kenn and I had failed. Again.

"Surrender. It's over. You can't succeed," a voice hissed from the dark.

Resigned that there was nothing left for me to do, I started to pass out again. I wanted to go away. I wanted this to stop. Like being alone in my apartment after *she* left, I didn't want to be a hero anymore. I wished Kenn had never conscripted me into his stupid idea. I'd told him he would get us killed. I wanted to disappear completely like Radiohead had. Cue some sad song, maybe some Lou Reed or Mazzy Star, and let me fade to black.

Just before I was cloaked in total darkness and lost consciousness again, I heard Kenn call over to me in a weak, beleaguered tone. Kenn was unbowed and launched another insult at our jailer. "Dude, that song is right; Henry Rollins is no fun."

9

Henry Rollins Is No Fun

This is Sid Itious at KQOO 90.9 FM. We all have an idea of what fun is. Is it something that brings you pleasure? Makes you happy? Or just carefree and improvised? What I can tell you is that it's not first-year civics and it's not my parents.

Chixdiggit! is a Canadian band with their view of a rock legend, Here's "Henry Rollins Is No Fun."

FCC transcript KQOO 90.9 FM 09.15.1998 0203

Operator search: "Rollins" or "Adolec"*

Operator's comments: Time not stated

Henry Rollins is no fun? Really, Kenn, still with the song titles? Given the circumstances, referring to a song by a Canadian band was pretty good, even if it was understated.

With Rollins's hands clenching into fists and then relaxing by his sides, I noticed one of his tattoos. In the webbing between his forefinger and thumb was a pair of stylized musical notes, actually a pair of triplet note beams, but laid over each other to look like a pair of capital M's. A menacing symbol we had seen before during other crossings upon those wishing to curtail musical freedom. It was like the patch on Mooseman's jacket, the lapel pins of the MBs in London the night we met Jerry Dammers, and what we had seen Lon wearing before.

Here we were spending days with Rollins; rather than being a captive audience, we were merely captives. Our rock 'n' roll dream transformed into a nightmare of corporal punishment. It was like we had become trapped in Edgar Allen Poe's "Pit and the Pendulum," except we were trapped with a clinically psychotic and hyperactive Henry Rollins. The horrors of being buried alive, strapped to a barrel in a whirlpool, or mocked by a talking raven were all manageable compared with being trapped in the past with Rollins torturing us. Strangely, there was an upside. My memory of song began to return and I felt like I was trapped in the Hoodoo Gurus song "In the Echo Chamber," because after all, the night was playing out in much the same way for Kenn and me.

I dreamed of the Cult anthem "She Sells Sanctuary," and then I thought of *her* and started aching. I had thought *she* was my salvation but *she* was my ruination.

She brought me complete isolation. Before I met *her* and fell in love, I didn't understand companionship. My ignorance of love shrouded me in a blissful blanket, like a warm fog covering the base of a mountain. *She* took the beauty of our love and harvested it for her own gain, leaving me bare like a discarded forestry cut block, selfishly exploited and left in ruin.

I dreamed of hatred and justified violence. Of protesters chained to trees or spiking trees that would tear through sawmills causing ripples of fear. I wanted peace but was willing to commit to any means necessary to achieve it.

Once again, the back of Rollins's hand crashed against my cheekbone, jarring me from my dream-filled state of unconsciousness. More than just pain coursing through my body was desperation and the knowledge we had failed.

Kenn was the scientist, but I was learning empirically about Newton's laws of motion and hoping not to live to learn from the tutorial. Action: a kick. Reaction: regaining awareness of my injuries. Action: pain searing through my body. Reaction: recoiling to protect injured areas. Action: covering new injury to prevent further damage. Reaction: leaving other part of body exposed. Action: exposing part of body to attack. Reaction: Rollins punches exposed abdomen. Action: sharp, heavy force striking bruised torso. Reaction: pain searing through my body and warm liquid running down my legs.

My eyes fluttered open as my mouth flooded with a rusty, metallic-tasting blood, causing me to choke. What would the other reactions be? A broken tooth? A split cheek? A cough and then a gag as the blood entered my throat?

There would be more reactions. Fear. Fear of asphyxiation on my own blood, spit, and vomit. Fears including images created by Poe and the Hoodoo Gurus as well as those of Hendrix and Janis Joplin. *I'm going to die like a rock star but without a legacy*, I thought in desperation.

Rollins interrupted my rumination by pounding me in the stomach. *Not really helping*, I thought as the air expelled from my lungs forced out the blood that was pooling in my throat. Wheezing, I tried to thank him for saving me from choking, but my words came out as gasps that seemed to satisfy him. As the room spun slowly, I realized that McCloy wasn't with Rollins this time.

Everything possessed a different intensity now. I couldn't tell if it was something about Rollins or if it was merely that we'd been captive for so long. Dehydrated, hungry, soiled, and in need of medical attention, I assumed that Kenn must be in a similar state as well. I knew that McCloy had sent someone in to attend to us, but that seemed like a long time ago, and whatever help was administered, it did nothing to dispel the desperation that I felt from the beatings I'd received.

Struggling to regain control of my breath, I saw Rollins towering over Kenn, who had now also been shaken back to consciousness, maybe even by the sound of Rollins striking me. I could see Kenn turning to look as me just as Rollins kicked over the chair he was bound to, forcing Kenn to the floor again, unable to move.

"Hey you, dick," Rollins sneered, while snatching Kenn and the chair off the floor and brusquely righting it again, "have I got your fucking attention yet?"

"Hang on a sec," Kenn managed to answer. "I'm trying to do long division. It won't be long, just like the list of your good songs."

Belligerent as ever, Kenn was still refusing to stand down. Even though he was somehow different now, somehow less accessible to me, always trying to prove something, I had to admit that he had my complete respect at this moment. I saw Kenn's head recoil before I heard him being struck. Watching helplessly in pained horror, I held my breath as Rollins's arm completed the long arc of its follow-through past Kenn's head, which was lolling to the side and slumping forward.

"Why don't you divide that then?" Rollins shouted, seemingly getting angrier. "That's like five fingers divided by one hand or some shit. You think you're a tough guy? Tell me what I want or I'll keep beating you until you do."

Still unbowed, Kenn said, "Go ahead, Rollins. You can be the guy that heard a message from the future or be remembered like the soldier who struck Christ, the weaklings who watched as the Nazis rose to power, the cowards who watched teammates being raped by their coaches. You're the guy who parks in the handicapped spot and then goes skateboarding. Let me die a martyr; you'll be reviled forever. You live with that."

Jesus, Kenn, I thought. *Really? You're going to keep this up and antagonize this monster?* But Kenn was right. Rollins had sold out. He no longer represented a change to the status quo. Rock 'n' roll was about people who took a stand like Lemmy and Billy Bragg. History was full of people who would become leaders of men by taking a stand, just like Joey Ramone. But Rollins was no longer part of this esteemed pantheon; he had changed sides from the guy who took a stand to the guy you take a stand against.

Somewhere, even though McCloy was gone, I sensed someone else was in the room with us. From beyond the light, I felt the presence of breathing or shifting of weight during the few quiet moments between questions or beatings. Something tugged at my soul, saying *"quit and let it pass."*

My mind wandered to other heroes who had come before, some like Socrates, who in life was persecuted and maligned by all but a relative few. It was in death that the elevation of the icon occurred. I thought that this would make for an interesting discussion with Kenn and Henry but decided that this wasn't perhaps the best time to raise a new topic when Rollins continued. "Well then, Jesus would have just turned the other cheek, wouldn't he?" he asked scornfully.

"Yeah, he would," Kenn added, struggling but able to turn a fresh cheek toward Rollins. "But probably because he was used to being hit by pussies like you. Maybe we can find a kid from the local elementary school to show you how to hit like an adult."

Kenn had been hit hard before, even before our confinement by Rollins, but Rollins was an idol to Kenn, or at least had been. For Kenn, this all must have been as shocking as a bride's wedding-night discovery of her spouse possessing child pornography.

Physically you could see that the beating was having an effect on Kenn, but Rollins was getting nowhere. As another torrent of beatings rained upon Kenn, I thought Rollins was killing him. Rage was electric on his skin, muscles straining like when Bruce Banner was losing control and turning into the Hulk.

Instead of becoming a green monster, Rollins turned away from Kenn and I felt a sense of relief. Kenn was safe, at least momentarily. Unfortunately, my relief lasted only until Rollins exploded upon me like a released spring and grabbed me by the throat.

His hand closed like a vise on my neck, just below my jawline, and I could feel the air and blood being cut off. Just as I was fading out, Rollins relaxed his grip, allowing air to start seeping back into my lungs; I stole short, quick gasps. I opened my eyes and my vision desperately ranged in and out of focus, trying to resolve the image.

"What's his name?" Rollins asked. His anxiety was palpably building as he was approaching his goal. I was always fearful of Rollins; his state of heightened anxiety wasn't any prettier. Even worse when you're within an arm's reach of this reverberating bundle of nerves and he's convinced that you have information he desires.

"Ww-whhoo?" I managed to weakly gasp.

"The guy who developed the time travel. You guys were talking about it in the van. I want to know," Rollins said, finally making it clear what he wanted. This was different. With McCloy around it was about the music and morality. It was about striking a blow against rock 'n' roll. Now, here alone, Rollins had his own agenda that consisted of learning about our time travel technology. I would never be able to listen to him cover MC5's "Kick Out the Jams" the same way ever again.

As I started to speak, Rollins grabbed me, tipped my chair over backward, and hissed, "Don't give me this bull about you two shitheads inventing time travel, or some video game thing. I don't buy your shit. McCloy thinks you're both full of shit, but I can kick it out of you. I want to know who developed the ability for you to cross."

Well, finally some good news. Now we knew what Rollins was torturing us for, and all we had to do was tell him the truth that he wouldn't believe and then this nightmare would stop. Right. Fuck.

"Let me make this clear," continued Henry. "If you don't tell me the truth, I'll leave you here to die."

Leave us here? Well that was an improvement to being beaten to death, wasn't it? Well, maybe not. Certainly not as much fun as it sounded to be "held at Her Majesty the Queen's pleasure," like when we were arrested kidnapping Billy Bragg, but better than being beaten to death. As I was being precariously held on the back two legs of the chair and feeling the absolute control that my former hero had over me, terror yielded to inspiration and I asked, "If I tell you, will you let us go?"

Henry's eyes glinted and, sensing that he was close, he said, "I promise. I promise I'll let you go."

Forget the fact that Kenn and I had been kidnapped and drugged by Rollins. Forget the fact that Kenn and I had been confined for days, all in the name of morality. Forget the fact that we had been transported across state lines and tortured. Forget the track "Liar" from Rollins's album *The End of Silence*. Forget about all of this. Because I did. I forgot and then did what anyone else would do: I started to cry. "OK, OK, I'll tell you," I said, sobbing.

"Stop!" Kenn groaned, but I ignored him.

"Chuck," I said. "It's Chuck Palahniuk. He has it figured out. Palahniuk showed us how to cross. But he said there were rules; he said we couldn't talk about crossing. Not to anyone. That was the first rule. But we thought we could trust you. You're just so punk . . ." I trailed off in sobs. I could see Kenn slumped in his chair, defeated and completely spent. Rollins was at the other end of the emotional spectrum, acting like a puppy with a new playmate, unable to contain his excitement and looking around hoping to find something more to play with.

"Where is he? How do I find him?" Rollins roared, now confident that he was closing in on his quarry.

Ignoring Kenn's groaning, I continued. "We don't know . . . that's rule number two."

"Listen, you're so close here. I'll let you go . . . all you need to do is to tell me where I find this guy. I already know who he is."

My plan was animated, forming its own shape, a clattering shuttle crossing a loom, perfectly spinning my lies. "You'll have to wait," I said, which only seemed to reenergize his rage. "I mean, you'll have to find him in the future. We've come back in time, right?"

Why did Rollins want to travel through time so badly? I mean, I knew that everyone did, but not to the point of obsession or torture. Rollins's fixation seemed extreme. Thoughts were reeling through my head: fear, hunger, and pain, prospects of our survival. Wondering if we would ever cross again and if we could somehow recover the cassette that we had failed to acquire at the Bowery.

Through the haze of my jumble of emotions, I thought about Billy Bragg. How calm he seemed when we took him to listen to the music in Park Royal. I felt shame not only realizing that he had retained his composure, but also that he might have felt the same terror at our hands that Kenn and I were feeling at Rollins's. Surely, this must have been different for him. Kenn and I weren't torturing him, just trying to show him what was right. What we were doing was important, and for the greater good. By contrast, Rollins just seemed to be in a rage, driven by some unseen demon. Maybe it was multiple demons with Rollins. Fuck, that was a vision: Rollins and demons occupying the same body. No thanks.

"How. Do. I. Find. Him!" Rollins roared, emphasizing every word, drawing me back to the reality of my captivity. I could still feel Rollins leaning my chair backward, tipping me so I could feel the precariousness of my situation. The sensation of weightlessness contrasting with his hands like granite clenched like a vise on my soiled shirt. "I'll let you guys go as soon as I have what I need."

"Oregon," I said. "The guy's a scientist who lives in Portland, but he publishes fiction under the pen name Chuck Palahniuk, that's how we know him. You can't find him yet. You'll have to wait for him to publish *Rant* first. That's when he learned how to do it. Please . . . please," I continued pleading. "That's how we found him. You said you'd let us go."

"Right." Henry grinned. "Thanks, that wasn't so bad, was it?" To this day, I still hate rhetorical questions. "OK, you want me to let you go?"

I started to nod weakly, sobbing, confirming that I wanted nothing more than to escape and be safe. For Kenn and me to go somewhere and hide. Eat something. Get medical attention and be alone with my feelings of embarrassment at our failure. Then I saw it. It was there in Henry's eye, a glint, along with the sly grin, the sign that trouble hadn't left the building. A hint or an inside joke that was amusing Rollins, something that told me we were still in trouble.

"OK," Rollins conceded, holding his hands up in front of himself. "A deal's a deal."

Rollins let me go and laughed. I was still tied to a chair that was leaning backward, and I fell for what seemed like an hour, while Rollins, roaring in laughter, slapped the front of his thigh. As I hit the cold, wet, concrete floor I could feel something break but couldn't tell if it was the chair or one of my bones. Maybe it was just my spirit. Shame, embarrassment, and pain washed over me again as urine soaked my pants and Rollins walked away. Slowly, hope that the menace was receding crept in and I tried to call out to Kenn, but sound barely escaped my parched lips.

As Rollins was stomping away, I thought I could hear the fall of hooves on hard ground. Perhaps the approaching Riders of the Apocalypse were coming to claim the ruin that Kenn and I had failed to prevent. I passed out, hallucinating about the old Western *The Magnificent Seven*, with Yul Brynner and Steve McQueen coming to our rescue.

10

The Magnificent Seven

Do you ever think about numbers? I'm really not very good with them. I'm weak at math, dreadful at science. Really, I can barely remember numbers, and yet they're important. Important in terms of symbols, or symmetry—even or odd, positive or negative. People have favorite numbers.

Numbers also aren't open to interpretation like words or colors. We know what 12362 is, but what's "meadow green"? Even colors defined by numbers make more sense like a television projecting light through a range of 255 shades of red, blue, or green. Combinations creating millions of discrete colors.

One is the loneliest number. Feist counts to four; Hendrix asks if six was nine.

This is KQRL Riverside 89.9 FM at 3:44 in the morning. The next number we're hearing is from the Clash. Here's "The Magnificent Seven."

FCC transcript KQRL 89.9 FM 02.22.2007 0344

The Magnificent Seven, heroes as tough and unflinching as the desert sun. In the movie, they were a motley crew of heroes assembled to defend Mexican peasants. Seven individual reasons, seven separate motivations; all inspired by a single purpose. The Magnificent Seven assembled to take a stand against wrongs in the world. I dreamed of being such a hero. Later I prayed they would descend upon Rollins, rescuing us and saving rock 'n' roll as we rode off into the sunset with smoke rising and the report of guns in the background. The dream looped like a maniacal eight-track and always ended with Kenn and me at the end of a rope, like in *The Good, the Bad, and the Ugly*. I wanted to sleep, to dream, but I also wanted the nightmare to end, to turn aside my outrageous fortune. I wanted someone, Kenn, anyone, even *her* to save me, to shoot the noose down so that I could just fall safely to the ground, even if into an open grave. Even the prospect of a fresh grave offered a welcoming sanctuary.

Light flickered throughout the room, telling me that I was still alive and regaining consciousness. As the restraints on my hands and feet came loose, I could feel the blood rushing into the previously isolated extremities, causing my arms and legs to ache. But the light wasn't flickering at all; rather my eyes were articulating like rusty shutters, letting in light and details of the room that would in turn register in my clouded brain. My arms were stiff, my tongue felt like a deflated balloon in a dirty ashtray, the pain was so absolute, it was as though I had been marinated in agony.

Where was Rollins? McCloy? I didn't see either of our tormentors, but now there was a figure moving cautiously through the room. What fresh hell was being visited upon us now? How was Kenn?

Slowly, as my eyes began to focus and the spinning of the room slowed like the last revolution of a carousel, my attention rested upon a curious-looking man. He was crouching, alternately studying Kenn and me with an invasive inquisitiveness. Our new examiner had a boyish look about him, despite his obvious years, yet his sandy hair was kept in a dated style reminiscent of either Phil Donahue or Lassie. But I guess we were still in—when? Nineteen eighty-four? Right. It was difficult to keep the references and styles straight.

I thought I could hear Kenn breathing, or coughing. I tried to focus my blurred vision. Eventually I could see that he, too, was still bound to a chair and helpless as this curious boyish man examined him. I tried to call out to Kenn but my voice failed me as though it had been stolen or

I had forgotten how to speak. Had we told Rollins too much? How had he known to be there? Was it Kenn's fault? He was so enthralled with the idea of being in the van with Rollins, drinking beer, racing through the night in the rain. There was always something with Kenn and his conspiracies.

No. This had started long before that. Kenn had rescued me from my post-Harpy trauma. He had shown me that rock 'n' roll had died and that the past had been stolen by the present, proving that things that were wrong needed to be undone. Kenn and I were in this together and we had failed. But why? Hadn't we meticulously planned the retrieval mission? Hadn't we known how it was going to end and what needed to be done? Hadn't we learned from our past?

As my eyes awoke, the peculiar-looking man was now face-to-face with me, stirring a silent giggle in my brain. This funny man-boy with his wire-framed glasses, denim pants, and plaid shirt showing under a corduroy vest occupied my mind, imploring me to answer his questions. But my mouth was dumb to sound and my words drifted into the air as silently as floating ash.

"Can you get up?" he asked in a soft yet firm, or maybe confident, tone. "I'm here to help you get out, but we need to hurry." I recoiled instinctively, as though he had struck me, and my giggle turned to a scream. "No, it's OK. It's OK," boy-man said, holding his hands up plaintively. "You're safe now. No one will hurt you."

Right. We'd been drugged, kidnapped, interrogated, and beaten, and now this Boy Scout gone country-looking joker was going to save the day—like maybe he'd sing about some dumb country road to take us home. "I cuuld uthz thome water, but I tthhink I'm ollwyythe. K-k-kenn?" I replied.

"OK, stand up and get your circulation back," our gracious savior said, helping both Kenn and me up and then handing us each a bottle of water. "I'm John Denver. You guys are safe now, but we've got to get that cassette back."

I glanced over at Kenn with a look of suspicion and shock. I mouthed

"John Denver?" in disbelief. Kenn fell back into the chair, and I thought I was going to as well. Clearly, whatever drugs Rollins gave us were still playing havoc on our systems. John Denver? Never.

My head was clearing, but I still felt stunned. We had been in the wrong time for longer than any other time we had crossed, and it was probably heightening my confusion. I was still suspicious and rightfully so. We had thought that Rollins was one of the good guys, and look how well that turned out. So now, John Denver of all people wanted to help us to recover a cassette from a Replacements gig? He probably thought that bootlegs were a new cuff style for his slacks.

"Where are we?" I asked, a question that had been bothering me for a while.

Denver looked surprised. "You're at a ranch owned by McCloy. How did you get here?"

"Rollins," Kenn said, as though the name tasted like an anchovy that had been surreptitiously placed onto a pizza.

"Henry Rollins from Black Flag?" Denver asked, seeming both surprised and impressed.

"Yeah," I answered, as I saw Kenn look away, decidedly defeated and hurt. I had only seen him like this around his parents, and that had been a while ago. "We couldn't believe it. He said he was there to help, and he had a van and it seemed like it was all going to work out. He said—" My speech was accelerating with each word. "Then he gave us a drugged beer. You know, we thought we could trust him. We thought he stood for the same things that we did. But then . . ." I trailed off just looking at the injuries that Kenn and I wore.

"Rollins. Hmm. I suppose that explains why he . . ." He left his comment incomplete. "What van? Can you guys walk? Tell me on the way. I want to get you guys some medical attention and get back to the city."

"How . . . why are you here?" I asked. "How . . . were you looking for us?" My confusion was cascading on itself. While I wasn't going to fuss over who was saving us, I had simply assumed that no one knew who we were or what we had been up to. Clearly, this was yet something else that I had been wrong about. "What city? McCloy said something about a country home. Are we still in Oklahoma?"

"So, really, how are you involved in this, Mr. Denver?" Kenn asked, being careful to be as respectful as possible to our most improbable liberator.

"Look, you're in California, outside of San Francisco. Chilton called me and told me what you guys were up to," he started.

"You mean Alex Chilton? You know Alex Chilton?" Kenn interrupted, appearing increasingly confused by the moment. Chilton was a singer, songwriter, guitarist, and producer of vast influence. As far as his personal musical efforts went, he had a relatively obscure indie career, carried by small labels. Despite the lack of commercial success, Alex Chilton drew a loyal following in the indie and alternative music fields, a fact represented by how often he was cited as an influence by many mainstream rock artists and bands. I was thrilled at the mention of his name as detailed memories started sprouting to spring buds with promise of new growth.

Bands that he produced included the Cramps, and because of this influence Chilton was the subject of the Replacements song bearing his name on the 1987 album *Pleased to Meet Me*, an album that, despite my recollection, would now not be recorded; an album on which Chilton was to be a guest musician, playing guitar on the song "Can't Hardly Wait." Without that influence, as Kenn and I had witnessed, the fabric of rock 'n' roll history would unravel like a loose hem.

"Alex? Sure, I mean it's not like we collaborate directly, musically, but we have lunch from time to time. He was supposed to be meeting us, but his plans have changed, making him unavailable, but all the same, we're unified in the cause," Denver replied as though he were merely explaining the difference between E major and E7 on his guitar.

He continued, "As it turns out, MacLeslie realized that he hadn't recovered the bootleg tape and also that somehow you guys were involved. Later he was talking to Alex about what a drag it was and how these things were ruining live music, but then also how to produce them if a good one was ever found. Alex and I are convinced that a good bootleg of a decent show would change the face of rock 'n' roll forever. A recording so poignant that it holds up music above other forms art. Live recordings have that potential, especially when recorded surreptitiously and not subjected to post-production treatment. More to the point, Alex thinks this could be that recording."

Kenn and I were nodding by this time. For anyone watching us, it would look like we were agreeing, rather than trying to comprehend what we were hearing. *Yeah, we knew. We really knew what the consequences of not getting that cassette to MacLeslie would be.*

I gave Denver the short version of what had happened, but without the time travel parts that we had told Rollins, about how we had seen McCloy's minion making an illicit recording of the show and what McCloy had said his plans were for the cassette.

"Alex," Kenn echoed wearily. It might have been the sedatives, or it might have been the beating he took, or the days of confinement, but Kenn did not seem to be coping with John Denver rescuing us, knowing Alex Chilton and Denver were pals, or the speed at which this was all happening.

"OK," Denver continued. "We've got to get going and meet up with the rest of the team."

Questions were exploding in my mind like flashbulbs catching Britney Spears getting out of a limo wearing a short dress. But Denver was right. We had to get going. "But, John, we came for the cassette. We should get it," I stated.

"Well, if I understand things correctly, you were chasing a tape, but you were brought here," he replied. "I figured that McCloy was the only guy with enough influence and motivation to carry off what Alex had been describing, and so it all sort of led me here to his ranch. He's got another place in town."

"Yeah, that was part of the plan," interjected Kenn, a little too quickly. "We were hoping Alex or you would get involved."

Ever gracious, Denver soothed us. "Of course, that was your plan. We expected you'd be brave enough to try a direct assault on the Evil, but the plans have changed, boys, and we've got to go. Look, Alex and I have a plan; we just have to leave here and regroup."

"But what's your part in this, John?" Kenn asked. "Why are you involved?"

"We are a human family; we have to look out for one another. The organized political process of this country is disgusting." Kenn and I looked at each other in disbelief. "The kind of money that is spent on campaigns displacing the rights of Americans is unacceptable."

"Uh, OK, but why are you here helping us, Mr. Denver?" Kenn asked with shock in his voice.

"Seriously," Denver said, turning to me, "is this guy an idiot?"

"Well, his marks in school were worse that Einstein's," I replied, ignoring Kenn's incendiary glare. "But in fairness, we've had a lot going on," I added.

Sure, I was making amends to Kenn. Of course I was, even if he had been a perpetual pain in my ass. Even if he reminded me of his superior scientific understanding, he was still my friend. My only friend, and had been for years. The humiliation, physical beating, and devastating disappointment that he experienced at the hands of one of his heroes had been unbearable for me to watch. Even worse was imagining how he felt.

"OK, fair enough," Denver conceded. "Let's go. We can talk more in the car."

As we quietly exited the stately ranch house that had served as our prison, there was a disarray of broken furniture, unconscious guards—some savagely beaten—and a general state of destruction and ruin. It was as though a tornado had run through an indoor trailer park.

"Did you do all of this yourself?" I asked.

"Well, I've had some training," Denver humbly replied. "You know, outside of music, and I have a lot of faith. It all helps."

"Jesus, fuck," I whispered to Kenn, shocked. "This guy is a fuckin' badass. He doesn't have as much as a hair out of place, and his silly-looking vest isn't even creased. And he's saying he's got *faith*."

"Yeah, it's always the quiet ones . . ." Kenn trailed off with a mix of trepidation, respect, and awe.

Outside there was a beat-up old pickup truck parked on the gravel pad, and we started running toward it. As Kenn opened the door to get in, Denver asked, "Kenneth, what are you doing?" Denver was sliding through the opened door of a sleek, shiny red Audi 5000s, with performance tires, tinted windows, and lowered suspension. The plate read "RKY MT HI."

Kenn and I stared at each other in shock as much as in surprise. Another example of how strange is only what you're not used to. I had only been able to picture John Denver in a pickup truck or an airplane, as fateful as that may be. Maybe I was still hallucinating, but maybe it was just the adrenaline that seemed to be allowing Kenn and me to overcome our rather worse-for-wear conditions to actually engage with Denver.

I tumbled into the backseat as an expedient to prevent some type of tirade or other infantile scene with Kenn. As Denver fired the engine, the dashboard lit up with controls and lights that I imagined worthy of a fighter jet. As I was staring in fascination at the interior of the car, he started to accelerate the automotive luxury that now was our sanctuary toward the open road. "Put your seat belt on, boy. I don't ride with anybody 'less they wear their seat belt. It's one of my rules."

"Hey, that's really good. That's Sy Richardson's character from the *Repo Man* movie," Kenn complimented, more impressed with every passing moment. "Is this really your car?" he asked in awe.

"Is your buddy really this thick?" asked an incredulous Denver. "I mean, seriously, didn't you see the plates? Do you think I borrowed this from Elton John and he's a 'Rocky Mountain High' fan?"

"Well, you know," I responded, trying to save some face for Kenn, "it's just this seems like a lot of car. I've probably only seen a couple, mostly in magazines," I lied. I had never seen this car. Fuck, James Bond hadn't seen this car. "Look, we don't mean to be disrespectful, but we're not really car guys."

"Yeah, well," a humble Denver said. "I've got some contacts, and it's sort of a special edition."

Yeah, like double-O special edition issued by "Q" sort of contacts, I thought. But the conversation had passed that point, and Denver continued accelerating away from the ranch. As he quietly brought the car to an improbable speed that seemed like we were orbiting and deftly handled it through a series of corners, along winding backroads, and local highways, a disquieted silence overtook me and I drifted in introspection, trying to heal and sleep.

My eyes flickered in the nether regions between degrees of lucidity, awareness, and unconsciousness. After a while, Denver slowed the Audi to a speed that was in line with the other traffic, if not the actual speed limit, as we gained access to Interstate 80.

Denver dialed his hands-free phone, which appeared more modern than I remembered for 1984. After two rings, the phone was answered, "Yo, dis is Luke wit' 2 Live Crew. Git' speakin' befo' I gots ta smack d' taste outta yo' fuckin' mowt."

"Luther, this is John Denver, and I'm here on speakerphone with a couple of colleagues. I'm driving."

"Oh, ahh . . . oh, sorry, I . . . Mr. Denver." You could hear the scrambled panic on the other end of the conversation. "I'm sorry, me and my missus . . . I mean my missus and I . . . and I mean she's a person and not really mine, but her and me . . . I mean—"

"Luther, it's OK. Look, I'm rather busy," interrupted Denver. "I'd really prefer you refrain from such nasty language. It reflects poorly on you, is a weak form of expression, and frankly is bad for your esteem."

"Yes, Mr. Denver. I just didn't knowed it was you callin', and you know I've got a certain image that I need to perpetuate," Luther/Luke Skyywalker replied, straining to sound more like he had been educated in a British grammar school, rather than schooled in Ebonics.

"Sure, Luther, I understand, but I can't say that I agree," replied a calm but stern Denver. "Look, I need a favor."

"You know I'm your nigg—I mean, Mr. Denver, you know I is always happy to help you. As always it's a privilege to be axed," said the suddenly demure musician. It was an interesting transformation for the producer from 2 Live Crew; he was the front man for a notoriously offensive hip-hop band but also in many ways a champion of freedom of speech and other musicians.

"I need a couple of guys to help me with a recovery operation in the Bay Area. Steady guys who can be trusted and who can carry themselves, on short notice. "

"Mr. Denver, you know I wish I could be there for ya', but . . . you know I've got this thing in Tamp—this thing in Miami, yeah Miami," he lied. Even over the telephone, you could tell that Luke felt that whatever Denver had on his mind was likely out of his league. I have to say, after seeing the carnage that he left in his wake liberating us, I didn't blame Luke, or anyone else for that matter.

Luther continued, "But you know I should be done in like seven or maybe eight days, and then I could jet on out. Would that be soon enough?" he asked.

"Hey, I know you would be . . . Luther, you've always been great, but I need someone who can get to their feet in hours, not weeks," Denver said, impressively stringing a graciously worded but stinging response.

"Right. Sorry, Mr. Denver," Luther said with a mix of relief and shame. "Do you know Anthony Kiedis and Flea from the Red Hot Chili Peppers?"

"No. I've never heard of them. Can they be trusted? This could be tough going. We might get wet."

There's the falling shoe, I thought. *Tough going* and *get wet*. I was pretty sure that Kenn and I had already had enough adventure to go beyond our capacity. This didn't sound like the conversation was about an afternoon on waterslides. No, and if now, after going "B-grade action movie" on our captors, Denver was describing something as "tough going," hopefully the team wouldn't include me.

Feeling the adrenaline draining from me, I looked over at Kenn. He was soft in the shoulders and wore his fatigue like an ill-fitting suit. My body rested, falling into a relaxed state only to be disturbed by spasms of pain and tension jarring my injuries. I could feel the relief of my rescue but failed to enjoy it. I closed my eyes and slid in and out of a sleep disturbed by visions of retreating horsemen. My instincts told me to resist, but I simply couldn't, and soon I slipped into tormented dreams and memories, vaguely hearing Denver's conversation in the background.

"Yeah, they're good. They've got a good act. It might take a while for it to take off, but they'll make it. In terms of your gig, these guys surf when they're not jamming, they're always up for a dare, and they're super fit and as cool as ice. I'd trust these guys," Luther represented.

"OK, how do I contact them?"

"Look, I'll have them call you. They're from L.A. but they're at Stanford this week for a couple of gigs. Leave it with me, Mr. Denver."

"Thanks, Luther. I won't tell anyone that you're a good guy." John signed off.

"My pleas—" as the line went dead.

Without anything other than tormented memories to molest my desired serenity, I slept as the sedan darted along the highways to wherever it was that Denver was whisking us away to. As we entered San Francisco, I sat up and shook my head, failing to marvel at the fiery red sun falling into the Pacific Ocean. I've always loved San Fran for the adventure it promises, the memories it hosts, and its constant enticements, but that night my reaction was different. I felt cold, and rather than appreciating the amber hues of the sunset, all I saw was that the light was casting long shadows, transforming the city into an energetic but foreboding place. My pulse quickened and injuries ached. We were near the Evil, and malice was burning within my soul.

As we entered a well-maintained but seemingly empty warehouse in the Presidio, Denver slowed down and killed the engine. "There'll be sandwiches and drinks on the table by that wall," he instructed. "Beyond the table are the showers and toilets; you'll see the door. Clean up now if you'd like, or wait until you've eaten. The others will be here soon, but I'll make sure the doctor sees to you immediately."

True to his word, food was set out and a doctor tended to our wounds, provided ice compresses and some type of saline-based intravenous liquid that cleared my head and settled my nerves. At the end of our treatments, Kenn and I were encased in a warm, soothing, pliable wax that smelled of lavender while we lay on cots, under thick woolen blankets. Quickly I slipped into a sleep, this time deeper and without my eyes flickering—just a falling sensation, falling through warm water. Falling, like I had when *she* left me, but this time I felt calm, knowing someone was there to catch me.

Waking from my deep but haunted sleep, I looked around the room that was dark beyond the immediate cones of illumination offered by hanging lights. I was on a low, military-style cot. Kenn was about five feet away from me, being attended to by a doctor. There was a makeshift canvas partition separating us from the rest of the warehouse, and there appeared to be a collection of monitoring equipment.

Finishing with Kenn and seeing that I was moving, the doctor came over to me, examined me for a few moments, muttered something, and removed the IV, saying, "You'll hurt for a while, but you and your friend will be fine." With that, he instructed a nurse or an assistant to remove my fragrant casing and to ensure we had showers, then walked off, leaving Kenn and me alone.

I would "hurt for a while"? It was true, and yet, graciously, the raw pain that once set off an electrical storm of activity when I was touched was yielding to the dull ache of healing.

The contrasts in life had never been more stark for me. I felt safe in the protection of Denver, but vulnerable and defeated because of McCloy holding the fate of our future. Even the water in the shower felt like thousands of glass shards descending upon my injured body like some Dante-esque torment. At the same time, the warmth and steam releasing lavender from my pores cleared my senses.

After we were dressed, Kenn and I were faced with a sensation that could only be described as strange, as we sat on the cots across from each other, each looking over the marks of the beatings that remained on the other's face. Kenn must have been feeling better, because after a few moments of silently regarding me, he just shrugged, rose to his feet, and started walking toward Denver's voice.

Somewhere off behind the distinctive voice that I knew to be Denver's, I could smell something. A nearly palpable aroma of idyllic America: of cooking dough, fried meat, and something sweet. Like Pavlovian dogs, we filled up our senses.

Without any regard for where he was going, I followed Kenn. I wanted to know what Denver had in mind, I wanted to go home, and I wanted more sandwiches. But mostly, I didn't want to be alone.

"Good. You guys are up again. I spoke to the doctor; he said you'll be OK in a bit of time. Make sure you drink lots of water and get something to eat. The sun's coming up and I've got cakes on the griddle. There's some bacon, too," Denver said, directing us back toward a table that was laden with hotcakes, Canadian bacon (yes, there was something that I did in fact love about Canada), juice, and fresh fruit. Life really was a funny riddle.

"Thank God, he's a country boy," I whispered to Kenn.

As we ravenously gulped down the pancakes, juice, and anything else that we could grab and shovel, Kenn nudged me with his elbow, alerting me to a newcomer. I saw a figure approaching us, dressed all in black, probably over six feet tall, but with rounded shoulders and a bit of a slouch. Not lazy, but as though he held an unseen burden that he couldn't retire. The man wasn't slight, but neither was he heavy; his black dress and somber visage made it difficult to judge. His voice was deep, measured with a touch of a southern accent. "Hellooo, I'm Johnny Cash," he said, introducing himself. "I understand that you'd like some help."

Before we could recover from our shock, other people started arriving as well. A couple of sinewy surfer-looking guys that Kenn and I knew to be Anthony Kiedis and Flea from the Red Hot Chili Peppers. Punk rock incarnate, although this was before they became a main attraction band. Still, the band was making a name for itself based on its originality and unbridled energy, especially live. Knowing the sort of live act that they would be thirty years into a future where rock 'n' roll hadn't died, Kenn and I were thrilled to see these guys in their raw youthfulness and relieved to have them on our team.

At last, from the dark edges of the warehouse emerged a figure whose presence was as vaporous and cool as the fog rolling off the San Francisco Bay. His swaggering gait was loose and powerful and he was looking from side to side, in a suspicious yet confident vigil. Like still river waters glistening in the night, waters that you know intuitively hide dangers that run deep below the surface. The man was wearing a black bomber jacket and dark, military-style pants, and glints of a gold rope chain were barely noticeable around his neck. As he neared, he nodded and made an audible yet incomprehensible acknowledgement. Everyone seemed to know who he was and welcomed him with guarded caution as you would any dangerous man, even if he was a friend. Ice-T, the Original Gangster.

"Thank you for joining us, Terrance," Denver started.

"Yo, you listen th' fuck up," Ice-T hissed. "You axed me to help you, so this is like a favor that I'm doin' fo' you. So you can respect me; call me by my motherfuckin' name. Yous can call me T, Ice-T, Ice, or Ice Motherfuckin' T, got it? Who da fuck is Terrance, my mother, and only my fuckin' mother calls me Tracy, where da fuck do yous git Terrance? I'm Ice-T. Unless of course yous don't think a brother is free to change his name. And if dat's so, I'd like to see ya try servin' dat shit to Ali."

Clearly taken aback, losing his composure for the first time since our rescue, Denver stammered, "Ah, OK, Sorry, I thought Tracy was. . ."

"Was wot? A girl name? Shit."

"No, yes, I mean I'm sorry, Mr. T."

"Whaa'? Does dis look like the fuckin' A-Team? I ain't no Mr. Fuckin' T, motherfucker. I'm Ice fuckin' T. Is it really that fuckin' complicated? Or should I jez go?"

"Sorry," Denver said, trying to recover. "Look, I'm sorry, Ice-T." The mere articulation of the name sounded awkward in his mouth. "I want . . . we need your help with this, but I'm uncomfortable with profanity. You know it's really just poor expression and lacks both creativity and clarity."

"*Creativity and clarity*?" asked Ice-T. "Are yous fuckin' kiddin' me? I didn't go to no fuckin' private school. My school was the street. Creativity was stayin' the fuck alive and gettin' paid by motherfuckers. I din't grow up wit' no motherfuckin' grandma's featherbed bullshit. My life was fuckin' hard. Dat clear enough?"

"Look," a cooler-headed Johnny Cash cut in, "we're all in this together if we're in this at all. You know, John, Ice-T is right; we all have different experiences and come from difference places. But you know, Ice," he continued, "John's right, too. It's not where we're from that's important, but where we're going. Finding ourselves here, we've got bigger problems. Fellas, we're at a real crossroads where we got to stand firm and do what's right. Because I tell you, if we don't stand tall, the Evil will win and we'll all fall together. But if we're going to work together, we have to take a moment and try to understand one another."

"Yeah, well a'rite," Ice-T said, backing down ever so slightly, "but if he tries dat bullshit on me again, I gonna smack the taste—"

Cash cut in again. "Fair enough, but you let me know first, OK? I won't put money down on either of you, but I sure wanna be in the room to see the dust kick up. You know, Denver is more than meets the eye, and—well, let's just say any scrap between you two, well, it'd be better than anything recent with Larry Holmes."

Laughing a short chuckle, Ice-T responded, "Well, dat's da truth. Larry. . . shit."

While the bristling anxiety and tension started dissipating through the room, Kenn and I looked around at the musicians and wondered how it was that such a group had been gathered.

"I still don't understand how this all fits together," said Kenn. "I mean, what difference does it make to you if the Replacements make music or not? Why is it this stand that determines if rock 'n' roll will continue or fall?"

"Look, guys," Denver started, "censorship affects us all." Turning directly to Ice-T, Kiedis, and Flea, he continued. "Sure, I'm not familiar with your forms of expression, or even your music itself. In fact, I only really know Johnny Cash's work, and while it rarely speaks to me, that's not the issue. But censorship? It silences the human spirit; it can't be tolerated. To me it doesn't matter if someone is cutting off or covering the naked genitalia of a sculpture, banning music, or burning books. It's all an abomination to humanity and an affront to the freedoms that are protected by our Constitution. Threats to music are threats to us all, regardless of where we come from or where we're going."

The room was silent, except for the soft noise of angry men shifting their feet on a concrete floor and the buzzing of overhead lights. Nothing disturbed Denver's monologue.

"When people link my lyrics, like 'Rocky Mountain High' to drug use, I get very cross. Censorship forced upon a people can't be accepted in a democratic society." Denver shook his head and then just stared at his shoes. Probably in the quiet contemplation of songs being banned.

"Cross?" Ice-T asked. He became quiet upon noticing the glare from Johnny Cash, a combined warning and a suggestion that respect was due.

Kiedis gave a playful, backhanded slap to Flea's shoulder and sort of bounced on the balls of his feet. "Look, we're just happy to help. This is awesome. The Replacements are a big deal; you've got to respect the artistry. Let's get going with this. You guys said that this all went down at The Bowery? We totally want to play there; it's supposed to be happening."

"Yeah, like, we're actually planning to do that this year," Flea chimed in.

I caught myself smiling. There it was, the inextinguishable energy and enthusiasm that the Red Hot Chili Peppers were known for. The very same energy that made their concerts a spectacle, possessing an awesome energy that could carry a major event without their instruments even plugged in. The sort of awesome that was both the slacked-jaw stoned surfer awesome and also the genuine dictionary definition of the word.

We were in good company. There was John Denver organizing and leading a team that included Ice-T, Johnny Cash, Anthony Kiedis, Flea, Kenn, and me. Looking around the room, Kenn smiled and elbowed me. "Hey, look, we're the Magnificent Seven."

It was true. Kenn and I had to be considered magnificent for our time travel discovery and general rock 'n' roll heroism, but the rest of our number was rock 'n' roll royalty. Well, I suppose it was Denver's rescue, and the fact that he organized the group represented his contribution. But the rest. Wow, the rest indeed would become legendary.

Denver turned and smiled. "Yeah, you're right, Kenneth. Like the Western with Yul Brynner or like the Clash song? You said that Rollins is involved in this? Well, we're going where eagles dare."

11

Where Eagles Dare

A lot has been made of being daring. We hear comments such as "He who dares wins" or that "Daring wins the day," but that's only part of the story. There is also commentary on "living to fight another day" or Shakespeare's "The better part of valor is discretion." So, what is it? Daring or judgment?

You have to dare to win, but a dead victor won't enjoy the spoils. Daredevils are notoriously quickly spent, like lit magnesium. Spectacular, but then reduced to memory. Like the Misfits song, never lasting long but leaving an impression by being daring. Whadda ya know? The Misfits is what we've got up next.

FCC transcript KQOO 90.9 FM 09.05.1996 0153
Operator Search: "Eagle" + "Subversive"

"'Where Eagles Dare'? That's a Misfits song," Kenn proclaimed.

Denver looked at him and replied, "Kenneth, I'm pretty sure it was Black Flag, with Rollins."

"I'm postive it was the Misfits," Kenn said, seeming to think that at this very moment, in this very place, and in light of everything that had happened, a key priority for us was to correct John Denver. At that moment, Kenn had no regard for our rescue or salvation. No consideration for the medical treatment and sustenance graciously offered and voraciously consumed. No, the only thing that occurred to Kenn was that he knew more about music than anyone else. *There's always something with Kenn*, I thought as I stood there in the bad kind of awe of him.

Denver's look said more than his words, but then he said, "OK, but Rollins made guest appearances with them, right? Weren't there various collaborations with Danzig and Rollins? And really, you knew what I meant, didn't you? Shall we get to business, or do you want to stand around and nitpick? If you're not finished eating, grab a plate and something to drink and head over to that storage container," Denver concluded, pointing to a large rectangular structure that extended into the shadows across the floor from us.

"Iron Maiden has a song called 'Where Eagles Dare' they released last year," Kiedis offered.

"Yeah, that's right." Flea was pacing while studying his hand as though he were holding something. "*Piece of Mind* is the album. Has anyone heard it? Maybe we should, you know, there could be something there we could incorporate. . ."

"Gentlemen, perhaps we could return to our task and leave the etymological discussion of my metaphor." Denver's tone seemed more patient than he appeared.

Both Kenn and I quickly, and submissively, conceded the insignificance of the point in rushed, quiet tones. I could feel the heat of Kenn's cheeks as his complexion flushed as though he had been discovered with a dirty magazine—you know, something with N'SYNC on the cover, like *Teen Idol*.

Denver led our new assembly over to the large, pale blue, rectangular container, which looked like it could be either the back of a truck or a boxcar on a train. Along an end, there were two doors that had an overlapping hinge, a large lever, and a small keypad the size of an eight-track tape cartridge.

John Denver's keystrokes generated a series of beeps and then a hiss as he threw his weight into moving the left door's lever. The mass of the door seemed significant, requiring John to jerk his arms toward himself while leaning back, using both his strength and his body weight to open the door wide enough to allow us access inside. As we stepped into the container, overhead fluorescent lights flickered to life, revealing the contents elaborately secured to the walls and in large portable containers.

Revealing guns. More guns. And even more guns. Metal boxes painted military green with yellow-stenciled words like "Small Arms Ammunition .50 cal. Belt. No Tracer," "50 count fragmentation hand grenades," and "9 mm magazines. 30 rounds. 1000 count." Words understood without knowing their precise meaning.

Guns seeming to come in every shape and size. I'm still not sure what I was expecting, but I never could have guessed that I was going to walk into some type of guns and ammo nirvana. "Storage container?" I whispered to Kenn. "This is a kennel for dogs of war."

"Small arms"? Kenn commented, reading aloud from one of the boxes that claimed to have something called .50 cal ammunition in it. "Why not large arms, like Uzis or bazookas? This is a serious problem. Rollins and McCloy aren't joking around. We're going to need *huge weapons*, not small arms." Kenn was sounding dismissive and putting on airs again, waving his arms to show how big the guns were that we needed. Obviously, he was feeling better.

I was about to echo his bravado, eager to demonstrate my virility as well, when Ice-T interjected, "Is yous fuckin' serious? Large arms? You keep coming wit' dat weak-ass shit and I'm gonna peel your cap back myself."

Ice-T's comments hit us like a Taser, immobilizing Kenn and me in a state of confused shock.

Stepping forward, Denver said gently, "Small arms consist of weapons below a certain caliber. Generally used by infantry units. By contrast, large armaments are deployed by aircraft or other mechanized military vehicles. The Uzi automatic that you may prefer," he continued, "utilizes a nine-millimeter round, which is still only two-thirds the size of the fifty-caliber. And the fifty-cal is considered a light machine and the top of the small arms class of firearm."

As the explanation continued, Kenn's head hung like an old tire swing in a field full of thistles, fastened with rope that had been bleached, frayed, and long, long since forgotten by the children that it had once provided so much joy to.

Cash showed us further compassion. "You boys have been turning the other cheek for a while, like our good Lord taught. There's plenty worse things than not knowing your way around a firearm. Stay close to one of us and we'll all be just fine."

I could feel embarrassment for Kenn flushing my face as hot as when Rollins had hit me; my heart broke as though *that girl* had once again left me. "Yeah, well, it's not going to matter," I said. "When I catch up with Rollins, I'll be using my bare hands. You can have a few shots if you want as well, hey, Kenn?" I added, clenching my fists while trying to cause a diversion.

A cold rolled across Denver, cold like the San Francisco fog or the steel that lay before us, inanimate yet poised for violence. "We're not going to be taking Rollins or laying a hand on anyone, I mean if we don't have to. The plan is simple: breach McCloy's home, remove and neutralize all threats with absolute prejudice, and recover the cassette and get it back to the 'Mats. Any questions?"

After a pause, Flea asked, "How we gonna know who's a threat?"

"Gentlemen," Denver added evenly, "look around this room. Anyone who isn't here now is a threat. We're not taking any chances, and we will be operating with absolute impunity. We won't be stopping to discuss a peaceful resolution. We can't negotiate with the Evil. They're terrorists, incapable of compassion and sworn to destroy everything that's right."

"Are you sure that this isn't too much?" I feebly asked, feeling like I had somehow just been transmitted from the victim to the bully side of the equation. "I mean, we're trying to get a cassette tape back, not invade Cuba."

"Check your resolve. The death of rock 'n' roll is close at hand, and if rock 'n' roll dies, our freedom will follow. It will be a cultural apocalypse. I'm ready to be judged on my life, but I'd be happy to wait awhile, too. If we stop the Evil here, we'll keep the Horsemen in the stable." Denver concluded his comments and turned back toward the weapons.

Without further discussion, the Magnificent Seven loaded up. Shotguns, pistols, automatic things, stun grenades, smoke bombs, knives, Kevlar vests, gas masks, special goggles for seeing in the dark, webbed belts for extra ammunition, and funny gloves with sticky pads on the palms. Everything but ham sandwiches wrapped in wax paper or any sense that this plan was going to work out for us.

As I contemplated our course, my stomach heaved, and I felt the room sway as my knees failed to support the increase in gravity. As far as I knew, Kenn had never fired a gun before; I certainly hadn't. Now here we were armed like some kind of joint John Woo/Michael Bay movie. To recover a cassette? Because the future of the world depended upon righting this wrong? To stop the apocalypse? Even I had stopped believing that rock 'n' roll had really died because of this bootleg. Things had gone too far.

This wasn't a plan; this was some type of feral black bag operation. Really? Really, was this the best solution? Steadying myself, I tried to regain the tenuous grasp I'd once held on my composure, hoping I would start thinking critically.

We needed to recover a cassette, a stolen or at least illegally recorded cassette from a show by the Replacements. Couldn't we just make an anonymous phone tip? Or appeal to some authority and demand the return of the cassette, as stolen property. Then there was also the kidnapping and torture by Rollins and McCloy. That had to be worthy of involving the police, I supposed, except for the fact that then some of the details would come out that Kenn and I really didn't want to face. Who were we? I could barely explain who I was under normal circumstances, let alone in the past or an alternate past.

I thought about all of this but failed to untangle the issues. Like the fact that Kenn and I didn't really exist, or if we did, we were only a few years old and living in Oregon. It would be more than a little difficult to explain how we'd traveled to a gig at The Bowery via a video game that was roughly twenty years away from being invented. There was also the detail of our escape, specifically the havoc that John Denver had wreaked upon the ranch, leaving a number of men dead or disabled. Right, we were on a course that wasn't going to be easily altered, but we were also in a past that was wrong, having come from a fractured present day.

Once again, Kenn and I found ourselves at the end of an album with a choice to make. We couldn't just ask to start over or to change the game; Kenn and I needed to see this through, just like the time we tracked down Lemmy from Motörhead in Nuremberg. Why? Because that was how we would become heroes, and since discovering time travel, we knew what had to be done, even if we didn't know how.

Again, I justified complacency as not having a choice. The justification was that changing the course of action was too difficult now. Required too much from us. Too many things had been set into motion, and it was simply easier to go with the flow. Easier to float than to swim.

"You know, guys, he's right," Kenn said, simultaneously breaking my thoughts and surprising me by giving me credit. "I don't need these weapons. My lethal weapon is my mind," he said, not only trying to extricate us from the possibility of participating in an armed fiasco, but also imparting lyrics to Ice-T.

Again, staring at my shoes, I felt embarrassed for Kenn's bravado; the comments rang clearly through the warehouse. "Yo, yous betta take a full auto, then, and maybe a couple of d'ose grenades," Ice-T snickered. "If he's on my team, I gonna want more Kevlar."

Everything told of an inauspicious start to active duty for Kenn and me. Once again, we were the odd men out. Not even the familiarity of being marginalized brought a sense of comfort.

"That's OK." The baritone of Johnny Cash filled the vacuum. "Kenn, I'll ride with you."

Making a mental inventory of the Magnificent Seven, I realized everyone had experience with hostility. Ice-T had served in the military.

Anthony and Flea lived in L.A. Flea had guns and violence in his home growing up. So it was reasonable that these guys could handle weapons and had witnessed violence, but Kenn and me, we couldn't even imagine what we were in for. The only side of violence that we had ever experienced was being under its thumb.

Maybe Cash wasn't as resolute as his reputation suggested. He was known to have been involved with violence, but even if the stories were only half-true, he would have a sturdy enough constitution that he wouldn't blanch at this operation. Johnny Cash: here was a guy so resilient in his personal and professional lives that he could only be regarded as a fucking badass. He lived hard and didn't worry if he had bruises to prove it.

As for Denver, at the very least we had to admit we were already surprised. He'd obviously had some type of intergalactic special forces training. A storage container that could provide an initial shipment for the Iran-Contra affair was merely something else that didn't fit with what I thought I knew of him.

"Kenn, I'm not really sure that I'm OK with this."

"Don't be a pussy. Cash said he'd ride with me. How bad could it be; we're part of the Magnificent Seven. Don't you want to settle things with Rollins and McCloy?" he hissed back at me. "Besides, this is an opportunity to plant the seeds of future events. We can make it an absolute certainty that great collaborations occur later. Maybe it's not about the Replacements tape but it's this intervention with these guys that's important."

Kenn might have been right. There would be no question later, for us, that we had planted the hints that set things in motion during our time in San Francisco that led to Cash's collaborating with One Bad Pig in 2001, and then later covering Nine Inch Nails, Beck, Depeche Mode, U2, and Soundgarden.

I still harbor a lingering regret for not suggesting a Leonard Cohen or Lou Reed collaboration. Maybe city and country just wouldn't mix, but I think that the "Man in Black" would have done just fine with either

Reed or Cohen. You know, something like "Endlessly Jealous" or a duet with Johnny and June Cash covering Cohen's "Never Any Good." In my mind, it's amazing.

Perhaps Denver sensed our anxiety, or perhaps my discomfort and fear were palpable. Whatever it was, he culled us out and designated us to travel with him, which brought some warmth to thaw the chill of our disquiet, reinvigorating us and allowing me to banish the menace and frustration of Ice-T's demeanor from my mind.

Despite Denver's support, being with men bent upon violence unsettled me. Possessing knowledge that our actions were sure to lead to the death of others, left me numb.

Everything assembled spoke of harm. It was as though we had walked into the Jam song "A Town Called Malice" to impose martial law. Our collection of weapons was vulgar. This wasn't new. Weapons have always come in different shapes and sizes, with those such as clubs and maces conveying an unmistakable promise of violence. These did not have the clean lines of a sword or the precision of a sniper, who would dispatch the victim quickly with a surgeon's detachment. No, these were close-quarters weapons of singular purpose.

There was no claim of self-defense; we were marauders setting upon a plan that contemplated extreme violence. Surely this was justified. I mean, we were recovering stolen property, setting the world right, and returning history to a proper state, just like when Phil Rudd tried to hire hit men to right wrongs. Justification aside, we were now the aggressors and preparing to return violence upon McCloy. However, despite any justification, the fact remained that we were simply angry men on a campaign of rage. Not the first boots to march along a trail paved with justification.

This was different, not like Lemmy's indictment of governments or rogue police forces. We had been directly engaged and seen the outcome of the Evil that was before us.

I wanted retribution. I wanted the restoration of rock 'n' roll, and I wanted to be even. I just didn't want the responsibility of violence. It would be easier, better, to deploy men of violence. I could hide behind vague directions and not be accountable for the actions of those who did my bidding. I wanted to claim the victory but not endure the sacrifice.

McCloy's acts had incensed us all. Each of the Magnificent Seven had his own reasons for answering the call to arms: to provide a bulwark against the Evil, to save rock 'n' roll, to right a wrong, to take a stand—a stand against bullies, against censorship, or to just stick it to the Man.

"Kenn, aren't we really perpetuating violence as a form of personal gratification? What if the rationalization is simply a device to let us move past the thrill of feeling an empty box collapse under a powerful kick? You know, the exhilaration that comes from smashing something, without threat of consequence. Are we really saving rock 'n' roll or merely searching for a cause that validates the course we want to take?"

"So, what if?" he replied.

Leave it to Kenn to miss my point and harbor his own animosity. I knew empirically what would happen if we failed to recover the cassette. We both did. Kenn and I knew that if *The Shit Hits the Fans* didn't hit the fans, then rock 'n' roll would die. But still . . . What if there was a different way of saving society? A means without violence? Was there really no alternative to armed conflict, or was it simply too difficult to imagine a better solution, because it takes longer?

I recalled conversations with Kenn about how disappointed our fathers were with our lack of interest in legitimate outdoor pursuits. Basically, anything involving hunting or firearms and putting animals in harm's way. Now there was irony in arming ourselves to defend rock 'n' roll. I wondered if they would appreciate the irony or merely reiterate the infallibility of their views. Maybe nothing would prepare us for violence against others; you're either prone to violence or you're not. Maybe there is a mineral in your blood that draws you toward or repels you away from violence, just like having a preference for certain foods.

As I looked around, it occurred to me that we are all capable of violence, even aggression, given the right motivation.

Perhaps sensing my unease, or conceding his own doubts, Kenn attempted levity. "You know the difference between a sociopath, a vigilante, and a hero?" When the silence became awkward to the point of being deafening, Kenn passively gave the answer: "Perspective and who's judging their motivation."

I looked at Kenn, his joke crashing like a cymbal on a tile floor. "Still not completely right, are you, buddy?" I asked, putting my hand on his shoulder. In quiet moments later, I would reflect on Kenn's joke and realize that he was probably closer to being right than he was funny; timing is everything. At the time, our course of action seemed the only viable option, but I suppose there could have been other solutions. Maybe in the end my motivation would seem slight to others, but at least for now, the Magnificent Seven seemed resolute, so Kenn and I drifted along with the stream of rage that was building in the warehouse, making both our mental and our physical preparations.

Certainly we had seen our share of shadow play up to now, but I wasn't sure that the actions of McCloy and Rollins justified ours. As my mind wandered through other historical events, I could feel the resonating of the bass line and the ethereal guitar track of Joy Division's "Shadowplay." Was that song reflecting who we had become?

I tried to tell myself we were just going to scare McCloy, the guns merely props. Despite my efforts, I knew it was a lie I couldn't believe. I couldn't. Denver had told us the plan; we had discounted other scenarios. McCloy ordering a laying down of arms with everyone throwing up their hands, disavowing his hatred for rock 'n' roll. Or the house being vacant, unguarded, with the cassette left on a desk. Arriving too late and discovering that a SWAT team, the Anti-Fascist Music League, or maybe the Vatican's Knights Templar had taken McCloy and Rollins into custody, leaving us to just nod our heads and keep rolling by, like an aborted drive-by shooting in some TV show with clichéd tropes reinforcing our views of urban gangs. The scenario that I was searching for was merely the proxy for denial that I always leaned on. Distraction, my preferred crutch; procrastination, my favorite vice.

We left the warehouse and, driving a circuitous route, arrived at the address Alex Chilton had provided about thirty-five minutes later: 3630 Jackson Street, Pacific Heights, San Francisco. Kenn's family might have felt comfortable in an area like this, but I certainly did not. So I welcomed the temporary reprieve of procrastination as we kept rolling past and parked about a block away from the house.

Kenn and I knew what would happen. We had seen the future; McCloy had revealed his plans to us. We knew that the tape would be doctored so as to cast such a pall over the band and rock 'n' roll in general that people would lose interest in the music. We knew that against all odds McCloy would succeed in destroying rock 'n' roll, and humanity would be forced to stagger on alone, in an unimaginable world without music or creation.

It was a stark humanity that we bore witness to, bereft of inspiration, emotion, and expression. Really, the Horsemen of the Apocalypse were incapable of worse. Considering all of these consequences, which Kenn and I had already seen unfold, steeled us to the task at hand. The repercussions of failing were the only thing that dispelled the trepidation I held about being surrounded by weapons. I felt the disquiet of having responsibility for these strange weapons, but we were also accountable for the future of rock 'n' roll.

"This is so fucking cool," enthused Kenn under his breath to me, as Denver parked and turned off the engine as we looked back at the house, which we later learned was the onetime residence of Abraham Rosenberg, the trusted friend and adviser to the king of Hawaii. The house itself looked like the set of *Pacific Heights*, the movie where Michael Keaton went all dark and disturbia in suburbia. In my mind, I could hear "Mountain Song," by Jane's Addiction, as we were walking down the street. Retreating into the rhythm and Eric Avery's attacking bass, I began to feel more menacing and less afraid than I deserved to.

"Kenneth," Denver said sternly, "I don't want to remind you about your language again. It's disgraceful, unimaginative, and fails to convey any real expression."

"It conveys my sense of excitement and awe pretty fucking well, I think."

"Kenneth," John reproached sternly.

"Kenn!" I hissed.

Except for Ice-T snickering behind us, we continued in silence, the Magnificent Seven starting to fan out in some type of attack formation. I started to absorb the details of the home in the early-evening twilight. The grounds were lush, with large leafy trees, manicured hedges, grass, and shrubs that appeared to be better cared for than most children. Maybe they were; maybe there were children pressed into indentured urban labor, clipping shrubs, pulling weeds, and cleaning fountains, maintaining the grounds. I suppose if you don't let kids listen to rock 'n' roll, they may as well do yard work.

More and more, while I wanted to speak out and admit that my heart wasn't really into our assault, there was a smoldering fire that wanted revenge for the torture Kenn and I had endured. I felt angry and malicious, justified but also conflicted.

"Sure." Denver spoke so softly that he was barely audible from where I was. "Sure, McCloy claims this is about morality. Or religion. He justifies his actions by protecting those who can't protect themselves. But it's not about religion; it's about control. It's about an imposition of morality and it's about people like McCloy. It's not about music at all."

Unsure if Denver was seeking comment from anyone, Kenn and I just looked at each other and shrugged.

"So? We gonna do dis or what?" inquired Ice-T. "I'm itchin' for somethin'."

"Yeah, this is the place. Alex says that the cassette is here," continued Denver. "So you all know what's at stake. Let's do what we came here for." Then he added, doing an impression, "There will be blood tonight!"

"He's pretty good at that," Kenn said to me in a shallow whisper. "Isn't that Mandy Patinkin from *The Princess Bride*?

"I think so," I whispered in response, "but I thought that was late eighties or early nineties."

"Definitely eighties. Besides, Denver seems to have access to stuff."

There were a few nods of agreement, probably to Denver's comments and not Kenn's, some concerned looks and checking of weapons. I noticed a look from Ice-T that suggested that while he had heard Denver, he might not have been really listening. Examining our teammates again, I realized we might be all heading in the same direction but on different paths. United by goals if not philosophies.

Conceptually, the plan was simple. The Seven would launch an assault on the Rosenberg house, with Kenn and me joining to ensure that the cassette was the genuine article. We were organized and armed heavily enough to invade Somalia. We had numbers and the element of surprise in our favor. This was not going to be like when we intervened at The Bowery when we thought that we had the element of surprise on our side, or even like the time when we were overpowered on Downing Street trying to rescue Billy Bragg. This time Kenn and I were with pros.

My confidence grew steadily as we walked up the approach to the Rosenberg house. Unlike 10 Downing, there was no fence. No posted sentry. No government significance. Just a private residence. Small walkway lights illuminating as we approached, sensing our presence.

Things that exist where science meets magic have always stuck me with awe, and motion-detection lights were such a thing. Photosensitive lights as well. Energy saving, inexpensive, discreet, and clever. Unfortunately, my fascination was also my distraction. As novel as motion-detection lights were, they were not widely utilized until well after the mid eighties. Another detail that should have served as a warning to us.

"Kenn, look," I commented, pointing to the lights, as Ice-T crashed a heavy foot into the front door, kicking it in off its freshly broken frame.

Kenn paused as the rest of the team poured through the door into a narrow foyer area . "C'mon, we gotta . . ." he started saying, before being drowned out by a siren.

Lights started flashing, covering the house and the grounds in a strobe effect while rolling steel shutters clattered down across the door and all the windows.

As Dick Cheney would again prove twenty-two years later, there was no animal more dangerous than a man with a gun. Kenn pulled the trigger of his machine pistol, a Bellini, I think Ice-T called it. The gun leaped like an angry rooster, spraying bullets and causing me to dive to the ground.

Something caused Kenn's weapon to stop firing; whether it was empty or jammed I'll never know. Kenn threw it into a bush with a mixture of revulsion and shock. As the siren was softening, I could hear a struggle of the rest of the Magnificent Seven inside the house, guns firing, men yelling, then silence, and then after a long sigh, the unmistakable voice of John Denver: "Fuck. Fuck. Fuck."

"I thought you said that was a weak form—"

"Shut the fuck up. Anyone says a fucking word, I'm going to fucking kill them. Try the window and door covers."

Sounds of escape efforts were interrupted by a voice and a hissing sound. "Hey, is that smoke?"

Without a word, Kenn and I returned to the door long enough to see gray smoke seeping from the chinks in the steel shutter and to hear the struggle inside subside with the sounds of dropping weapons and dull thuds on the floor.

"Kenn, run!" I said, shedding all of the gear that we had so fastidiously donned merely an hour ago. "We can't help them now." And with that, we were crushed with the realization that we had failed rock 'n' roll again, that we'd failed to gain control of the cassette and also contributed to the capture of our only allies. Rather than hearing music in my head, I heard voices. The pleas of the trapped Seven, the admonishments of teachers who told me I'd always be a failure and of the bullies who tormented my past.

Kenn and I were on the run again. Panicked and without support. While I should have been thinking about the fate of the rest of the Seven, or the pending demise of rock 'n' roll, I couldn't even overcome my own fears and self-loathing.

Kenn and I fled, terrified, fueled by adrenaline and panic. We ran through dense trees toward the Presidio and then walked when we could no longer sustain our desperate flight. Skirting the open parks and baseball fields, we tried keeping to the shadows even while remaining terrified of our own. Words between us were sparse and flat, devoid of emotion like dry crackers. Normally incapable of rapid agreement, we were united by a common threat, so concessions were quickly found.

Once we were convinced that our immediate peril had abated, Kenn said, "We have to get to the wharfs and as far away as possible from Jackson Street as we can."

There was no discussion or even a hint at discussing a new plan. There was no need to argue or juggle whose assertion was stronger—we simply needed to escape and find help.

The limited money Denver had provided wouldn't last long. We had no allies, we would be getting hungry, but at the time, none of these thoughts even entered my mind. All I could think about was that I just needed to find someone to gimme shelter.

12

Gimme Shelter

Shelter. A human necessity that provides both physical and emotional satisfaction. Sometimes shelter is a kind word, a warm sweater, or a hearty bowl of soup, while other times it's a structure that keeps threats at bay.

Shelter also polarizes people or interests. Tax shelters . . . harboring aliens or criminals. Sanctuary sought but not found. A need or a choice.

This is Sid Itious, Monday morning at two thirty-seven, March second; you're listening to KQRL 89.9 FM, Riverside, California. I hope that you find whatever you're in need of, perhaps even on this show. Here's the Sisters of Mercy with their take on a Stones classic.

FCC transcript KQRL 89.9 FM 03.02.2015 0237

File under: Suspect [redacted]

"Gimme shelter," Kenn moaned, articulating my thoughts.

Shelter. Sanctuary. Safe passage. Our most pressing need. A quick inventory of our situation made the Bay of Pigs invasion shine as a wonderful success. Trapped in our past, separated from people we could trust to protect us, and no immediate prospects for the recovery of *The Shit Hits the Fans*.

My mind was reeling, searching for solutions, for options or simply shelter. "What about the offices of the Alternative Tentacles?" It seemed to offer potential. Alternative Tentacles was the Dead Kennedys' label, which was making as much noise with the bands of the emerging Bay Area punk scene as it was with its political views. Perhaps sanctuary within the headquarters of some other local musical advocate, someone who had a penchant for adversity and taking up conspiracies.

"Jazz bar," he said despondently.

"Sure, or a jazz bar could be a start." For Kenn, sanctuary meant something else. It was about a girl. Kenn wanted to return to the martini bar where he had been Tasered by a girl. A girl who would someday get a dragon tattoo, who four years from now we would watch shake martinis with the energy of a primal scream. And at that time, like now, Kenn would be of singular focus and like an unstoppable force. Events that would lead to my being unceremoniously unbidden by Kenn after a Tracy Chapman gig. I wasn't prepared to be the immovable object that was going to stand in his way. I would have been happy to sit anywhere, and if we could have a drink or several, so much the better.

Seeing the Golden Gate Bridge looming before us, I knew we were within the Presidio. Even in our rightfully perplexed and panicked state, we could follow famous landmarks. Bridge to piers, along the piers to North Beach, and then navigate toward the Transamerica pyramid, across the street to the bar, the jazz bar Kenn was talking about, or at least sanctuary in another form. I loved San Francisco for its architectural cues. It was as though I had spent an entire life in the city. But tonight, even with the conveniently placed architectural beacon, familiarity didn't bring comfort; I was ill at ease.

My disquiet swirled in the confluence of the knowledge that we heading back to the bar where Kenn would be assaulted in a few years, and the accumulation of our failings. As we walked in a somber silence, my corrosive self-loathing was interrupted only by the most spartan of comments. I had lost track of time and even lost the sense of the confusion of my reality.

"Do you think they're OK?" Kenn asked, then continuing in my hesitation. "What do you think is going to happen . . ." He trailed off, either distracted or afraid of what the answer might be.

I tried to think of an answer but just sighed. My thoughts drifted among the fact that we were lost, the memory of being tortured by Rollins, and the enormity of losing not only the cassette, but potentially other sources of rock 'n' roll inspiration in the rest of the Seven.

"I'm such a fuck-up," Kenn continued. "My father was right, I should have just listened to him . . . Then it wouldn't have ever—"

"Kenn," I interrupted, "we don't need to do this." Fatigue permeated my thoughts and delayed my movements. Although the medical treatment and sustenance had helped, my body ached and was probably visibly bruised from Rollins. And I was scared. Looking at Kenn, I could see he was tired and wore the marks of his beating all over his body. As bad as it must have been for Kenn, having worshiped Rollins, he was now digging up past experiences with his father. It was too much.

There was no doubt that being rescued by John Denver had saved us, but our failures were stacking up quickly. The anxiety and the stress continued to bear down upon me and I felt as exhausted as Atlas sustaining the heft of the world.

"I never wanted any of this," Kenn admitted. "I just thought that we would go see a bunch of great shows . . ." Of course, I suppose people rarely set out to become heroes. Even adventurers don't seek out the kind of drama that we had stumbled upon, but consequences operate like ocean currents: even if they are predictable or anticipated, they can still overwhelm you.

"Kenn, things have escalated beyond anything we could imagine." Screaming in my mind like an incessant fire alarm, were all the things that defied my comprehension, words I spoke were as much for Kenn as they were for me. "You were right before, buddy; we just need to find shelter. Let's find the girl."

"I thought this would be a relatively straightforward intervention. You know, identify the bad guy, get the cassette, return it to the Replacements, save rock 'n' roll, and be heroes. Why does everything I do always get so fucked up?"

He was right—well, at least about the first part; this hadn't been that kind of adventure. How had it turned into something so much more?

Somewhere, something that seemed easy had turned into a mission more like Special Forces stuff. You know, with the gruff yet compelling George Peppard–type character barking out, "OK, boys, I need you to travel through time and kidnap General Rommel and replace him with Jim Henson so that the Nazis' Panzer Division will operate Oscar the Grouch as a puppet dictator. Oh yeah, and bring me back a nice bottle of scotch or maybe some German schnapps." *What. The. Fuck. Were. We. Doing?*

But here we were, in San Francisco by way of Oklahoma City, and after a slight case of kidnapping, some torture, a rescue, and some botched recovery attempts, we were back to that night after Tracy Chapman. All Kenn could think about was a girl. It was always about a girl. Maybe even when it wasn't.

"Kenn, seriously," I started.

"Look, I am serious, don't project your shit on me," he interrupted. "This isn't about her. Yeah, sure, I do want to see if she's there again, but it's more than that."

More? OK, Kenn had my attention. It had to be good to convince me, but I suppose that this is when Kenn was at his best: when I didn't think he had it in him to rise to a challenge. But then, really, he always did rise to succeed. My friend that I was tired of. My friend that I needed now, as I so often had.

I had been so utterly exhausted by Kenn's garbage. Weary of fighting his insatiable need to run ahead or claim credit. Overextended, but not bankrupt. Realizing that Kenn had persevered against improbable odds to do what was right was more than rock 'n' roll or the time that we had spent together as friends; it was the realization that Kenn was a hero in his own right.

Kenn didn't need me to be a hero; he already was. I was at best his sidekick, dangling desperately from his cape. It was through Kenn that I understood that anyone willing to take a stand could be a hero.

"The logic is the same as it was last time we went to that bar," he stated, as if it was an indisputable fact.

"Yes, we were stuck in the past. What else?" I asked, trying to anticipate where he was heading, other than to discover more electrical burns on his torso.

"When we were last there it was a jazz bar. There was a group of Scientologists across the street trying to raise money and awareness for their proposed new center in the old Transamerica building, and we went in because we needed a drink and a place to hatch a plan."

"Right," I agreed, "but that will be four years from now. It's a long shot that she'll be there or that anything else will be, either."

"Of course, but I have to see her again," he conceded, "and if not now, then later. We've also got to get reorganized, have a drink, some food, and figure out how we're getting out of this disaster. The last place that McCloy will look for us is anywhere that might have jazz or Scientologists."

And just like that, in a stroke of sublime lucidity, Kenn was right. Despite the turmoil we were facing, his judgment was intact, his focus and resolve singular and clear. There really wasn't any argument; we returned to the jazz bar in search of some food, a drink, and a girl. It was an ideal shelter.

As you might have anticipated, the girl was not in fact behind the bar. So Kenn and I found a table off to the side and noticed that the bar was quieter than it had been previously. The corner set up for the jazz band was still there, but tonight it was just instruments cluttered against their stands like vagrants waiting for something better, somewhere to go, or a reason to move along. Among the instruments was a tired-looking upright bass with cracking lacquer, fading where various palms had rested alongside the strings, and a drum kit that was approaching the end of its useful life.

The waiter came over, and although lacking the appetite and inclination to do so, intuitively we knew that we needed to eat. Even the relatively simple task of searching the menu and making a decision filled me with anxiety and despair. The menu itself was only one page, containing a spartan selection of basic items, but in my mind it stretched before me, the way a desert might before an agoraphobic.

"Just a couple of Tanqueray and tonics," Kenn said, trying to make a decision about food, "and maybe just something to share. I don't know. What's good and easy?"

The waiter, seeming impatient, annoyed by our combination of dithering and vacant pauses. "Good and easy? To share? Well I am, sometimes. Sometimes good, but always easy. And with you two I'd be happy to share . . ."

"Ah, yeah," I said wearily, "right. Maybe something from the menu for now. We've had a long day and could just use some chow."

"Chow? Maybe the Tex-Mex place on the pier?"

"We're happy here. Maybe if we could just have a couple of minutes, or is there something you'd suggest?" Kenn quickly interjected.

"So, boys," the waiter said after repeating a mixed selection of recommendations, "I'm Joee, with a double e. Yeah, it's that way because I'm different. It's like meeee." Then without missing a beat, he continued, "About that a little earlier, don't you mind, but if you fellas are looking for something else, off the menu, let me know. Maybe you want an adventure tonight or just a quiet night? I'm just getting a sense of the both of you; you've got a look about you that says you're close and that you might like the rough stuff. Just so you know, a couple of my friends have a little after-hours place that's just a skip away. Very discreet. Very." With that, Joee left with a slight skip and then returned as soon as he placed another table's order at the bar.

"So, have you decided? About food or more drinks or anything . . . just let me know. I'm meeting my friend Serge, you know, like the sewing machine—we call him that either because he does decorative seams or because he cuts as he goes; you decide. No? OK, I'll be back." And with that, he turned a sort of half spin on his heel and did another little skip, leaving us more confused than ever.

"He thinks we're a couple. Fair enough, I suppose, for San Francisco in 1984." As my mind wandered to why Kenn and I might look like a couple, or the conclusions that people might draw about our obvious injuries, I started to contemplate a response. I managed to check my wandering mind. We needed to focus; the last thing I needed was to sort out what the hell Joee had meant and what the fuck his friend's name had to do with a sewing machine. Gay men really were too complicated for my sheltered existence.

"Are either of the e's capitalized?" Kenn asked in a flat monotone, sounding like he himself didn't understand the question, but by this time, Joee was out of earshot. "That would be different."

I tried a joke. "Well, there you go, Kenn. Joee is different, just like you." It would have appeared that Kenn had ignored me, but for his shooting glare.

Looking around the bar, waiting for Joee to return, we saw her again, the bartender from the last time. The very same girl who had Tasered Kenn before uttering a single word to us, was now arguing with a pay phone by the fire escape door at the back of the bar. Her tight black dress juxtaposed against the heavy boots that were covering her calves reminded me of how captivating she had been when we saw her the last time. Lacking the tattoos she would have years from now, it was unmistakably the same girl. As she leaned against the wall, the muscles in her shoulder and back appeared taut, rippling as she tapped the fingers of the hand extended above her head.

The conversation sounded animated, to say the least, the bartender's previous balance of insouciance and vigilance tipping into unfettered hostility. Still, without heed to what might have been obvious warnings, Kenn and I approached her.

"Look, Grandma, I know that you had children by the time you were my age . . . What? My mother had a cesarean because I was in crisis; that doesn't make her any less of a woman. I know that all your children were born naturally. Yes. But the only difference that makes is that—" and with that she let loose a tirade of such explicit profanity and visceral description that Kenn looked away while I stared at my shoes uneasily. Sure, we should have already been somewhat wary of someone who had used a Taser on him twice, but that was how things worked with girls. Kenn and I always seemed to have short memories when it came to matters involving women.

I could see that even now, without the Taser and significantly fewer tattoos, this woman had again incapacitated Kenn, but we needed help, and somehow she still drew us like moths to a flame.

Surely the moth must know the danger of the flame. All the signs are there. The light, the heat, the sound should all be a warning, but warnings are often unheard. I think back and I think, *Yeah, that's probably right, and I also realize, Yeah, I recognized that at the time, too.*

Kenn knew the danger as well; I watched him massage the scars beneath his shirt that he would receive in four years' time, I was certain he recalled the pain. How would minds such as Einstein and Jung explain faded scars from the future?

"Just because my father left doesn't mean my mother is a lesbian," the bartender spat into the phone with nearly visible venom.

Oh, really? The l-word! Kenn and I slowed our retreat, you know, just in case.

"Well, maybe that is what I really need; a couple of hot young lesbians to crawl all over me until I pass out from exhaustion! Hey, wait, there's a couple of guys standing here." Looking at Kenn, I suddenly felt nervous and awkward, like voyeurs at a windowsill caught in a floodlight. We froze in place, as though our feet had been cast in the very concrete that the floor was made out of. Fear of our future encounter crept up on me; my only reassurance was that I could see this girl's hands and they contained only a telephone and not a Taser. I wasn't sure it was any less dangerous.

The girl continued, "Should I ask them if they'll watch and maybe take some pictures for you?" Yeah, so now that certain male fantasies began reeling through our minds, we weren't going anywhere and in fact started moving closer to the phone. Kenn was nodding to confirm his willingness.

Kenn nudged me and said, "This is going to be awesome." Still I thought of the flickering flame and the hovering moth; this was a danger that I couldn't resist. Wasn't there an expression about courage and valor?

As we approached, she covered the receiver on the telephone and spat, "You assholes." She seemed to be talking directly to us now, causing optimism to swell in me.

Kenn and I looked at each other as she hissed violently toward us, "It's not happening. Not now, not ever, so fuck off. And fuck off now!" And with that, she returned to her conversation. Indeed, it was now clear that she was talking to us. Not perhaps the most auspicious of conversations, but strangely a vast improvement from our prior experience with her.

Ordinarily, Kenn and I might have considered holding our ground better, but I suggested, "You know, this is clearly a private matter. We should leave."

Kenn offered feeble resistance, commenting about the conversation being played out in a very public forum, but we really had more than enough failure on our plates and another ass-kicking was the last thing we needed.

With more than a measure of dejection and confusion, we returned to the bar, changed our drink order to a couple of martinis from Joee, accepted his food recommendation, and returned to our table. Wallowing in silence, our thoughts were interrupted by the arrival of Joee acting like a mother hen with our drinks and some type of food. "Here you boys go," he announced with polite ambivalence. Then in a hushed tone, which accentuated the pronunciation of "s," he offered, "Tsk, tsk, I should have known you were into the rough stuff, but I just have to tell you, thaaat one"—motioning over to Taser girl—"is really rough. I think you'd be better off with me and Serge. Give it a think." Finished with both the delivery of our drinks and his warning, Joee turned with his little half spin and skip that were quickly becoming familiar, leaving Kenn and me relieved that at least one of our concerns had been resolved. We retreated back into our silence. Unfortunately, our silence allowed our thoughts to echo through the recesses of our minds, where seeds of doubt grew into fiendish specters.

How were we going to get the tape back? We were now separated from John Denver and the rest of the Seven and here in San Francisco, essentially lost; well, certainly stranded and without a plan. The only thing worse than being lost and facing failure is the realization that the only means of escape are beyond your reach.

For Kenn and me, there was no return until we had completed what we had crossed for. While we had come to learn that once we crossed, we would remain until the end of the show, or until we set right what was out of place, we didn't understand the consequences of this. At least we hadn't understood until now. We had been given multiple chances with Billy Bragg, but something was different with Rollins. Something that we couldn't understand, perhaps because when we tried to abduct Billy Bragg, we had remained conscious when we passed through doors or maybe because we remained in London. Or maybe because the world that Kenn and I occupied still was largely intact. But whatever the reason, this was another aspect of time travel that existed beyond our understanding. Maybe the secret was that rock 'n' roll was the energy that sustained us and facilitated time travel.

Although Kenn and I lacked the understanding of how or why, we had gained other knowledge. I realized that our actions were actually contributing to the demise of rock 'n' roll, rather than saving it. We were making things worse, and so it now appeared that we were going to float through 1984 until we got the recording back to MacLeslie.

I had started to speak a couple of times and then stopped. The reality was that I didn't really know what I could say. Well, I suppose I could have said what I had been thinking when Kenn said we should find the bar. I could have told Kenn that he was a hero, but that seemed too much for either of us to manage at the moment. So, instead, I did what close friends and cowards always do. Nothing. Nothing at all. I sat in silence, watching my friend in anguish.

"My dad always said I was a fuck-up," Kenn started again. "Maybe

I should call him and tell him I'm sorry. That I'll try harder. I could talk to him; he's still alive now, right?"

Yeah, Kenn was right. His parents would still be alive in this time line, and they always had been pretty hard on him. Maybe all parents were, projecting their own views as to what was best onto their children. An eternity of saddling children with their own unrealized ambitions and dreams, the ultimate adult repression. The endless histories of parents wanting the best for their children and the children failing to reach the highest of branches.

Certainly my family didn't accept what I had done, what I was doing. I could always do more. Be a lawyer. Be a doctor. An engineer, an accountant, a teacher; something important. A leader of men. Something that would make them proud. Nothing related to rock 'n' roll. The sooner I gave up the silly distraction, the better I would be, at least in their eyes. I just needed to obey them.

Kenn had a path to follow but refused a single step. His father tried every conceivable means of enticing Kenn into business: allowances, promises of cars for graduating, trips, and even consequences that removed all privileges when Kenn refused. But in the end he never tried to show Kenn support, love, or direction out of the rut they were in. The conflict intensified. Kenn didn't want to be called "Jr."; his father took insult, because it had been good enough for him, until his father died and the title slid from one son to the next. The men were different, yet the same in their desire to do things on their own terms or not at all.

Kenn had no chance. Both his parents died without resolution to their issues, and Kenn retreated into rock 'n' roll at an early age. For most people music was entertainment. A distraction. Background noise or color to set the stage, to enliven the party. For Kenn it was more than that. It was his shelter. Later it became my sanctuary as well, but like crossing, it was Kenn who had first discovered it and then trusted me enough to share it with me.

Initially, the music was simple escapism. The rhythm. The beat. The tunes. These elements hooked him quickly. They took hold of his soul and imagination and later, when he started listening more intently, he heard patterns and learned about a world called rock 'n' roll. Then it was the information, knowledge about the bands, artists, tours, and record releases. He shared rock 'n' roll indiscriminately with me like a dirty syringe. Predictably, I was contaminated with Kenn's infection, hooked on his addiction.

But still, we were trapped in the past, and all our future accomplishments counted for nothing. Changing history was a big deal. But now all of that was gone, because we had failed and had allowed rock 'n' roll to die. Staring through my gloom at the table, I heard a foot scraping across the floor.

"OK, what do you two shitheads want?" she asked, sliding into the booth beside Kenn and locking gazes with me.

"Ahhh . . ."

"Who are you?" I asked, my jaw agape.

"Oh. I'm Brandy," she said flatly. "Brandy Alexander."

"Right, you mean like—" Kenn started to say, but I cut him off by softly saying, "Kenn?" and pointing to the place on his chest that was still hairless. "Don't forget, dude."

"You might want to consider changing your name to something else," I suggested as gently as I could. "I mean, a bartender named Brandy Alexander?"

"I'm not going to be a bartender forever," Brandy said with a blended serving of scorn and indifference. "I'm a jazz musician. Bass," she added, proudly motioning toward the instrument with her head. "Besides, like the drink, I go down easy."

"You'll need more work on that Hofner," offered Kenn.

"I wish I had a Hofner. I just borrow what I can for now," she said with a tone that was becoming pliable and soft, almost tender. "But I'm at Berkeley Law. I'll be done in two more years. Five if I only go part-time."

"Ah," Kenn said, assembling the parts to make a whole. "A law student, thus explaining how you can talk to Grandma like she was something expelled from hell."

"Yeah, well, you give it a try." Brandy's retort was that of the girl we had first experienced—as visceral as a car accident and brazen as a Teamster. "That bitch is a fucking c—"

"*Country*," I interjected, trying to turn the conversation to other topics. "We don't need the entire *country* hearing what you think of Grandma. So you're a bass player, a bartender, and a law student?"

"Yeah," she replied, still agitated. "You two seem to have it all figured out. So what? Do you think you deserve a handjob?"

Raising my hand to Kenn and turning back to Brandy, I said, "No. No, thank you. I've seen you with a martini shaker." Kenn and Brandy reacted simultaneously.

Brandy looked at me, her eyes narrowed as if studying mine. As if in doing so she could read my mind or discover my secrets. She paused to absorb what I had just said and to try to control the moment. She couldn't. Her perfect mouth flickered, betraying her, and then flickered again. Brandy's brown eyes sparkled and then all was lost, at least for me.

Looking closely, you'd find it there: a coy recognition along with an approval now echoed in her eyes. A satisfaction. Brandy retained the facade of control, but I had been accepted. Later, as a friend, she would look at me with eyes that laced sutures through my soul. I was bound to an ideal.

Having barely noticed any other sensation, I realized that Kenn had snorted his martini all over my side of the booth and was now coughing. The moment in which Kenn was choking and soaking things with nasal-propelled alcohol passed almost instantly, whereas the moment between Brandy and me has stayed with me to this day.

Brandy ordered us a round of drinks and some more food from Joee, who seemed to give her a wide berth and now regarded us with a mixture of ambivalence and curiosity. Kenn barely noticed Joee's presence. We were talking about rock 'n' roll, and Brandy held his attention with steel pincers.

"You know, you should consider taking more of an edge on with the bass," I suggested. "You could find yourself playing pretty good rockabilly, you know, if you think you could handle something other than making it up as you go with a jazz group." The classic jazz criticism, meant as a means of goading her along. Jazz wasn't bad, just not my thing.

"You mean ol'-school like the Blasters or Brian Setzer?" Brandy asked with the first glimpse of enthusiasm that I had seen from her. "I'd trade anything to see them live . . ." She trailed off, graciously catching my hand signal, which wasn't particularly obvious but was effective because Kenn's attention had fallen from her to his drink like a stalled helicopter. "Wait, have you seen me play?"

I looked nervously and sympathetically at Kenn, who still seemed lost in his brooding. The Stray Cats were one thing, but my heart still fluttered, hoping that Kenn had missed the reference to the Blasters. Kenn had long been a Blasters fan, but seeing them live changed all of that. It might even remain as the worst night of his life. Rock 'n' roll had that sort of effect and power. It could change people and experiences in ways that were unexpected and unpredictable.

If forced, he would freely admit that the Alvin brothers, both as the Blasters and contributing to other bands, were an immense talent. They were an act that stood the test of time and made its mark. Unfortunately, the mark was also left on Kenn, and it was a subject that I always steered the conversation away from.

"Ah, yeah, the last time we were in, we caught part of your show. You were bartending, too."

"Hmm, I suppose I don't really notice unless you're at the bar."

"Maybe you could help us. We need to find some punks that are up for a challenge," I suggested, changing the subject.

"Right," Brandy said, "any challenge you guys would be up for, I should be able to find you some help. I think that there's a day care halfway down Columbus. They'll be open again in the morning."

"Nice," I said, watching Kenn. "This is a little different. We were at a Replacements gig a few weeks back and saw a guy boot a cassette, but the recovery of it has escalated from a dare to a bet and now to something more."

"Aha," she said, disbelieving.

Kenn told Brandy a version of the truth that was believable. "Look, we almost got the tape, but then we got caught and beat up." Easy to believe as we had the marks to support the story. Brandy's body language became pliable again, and she leaned toward the table, her eyes telling us that she was becoming a believer.

I struggled to hold her gaze but became uncomfortable and found myself looking at her cleavage. "But while they were beating us, they said they were going to use the tape to break up the band," I continued, "and demonstrate the immorality of rock 'n' roll. If they succeed, this will be the end of the band and will become a firebrand to rally around while marginalizing rock 'n' roll. We need that cassette back, but the house is heavily guarded."

"We're fucked," Kenn said dejectedly. Of course he was dejected. Of course he thought that all was lost. Despite ideals or wishes that we are all created equal, people were different. Each person, unique to himself, possessed his own limits and threshold, beyond which waited a breaking point.

"We're fucked, and there ain't a hoot to be done about it."

Suddenly I sat up with stunned enlightenment and blurted out, "Kenn, that's awesome. You're a genius! We need to have a hootenanny!"

"A what?" replied an incredulous Brandy.

"Ignore him. We're fucked and have had a long few days," Kenn added morosely.

"No, this is perfect," I enthusiastically continued. "The answer to the problem is a hootenanny."

13

Hootenanny

This is KQSF 90.9 FM, July 5, 2011, 8:44. You're listening to Transmission with Sid.

Freedoms are rights, entitlements, things that people are allowed to do. For a freedom to have value, it must be inalienable, protected. In fact, it needs to be protected from the party that has the most to gain from violating the right.

Freedom of assembly is a right that causes the most concern. It allows contagious ideas to pass unchecked, like a shared cigarette. Assembly provides an exchange of wills to strengthen resolve and cast aside doubt. Last weekend I saw legends of rock 'n' roll assemble at a hootenanny. The big guns were there. The Reverend Horton Heat, Supersuckers, Mojo Nixon, Dropkick Murphys. Thank you, boys. Here's a Replacements track for your troubles.

FCC transcript KQSF 90.9 FM 07.05.2011 2044

Operator's comments: subversion suspected

File as: "Monitor"/"Yellow Flag"

Hootenanny. It was perfect.

"What's a hootenanny?" Brandy asked.

"The solution to our problem. The perfect solution, in fact," I replied.

Hootenanny was originally an Appalachian colloquialism used for things whose names were forgotten or unknown. Dead things. Dead and forgotten like rock 'n' roll was becoming. A form of linguistic laziness for something on the tongue's tip, as in "Hand me that hootenanny."

Rock 'n' roll was becoming a forgotten word. Something like an exotic species resident only on the Galapagos Islands. Kenn and I were forgetting the songs that had once defined our lives. Time was erasing experiences that we had lived, in a different existence. Sometimes, like an old injury when the weather changed suddenly, we were reminded of what had made us who we were and who we wanted to be. Like faded scar tissue, definitions of words and clips of memories offered faint beacons back into the recesses of our memories. Memories of music and terms with multiple meanings, like *hootenanny*.

Hootenanny later became a country word for a party, and more specifically a folk-music party. A gathering of musical celebration; live music for a cause. But the relevance didn't end there.

During the late 1930s, *hootenanny* was also used by Hugh DeLacy's New Deal Democrats to describe periodic music-based fund-raisers. Woody Guthrie and others used *hootenanny* to describe their weekly rent parties, which featured many notable folksingers. Ironically, it was the collective and cooperative spirit of the hootenanny that DeLacy's opponents targeted, tarring him as a communist. It was one of the first times that music would be connected to concepts of socialism and un-Americanness and thus immorality. Sadly, rock 'n' roll too would have its detractors, those who claimed it was evil. People who didn't try to understand but would rather attempt to view the world through closed eyes. People who found it easier to label things to suit their own agendas. People who were actually themselves immoral and evil, intent upon misdirecting popular sentiments away from themselves and onto targets like homosexuals, socialists, and rock 'n' roll.

This is the struggle that rock 'n' roll has always faced. A struggle shared by other forms of art and expression that we all encounter and must overcome. Fear of change is an irrational dread.

"Kenn, we need a hootenanny."

"Great idea, genius. We need a gig to really whip up McCloy's fervor. He hates music enough already and you'll just incite him further. We're fucked."

"Irrational fears spur desperate acts. History proves this: women burned as witches, Congress forcing people to name names in response to the specter of communism. Censorship has been the death of rock 'n' roll, and yet music has never been a real threat to society. A hootenanny will play on McCloy's fear and cause him to lash out. McCloy thinks music is un-American and as much of a threat as McCarthy thought communism was."

Brandy said, "I'm not following you. How can something be considered un-American?"

"Maybe the problem is that we don't really understand what being American means. Kenn, consider how history changes through differing interpretations of related actions. Presidential apologies for interned Japanese families, some in Oregon that we know the grandchildren of. Irrational fears of yesterday become the reparations of tomorrow."

"You're in shock, dude," Kenn told me. "Brandy, can you get Joee's attention so we can have another round of drinks?"

"Kenn, I'm fine. Just hear me out. Change takes courage."

Brandy, returning with a tray of drinks asked, "Un-American? Immoral? Subversive? Aren't these just judgment-laden labels applied to things someone wants to oppose?"

"Exactly," Kenn said. "It's a way of labeling immorality, but the question ends up being *Immoral to who*?"

"You mean to *whom*," Brandy corrected, reaching toward Kenn and taking his drink, allowing the muscles in her shoulders to dance and flicker in a stunningly distracting manner.

"I mean we've had a hell of a week and don't need a grammar lesson," I replied.

"He means labeling people like Madonna, Lady Gaga, David Bowie, the Cramps, and Katy Perry. But never with an explanation as to why."

"Who?"

"Whom."

"Lady Gaga and Katy Perry." I scrambled on his miscue. "Sort of obscure acts that have caused a bit of a backlash for behavior some consider outrageous."

"Like what sort of behavior?"

"Yeah, well, you know, Katy claims to have kissed a girl. Actually, she kissed a girl *and liked it.* Can you imagine? Expressing an emotion publicly, either real or imagined, as scandalous as liking a *kiss*? In America?"

As perilous as it was discussing the future with Brandy, I reluctantly felt compelled to finish what we had started. "Regardless of whether or not Ms. Perry actually kissed a girl and liked it, her song caused a stir and proved that she's rock 'n' roll. Sure, Indigo Girls had previously covered this ground, just not in the same manner. Why? Indigo Girls were consenting adults, independent women who sang about issues of humanity and women's struggles. Katy Perry possesses the sensual yet wholesome pin-up-girl-next-door look. Rather than young adults who had determined that they were lesbians, here was a young girl exploring her curiosity, merely for her own gratification. Trying something for the sake of just seeing what it was about is the essence of rock 'n' roll.

"I know I'm rambling," I continued. "I keep hoping that you'll remember what we're after. But you don't seem to be getting there, Kenn. What is it that we're after?"

"A Replacements bootleg."

"Right." My response was measured. Aware of Brandy's presence and the likelihood she wouldn't really believe that Kenn and I were from an alternative future, I said, "Consider a world in which music isn't repressed, where a hootenanny festival features various acts. "Conceivably, there could be songs about hootenannies and albums of the same name."

Nodding, Brandy asked, "So what?"

"So, the Replacements had both a song and an album titled 'Hootenanny.' Both were recorded and released in 1983 before the album *Let It Be* and, more important, before the gig that the cassette was taken from. It's perfect. A hootenanny can become the very thing that would raise McCloy's ire and distract him and his brethren. This will give us the diversion we need."

Kenn started warming to the idea, and his malaise began thawing like frost in a spring sun. I could see obvious signs of him coming around; he would be back in action soon. Brandy, well, she was seemingly always ready for a fight, so she said, "Fuck yeah, what can I do?"

"Sorry, Brandy, this is rock 'n' roll, not a jazzy thing," I taunted her. "Thanks, but I think we're better off on our own again."

She reached across the table and as the firmness of her breast brushed against my arm, she immobilized my wrist in a firm grip and started reaching for what I could only assume was her Taser. "Call this whatever you like—a direct action, a hootenanny, or a circle jerk—I want in."

"You want to watch us circle jerk?" Kenn asked with more than a hint of hope.

"Watch out, Brandy 'n' Rocks." I smiled, having subtly planted what would later prove to be her stage name and persona. "You might be rock 'n' roll after all."

"Fuck you," she hissed, only half serious, as if warming to the idea. "Censorship affects all art, and personal liberty."

Right, here we go, I thought, having forgotten she was also a law student. Pausing to imagine her in a law school lecture, I could envision her as hell on wheels and running on nitro. Terrifying and mesmerizing all at once, far too much for the average law school class to contain.

"We'll need some bands," Kenn said, independent of the conversation that Brandy and I were now having. "Locals, guys passing through, anyone available. Right now, punk is stretching its legs," Kenn added, now fully engaged in the solution; you could almost hear the gears working in his brain.

"We should start calling on bands like the Dead Kennedys," I suggested.

"Maybe, we should try to contact Jello Biafra," suggested Kenn, back at trying to show off. I nodded in agreement, somewhere between tiring of him and being impressed. He was shouldering the task and thinking quickly, but still it seemed to always have to come at my cost. "He'll know who's around and up for a show. We'll tell them whatever we need to in order to get these guys assembled."

"Great idea, good thing I didn't suggest that earlier," I added, yet still impressed with Kenn's turnaround. "I'll call the local radio stations and the clubs so that we can have the press involved and come up with some red herring venues, and Brandy, can you get us a list of places outside where the bands can play? Then we'll coordinate a start time."

Joee orbited back around as celestial as ever and said, "I couldn't help but overhear your earlier discussion and while you're clearly not interested in Serge and I, you know, whatever, there is still a lot I can do." Pausing for effect, Joee leaned forward and continued in a conspiratorial tone, "I've made a couple of calls for you and Mr. Biafra is good to go. We're close. He's actually a cousin of mine."

Stunned, Kenn and I exchanged looks. "Fuck, Joee, that's great. That's huge. Thanks."

"I'm here to help you boys, always," leaning closer and now whispering across the back of his hand he continued, "just keep your eyes open, I can't always be so obvious in trying to get your attention. Keep an open mind about who you meet."

"I'm going to invite some girls, too," Brandy injecting herself into our pause. Kenn and I were learning, albeit slower than you'd think, that there was no sense in arguing with Brandy.

"Sure. Girls are usually cute," I added with a mocking confidence, now that she had something other than my numb wrist and her Taser to occupy her attention. In response, Brandy pulled a face, gave me a glare, and set off on her self-appointed tasks. "Back here in an hour, Ms. Alexander," I called after her. She wiggled her firm ass while flipping us the finger to acknowledge my comment as she walked away.

"You know, dude, I think she's beginning to like us."

"Don't worry, Kenn, I'm sure she'll get over it."

An hour later, we were back with a round of beer, strange little bite-size pizzas, a frosty reception from Joee, and the formation of a pretty good lineup. Our hootenanny was coming together: the plan was simple but required coordination.

Multiple bands simultaneously playing multiple venues. A concert of concerts. It was all to kick off after the Dead Kennedys' first salvo to lead the charge. All the advertising spots on the radio, the only thing we could arrange at short notice, were mentioning various free gigs at notable rock bars such as the Farm, the Warfield, Club Foot, and the Elite Club, this serving as the first of several diversionary tactics, as all the gigs were going to be in open public parks.

Brandy came up with the legal angle for us. Because they were free, there was no licensing, no permits, just honest Americans exercising their freedom of assembly and expression, as protected by the Constitution. Further, because they were all held in public parks, there was no worry about nuisance or obstruction issues, just music for all. Brandy was becoming as invaluable as she was distracting. I suppose it's always good to have a lawyer around, or at least a lawyer to be.

Between the red herring locations and the real shows that we would later call "Spontaneous" or "Guerrilla Gigs," this would create enough chaos, distracting law enforcement resources and enabling us to recover the tape and rejoin the Magnificent Seven. With some luck, we'd be able to lure McCloy away from his house and then enter without any further use of force, drama, and most important, failures on our part.

There were a bunch of reasons to let the Dead Kennedys kick the hootenanny off. First of all, Alternative Tentacles was their label, they were local, and on a rising star, but also because they managed to make contact with the various bands over an incredibly short period of time and to conscript them into the cause. However, what was perhaps the most compelling reason, even more compelling than the insistence of Jello Biafra, was that the band agreed to open with "Holiday in Cambodia."

The ominous bass line, the eerie jangling guitar, and crescendo opening to the song would all but guarantee that the crowd would launch into a fervor that would be commensurate with a great rock show.

Our hootenanny was going to be timed so that immediately after "Holiday in Cambodia" was finished, a cascade of other bands would start throughout the city. Because we had given out fake press releases, we expected that McCloy and his nefarious bunch would be raiding various venues throughout the city looking to extinguish rock 'n' roll once and for all. Pull the grass out by the roots, as it were. We would use this opportunity to plant more seeds and mow his lawn while he was away from home.

McCloy wouldn't be able to enlist the assistance of the police, as they would be attending to an unprecedented number of congestion and public gathering complaints due to the droves of music lovers flocking into the public parks. A key objective was to make sure resources were stretched, allowing Kenn and me to move unencumbered amid the chaos. In short, we would create a diversion of epic proportions for our mission. We would create a white riot.

14

White Riot

Time stands still. It allows us a gap to exit or to enter the theater of the world. Like when your cassette player eats a tape while you're driving. Everything stops. Life remains frozen as you carefully extricate the tape from the maw of the player. The passengers of the vehicle collectively holding their breath until the tension dissipates as the condition of the cassette is revealed. Is it all right? Can it be saved?

I bet riots are like that, too.

Riots come in many shapes and sizes. From the property-damaging rampages of drunken sporting fans—yes, Detroit and Vancouver, I'm talking about you—to misguided acts of civil disobedience. I'm Sid and you're listening to KQRL 89.9. It is now 2:33 in the morning.

This isn't the bread line riots, or the coal miner strikes, the race or class riots that are destructive, but rather it's supposed to be the good sort of riot. Like when people say "He's a riot" or "We had a riot last night." The uncontrolled, unbridled sort of fun that can't be contained and just needs to run out of steam like an excited four-year-old. Here's the Clash.

FCC transcript KQRL 89.9 FM 09.05.1987 0303
Operator's Comments: Incorrect time, flagged

"White Riot Causes Chaos!" the headlines read in the morning: It was awesome. Without a doubt my finest hour.

Well, maybe it wasn't really a white riot, but the denizens of the greater San Francisco Bay Area were in the streets. There were punks and rockers from Stanford to Oakland and Berkeley, up to Vallejo and San Rafael, all found at our spontaneous hootenannies. With the Dead Kennedys leading the charge in front of a crowd along the Golden Gate Promenade, things rapidly hit a boil and vaporized as superheated steam. Washington Square was hosting the Suicidal Tendencies, who happened to be up from L.A., as were the appropriately named Minutemen, who we had thundering away in Union Square. Head On was at the Berkeley campus; Agent Orange at Lake Merced Park; and the largest draw of them all, Crosby, Stills, Nash, and Young, had filled up Alamo Square. The entertainment was epic, but more important, it choked off traffic for blocks around, crippling the central part of the city and many of the surrounding regions.

Kenn had planned it perfectly. The result was a phalanx of rock 'n' roll detonating at different times in seemingly random locations in order to maximize havoc. It was like fireworks or popcorn left under a hot piece of metal, exploding unexpectedly and popping up unpredictably. These fireworks caused sparks of excitement, scrambling the police across the city, but more important, McCloy and his minions were propelled into action.

The guys from Alternative Tentacles and the radio stations we had contacted managed to reach out to everyone currently in a band in the greater Bay Area. Even people who had once been in a band or even considered forming one responded to our plea. There were musicians in the streets and parks everywhere. Even more interesting was the outpouring of rock 'n' roll fans. There was always an audience, someone to help set up, or just some random guy with beer or something of value to offer our cause. It was all pretty random, the things that people brought out: amps, generators, and coolers full of cold drinks. Someone even brought a police scanner along, allowing us to learn that traffic was halted, paralyzing the city. Within forty minutes of hootenanny mayhem, you could feel the tide of our success flooding through the streets. The police and emergency services were struggling to retain order, and reports were coming in that McCloy was frustrated at every turn.

A large part of the success of the hootenanny diversion was predicated on audience participation—specifically, the type of audience we expected to attract. Anarchists, all prewired for rebellion and civil disobedience. Unable to enlist the police, Lon had to deploy his own teams to the various nightclubs so that he and his goons could try to intervene and prevent bands from taking the stage. Tough times when you have to do your own heavy lifting. This was a particularly deft touch in our plan because there were no scheduled shows, and all the venues claimed that bands that were supposed to show had instead canceled at the last moment, without justification or excuse. While this was a fact that would have ordinarily pleased Lon immensely, I imagined that he would have sensed that something else was going on, torturing his need for control. What Lon had thought was going to be a simple capture turned into a bottomless barrel of red herrings.

Helping the cause, Brandy was up to her own tricks as well. Brandy could stop traffic in her own right. But she did so by setting up two bands, Rude Girl and the Desperate Teenage Lovedolls, on Lombard Street. Actually, I had to admit that she had a brilliant vision for aesthetics. Two all-girl acts taking advantage of both the acoustics and the striking visual presence that the steep incline of the famous switchback roadway had to offer. It was a pure rock 'n' roll move, but who doesn't want to look up at a bunch of immodest girls in short skirts and Dr. Martens boots who were throttling guitars, bludgeoning drums, and berating the mic stand. It was a spectacle that Kenn and I simply had to see. We were awestruck. We told people that we had a responsibility to make sure that the hootenanny was progressing as planned, but the truth was, we were just looking up skirts. Just a white lie, and really no harm caused, right? Besides, if the girls didn't want people looking up their skirts, they would have worn something different, right? At least that was my justification.

I think it was at that moment, peering up at the raucous short skirts and thundering version of rock 'n' roll, that I began to lose my view that girls were only the downfall of rock 'n' roll and the corruption of humanity. Looking past the sparse hemline, I noticed that Brandy was impressive, musically; she had a sharp sense and great instincts, not to mention that she was hotter than summer lightning.

"Since I seem to terrify and distract you guys," Brandy said sardonically, "what's next?"

Brandy was right. As tempting as sitting back and basking in our eventual success might have been, or even remaining in San Fran, going from one venue to the next watching the various bands that had come together in aid of rock 'n' roll, we knew it wasn't to be.

Even if we could control crossing back to our time, which we never had managed, we still had to find MacLeslie and physically return the cassette to the band.

So Kenn and I skirted around the edge of our mayhem and sped off to rescue the remaining Magnificent Seven so we could return the cassette to the Replacements.

Reflecting upon our achievements, Kenn and I were content returning to music without recounting the specifics of our adventure. There was no discussion of our standoff with Rollins or McCloy, of subsequent crossings, or even of the Replacements. The solemn enjoyment of being reunited with our music and some passing musings about Brandy was all that remained of saving rock 'n' roll.

"What did you say to Brandy as we left?" I asked, recalling her sarcasm and taunting question.

"I don't know, memory is a complicated thing, something like; 'Well, Brandy,' I said," Kenn said, recreating his mocking tone. "'It's complicated. Let's just say, today your love, tomorrow the world.'"

PART 3

CEREMONY

Ceremony:

A formal act or celebration conducted according to a specified
   ritual or custom.

A conventional social gesture designed to mark an occasion,
   achievement, or rite of passage.

An act having social or religious meaning through its observance or
   practice, even if the substance of the act itself appears superficial.

A song by Joy Division released on the live album *Still.* The recording
   was made sixteen days before the suicide of Ian Curtis on
   May 18, 1980.

A song covered in 1981 by New Order, the reconstitution of Joy Division,
   after Curtis's untimely demise. "Ceremony" was released as New
   Order's first single.

A song covered in 1989 by Galaxie 500 on their 1989 debut EP, *Blue Thunder*.

A song covered in 2007 by Radiohead for their *Thumbs Down* webcast.

15

Today Your Love, Tomorrow the World

The Ramones changed the world. They changed the world one song and four chords at a time. Nothing ambitious. Nothing arrogant, merely a collection of disparate parts with a shared view of music. A perfect example of how important the little things are.

The Ramones changed the world by making music that they wanted to hear. Music that they loved and that meant something to them.

The Ramones represent the musical equivalent of Maslow's hierarchy of needs, where basic needs, such as food and shelter, must be met before higher needs such as self-fulfillment can be.

This is Sid here at KQRF 89.9, the time check is 4:33 a.m. Look around you. Can you see the convergence of Maslow and the Ramones? After all, we've all heard the expression "first things first." We need to feel safe, secure, content before we dare to achieve more. If you're looking for an example, up next is "Today Your Love, Tomorrow the World."

FCC transcript KQOO 90.9 FM 09.15.2011 0433

Operators Comments: station ID FAIL

Search Term: "mind control" + "maslow"

"Today your love, tomorrow the world?" I repeated, in shock, yet starting to laugh. "Really? Really, Kenn? That was what you left Brandy with?" We had returned to Kenn's, having ensured the bootleg cassette was safely in MacLeslie's and the Replacements' care.

Kenn and I were exhausted. While our physical injuries had all but vanished, as they often did when we returned home, the stress still weighed upon us, creating as much lassitude as physical trauma would. But even as fatigued as we were, the elation of our success made us dizzy.

"Should I put on some U2?" I asked.

Returning to Kenn's basement felt like the sort of homecoming that you see in airports. The kind where a travel-weary person shambles with uncertainty into the brightly illuminated concourse and at the last moment sees the blur of someone rushing to greet them. Kenn and I were both on the cusp of tears as we witnessed the bounty of his fully restored music collection. The world was as it should be.

"Fuck, man, I didn't really know what else to say," Kenn said, shrugging off my comment with a smile but still a little chagrinned. "I thought it was clever, and besides, the Ramones said it first."

"You'll be remembered, buddy." Actually, it was a pretty cool parting line, especially for Brandy. It was sort of mysterious and ambitious, like rock 'n' roll, and yet complicated like Kenn and me. Actually I told Kenn that he had done remarkably well during the recovery operation and that I wouldn't have been able to shake out of my funk without his intervention. It was then that I finally had the courage to tell him that he was a good friend.

Kenn and I opened a couple of beers, ordered pizza, canceled the order, and then ordered Chinese instead, while we talked. We canceled the Chinese order and reordered the pizza, and then finally settled for half orders of each.

"OK, desert-island discs," Kenn said. "Our music collection is restored; what do we listen to first?"

People write about the things they miss. The first meal they'll have when they return home, friends they'll see. A baseball game, maybe.

Kenn and I couldn't decide what to listen to first so we just started playing things randomly. The moment washing over us, serendipity taking control.

"What a genius," Kenn sighed.

"Me?"

"No, the genius who invented random song shuffling. I hope he got a Nobel Prize."

"I don't think that the Nobel Committee concerns itself with stereo settings."

"They should. Why would you think I was talking about you?"

"You call me genius enough so I never know who you're talking about," I said, "but, yeah, the inventor probably didn't get the accolades he deserved, much like whoever created the takeout container or drive-through window."

"Life is harsh; the world unfair."

As we were pushing our remaining food around and nursing the remaining beers from Kenn's now barren fridge, I realized Kenn was right. We could take on the world. In fact, we already had.

Even from the beginning of this story, you already knew how it turned out, but now you know *why*. That's the important part. Isn't "*Why?*" the eternal human question?

Ultimately this is a story about a girl. This is a story about redemption and love, about learning something from Pyrah, and mostly about myself.

These are the details of how our story ended.

I was standing beside Kenn, lost in the rock 'n' roll moment, confused by my emotions and the gathering of great bands that we had organized. It was Brandy who shattered my reverie, shouting something like, "We've established you're not waiting around for a handjob from me. Haven't you idiots got something meaningful to do?"

Right, the diversion was only the first part. We needed to get back to McCloy's house in order to free the rest of the Seven and recover the tape. We still needed to get Denver, Ice-T, Johnny Cash, and the Chilis back to safety; maybe that would allow Kenn and me to go home.

Hadn't we achieved enough? I mean, we had proved that rock 'n' roll would stand in the face of adversity. Kenn and I had created the concept of spontaneous or guerrilla gigs, which would later become flash mobbing, but only after bands like the Black Eyed Peas, Get Cape. Wear Cape. Fly, the Rheostatics, and U2 had emulated what Kenn and I started in San Francisco.

"Yeah, Brandy." Kenn nodded with menace in his eyes and confidence in his posture. "We're gonna come out swinging."

16

Come Out Swinging

Following the last set, which ended with Chixdiggit and their view that "Henry Rollins Is No Fun," here's the Offspring and "Come Out Swinging."

FCC transcript KQXF 92.9 FM 01.21.1999 0513
Operator comments: Intervention fails all license requirements

"Come out swinging?" I asked Kenn, feeling the excitement of our success drain away, leaving me awash with new feelings of confusion and apprehension. My stomach began to list again as it had in John Denver's warehouse. Although it was clear what we had to do, I started compiling excuses. I knew what was at stake and everything that Kenn and I had endured, but still it was facing demons that challenged my resolve. McCloy, Rollins, the fact that we had already failed so dramatically and that really Kenn and I were out of our depth, especially as things were likely to become violent, were all barriers that existed in my mind, discouraging me from continuing.

"We need a car," Kenn said, "or a lift back to the Rosenberg house."

"Here," Brandy offered, throwing a set of keys to Kenn. "Borrow my roommate's; he'll be cool with it."

Kenn shrugged and grunted a form of thanks for her help and the gracious loan of her roommate's crappy little Mazda GLC. The car was resting on worn tires and covered with so many stickers of punk bands and Southern California universities that you could barely see the blue paint under them all.

"You sure this is OK?" I asked.

"Meh. What's he going to say? He probably won't even notice."

"Is that him standing over by the lamppost?" Brandy and Kenn turned toward a forlorn-looking guy who appeared as though he wanted to say something but thought shifting his gaze between his car and his shoes was more interesting.

He was a skinny, nervous-looking guy. Perhaps a classmate as well as her roommate, but he appeared to have access to money. His clothes were clean and new, even though they had that retrograde punk rock look to them; it wasn't the punk of the streets but rather a stylized punk. A look that was *organized* rather than created. His was a look that showed as a fragile familiarity with the scene but lacked the casual comfort. I wouldn't say that he was disingenuous, but he lacked the aggression that a strident Mohawk and the facial piercings suggested. His angry veneer was betrayed by the sensitivity in his eyes. Perhaps more contrived than genuine. He seemed like someone who would remain on the periphery of things his entire life, without entering the fray. A participant who would remain detached, at an arm's length, standing at the edge of the mosh pit but never slam dancing. Not bad, nothing to be ashamed of, just talking the talk, but then, living alongside Brandy, caution was likely prudent.

Although I envied the roommate's proximity to Brandy, I suspect that life as her roommate would be like being on opposite sides of the same tether. I could envision wanting Brandy romantically but also being afraid of her, and more anxious of her Taser; it would be this fear that would prevent any unsolicited advance. I could only conclude that everyone else felt the same way about her.

Her roommate's stringy wet hair, faltering at half-mast between a defiant electric-blue Mohawk and a flaccid comb-over, embarrassed by its very existence. The wet, defeated look of his hair suited him.

He seemed chilled by the rain, which was probably compounded by Brandy's extracting any sacrifice from him that she desired. It was difficult to be certain, but through the gloomy night air, the Gothic script across his shoulders seemed to say "*Unrequited.*"

Racing back to the Rosenberg House in a car that blurred the line between stolen and borrowed, Kenn looked across at me. "She's something else," Kenn said, reading my thoughts, which must have been painted on my face.

"Uh-huh," I replied, vacillating between a preoccupation with Brandy and thoughts of what would be waiting for us at the Rosenberg house.

"What do you think? Did Brandy get permission from the guy?"

"Doubt it. He looks like he's been reared on a diet of losing control over anything in his life that has the slightest connection with Brandy."

"Talk about being hardcore"—the respect for Brandy glowing from Kenn—"I bet she shaves with a straight razor."

"You know, Kenn," I replied in distracted astonishment, "you absolutely amaze me. How do you even come up with this shit? Now I've got the image of Brandy shaving her legs with a straight blade." In my mind, she would use an implement that had seen better days. A long bone handle, cracked and chipped, and a blade that, although stained and bearing flecks of rust, had a gleaming edge as sharp as Brandy's wit. Both equally deadly.

"I wasn't thinking about her legs."

"Stop it!"

"What?" Kenn started incredulously. "You don't think so? Try to tell me that you've never given it any thought."

He had me there, because I was now in fact, for some inexplicable reason, thinking about Brandy's grooming preferences. "Fuck, Kenn. She could shave with a broken whiskey bottle, for all I know. What's the matter with you?"

"I lack judgment and the ability to filter comments."

"That's not your only problem. Can we just drive? Please?"

Kenn silently nodded, seemingly enjoying the image of Brandy with her leg on the edge of a bathtub, drawing long strokes with a broken bottle of Jack Daniels against her soapy skin. We turned onto Jackson Street, two blocks away from McCloy's, but in the opposite direction from where Denver had parked. Kenn pulled over and silenced the engine. Together we sighed.

After a moment's pause, Kenn looked at me and nodded. "OK. Let's see how this goes."

While I never actually knew, I suspected that Kenn was as apprehensive as I was about returning to the scene of our previous failure. Some people just project things differently, based upon their own capacity for perseverance.

Returning in silence to the Rosenberg house, where Kenn and I had abandoned the magnificent part of the Seven, we prepared ourselves for another assault. This time it was more than confronting the Evil in order to prevent the rock 'pocalypse; we were also trying to exorcise our own ghosts. Specters of our own failing, taunts that whispered in our ears from a night's wind, torments of our expectations perpetually being out of step with our abilities—these were the monsters that we faced and needed to overcome.

Unlike our previous and spectacularly unsuccessful effort, we were unarmed, alone, and without the effervescent optimism of being with rock 'n' roll luminaries. Not just rock stars, but legends that were doubling as an elite paramilitary assault team.

Unlike previous crossings, Kenn and I dispensed with developing a plan for the actual assault of the Rosenberg house. I really don't know why. Proceeding without a plan didn't seem like a great idea, but lately our plans had been such abject failures, and really we had expended all our imagination coming up with the diversions. Either this was going to work or it wasn't.

Entry into the house was straightforward. The house was unguarded and unlocked, with signs of a hasty exit.

"I hoped that this would be easy," Kenn said.

"This place feels like a tomb."

"A pretty swank tomb. Maybe Brandy will dress up like Lara Croft and meet us later?"

"*Tomb Raider* hasn't been made yet, so probably not. Seems that McCloy left in a hurry. Still, wasn't the house locked down remotely last time? I bet he's pissed at us." The thought of Brandy as Lara Croft distracted me, and I began thinking about how long it had been since I'd even played a video game.

"Fuck 'im, I'm not all that pleased with him either right now. We hoped the diversion would make things easy, but . . . here, let's head this way."

We headed down a corridor, opening doors that entered into sitting and meeting rooms, places where men would smoke cigars and others where women would drink tea. The only living sounds were those of an operating house—water pipes, fans, other mechanical processes; no people, no music or television or even radio.

The house contained numerous large rooms that sprawled past their leather furniture, swallowing expanses of tapestries and embroidered carpets. McCloy appeared to be someone who protected the status quo because that also protected his way of life. The trappings of a life ordered to please himself and celebrate his achievements and station. A ceremony of possessions. Finally, behind the fifth door in the corridor, we found the Magnificent Seven.

They were all gagged and bound to chairs. They appeared comfortable, resigned perhaps to their confinement. Their confinement hadn't included torture like that of ours; in fact the room was well lit, and they were in comfortable stuffed leather chairs, just immobilized.

"Let's get these guys loose first, Kenn; then we can search for the cassette."

"Sure—" Kenn started to say.

"Hey, how cool is this?" Brandy interrupted. "I thought I'd follow you guys so I could help, and look who I brought! Totally badass!"

The shock of seeing Brandy was compounded not only by the fact that she was not dressed like Lara Croft, but by the fact that Dave Alvin was in tow. Kenn shut down instantly, turning his back. He began pacing on the other side of the room, clenching his fists and expelling deep breaths.

I quietly explained to Dave and Brandy that Kenn couldn't cope with anything related to the Blasters. While there was no argument that the Blasters and subsequent projects by the Alvin brothers provided the foundation of rock 'n' roll and specifically rockabilly, it wasn't about the music. For Kenn it was a personal torment. A complicated history that we just didn't talk about anymore. Kenn simply couldn't.

It wasn't a case of Kenn brooding or being sullen, but rather a case of him being agitated. I knew Kenn's history, and the only way that Kenn could cope was to ignore Alvin's presence altogether. I started wishing for a distraction. Fortunately, my pleas were immediately answered in a manner consuming all of Kenn's emotion and narrowing his focus like that of a surgical laser.

As Kenn stepped onto an area rug to start freeing John Denver, lights began to flash, the door swung shut, and the window shutters slid down with the distinct sound of locking mechanisms engaging.

"Fuck," Kenn said as John Denver's head slumped forward, retreating from his newly discovered optimism back to resignation.

"Kenn, I'm sure it will be fine," I said as I looked around nervously. "Let's get everyone unbound and figure this out."

We nervously removed the gags and untied the Magnificent Seven, helping them up, making spartan conversation while looking around for some means of escape. The flashing light had slowed to a rate that I would describe as mildly irritating, but considering that I was losing track of how many times I had failed on this crossing, a flashing light seemed like just another torment in hell.

A muffled shout from outside of the room caused us to pause.

"Can you hear me? Get away from the door. Do it now!" The door to the room exploded open with a black skateboarding shoe and a tattoo-covered leg following through its powerful kick. "I've got the cassette!

I've got the cassette! Let's get out of here. My van is in the carport."

Rollins. Fucking Rollins had the cassette now and was joyously waving it above his head. Once again Kenn and I had been duped into failure.

Despite the noise created by the efforts to liberate the Magnificent part of the Seven, the distraction of Brandy and Alvin and the broken door raining splinters of wood onto the floor, an uneasy hush fell over the room. All eyes turned to Rollins, offering him only indictment and demanding an explanation. The cold, damning stares of those who were once his peers and shared inspiration caused Rollins to soften and appear as uncomfortable as a school bully having been called out before the principal.

"Ah, hey . . . right," Rollins started. "Look, I probably owe you guys, a . . . well, I do owe all of you guys, but especially you and Kenn, an apology," he said, turning to me. "It wasn't right. I can't pretend that I didn't know it was wrong at the time, but I was confused. You said you had discovered time travel. I needed to make some things right. Correct the past. I'm sorry. I'm so sorry."

The mighty bulk of Henry Rollins sagged, bowing his usually rigid posture as though the weight of his sin was too much to bear, as though the words themselves had been propping him up. "Here," he said, handing me the cassette. Rollins turned to Kenn and said, "Look, I know that I let you down. You're obviously a fan, I could tell by our conversation in the van. Really, I'm flattered. So I can't imagine how it must have been for you—you know, later, when . . . well, because of how I acted."

How he 'acted,' I thought. Did he mean the drugging, kidnapping, lying, beatings, deprivation of food and water, and extended confinement? Is that what that was? An act? Or was this simply part of a past he wanted to change?

"I want to make this right. I need to make amends, so that's why I'm here now. To get the cassette back to you guys so you could decide what to do with it. And, Kenn, you get to give back what I gave you. I'll let you even the score," Rollins said, settling to his knees and raising his palms in supplication, the lion becoming a sacrificial lamb.

The room was in silent shock. Kenn and I cast awkward, embarrassed looks at each other, not knowing where to look or what was going to happen. Kenn moved alone toward Rollins. "OK," Kenn muttered, "let's see." He found and unsheathed a long knife from the desk and laid it down in front of Rollins. Then he found a large piece of timber from the shattered door, removed his thick leather belt, and took a large glass object off a side table and placed these objects on the floor next to the knife.

"So, I get to strike back at you for confining and torturing us," Kenn started, dragging a chair behind the kneeling Rollins, the room mesmerized by the spectacle unfolding before us, silent but with a palpable feeling of discomfort. "What about the drugs? Or the kidnapping?"

"Kenn, you don't have to do this," I said, knowing that I wanted to as well, but feeling ill at the prospect. "You can—"

Kenn held his hand up to silence me. "And if I strike you back. Now. Here. This will make us even, for your betrayal. I'll still have my injuries, but this will make *you* feel better, because then *I'll* be the same as you." Kenn's voice was cold and detached, like a chisel on stone.

"Well . . ." Rollins tried to reply, with anxiety building in his voice and his body starting to tremble. "That wasn't really what I meant . . . but I thought that maybe . . . I don't know . . . that maybe you would forgive me. Maybe I could . . . or you might—"

Kenn interrupted. "So, I could use this knife and what? Cut you? Leave a scar, maybe remove a finger? Or should I crush your hand with this desk piece?" he asked, testing the heft of the glass object. "Maybe I could strangle you with my belt, or smash you with the chair. Maybe I should get acid to burn off those little notes that you've got tattooed on your hand to remove your badge of shame. What if I break your knee? But just one, right? Just one and then we're even?"

Rollins was looking around the room, hoping that someone would intervene and save him, that someone would offer him some sanctuary, but knowing that he was alone. Alone in the judgment caused by his actions. There was a palpable ripple of shock passing through the room, turning us into rubbernecking witnesses, unwilling to do anything but look on and absorb Kenn's words, yet still beyond the shock there was a coldness in all the eyes that held Rollins.

Would retribution make it even between Rollins and Kenn? No. The expression on Henry's face said that he knew it wouldn't be even. Sure, while the tallies on the scorecard registered for both sides, that retribution doesn't make amends.

"Look. Please," he started pleading, "I just wanted to change the past. I want to be sorry and be forgiven."

"Well then," Kenn countered, with a calm so controlled that it flushed cold air through the room, chilling everyone. Even Rollins had goose bumps, although he was sweating and breathing heavily. I wanted to look away but couldn't, gripped by the sort of feeling that causes nausea when you witness an accident or public humiliation. I was transfixed by what was playing out between Kenn and Rollins.

Kenn grabbed the knife and rolled it in his hand, circling behind Rollins's back. "This seems to be a lot about you. I should help you feel better by lowering myself to that of a common torturer. Is that it? Is this the best that we can do? We know so little about ourselves that we don't know how to repair the damage caused by our atrocities, so we simply allow others to seek retribution instead? You know, Henry, it's not the past that's difficult to change but the future." Kenn let the knife drop, and Rollins collapsed forward to the floor, broken and exhausted. "I'm not going to forgive you, nor am I going to strike back at you. You decide what it is that you want. You choose what your future will be. Change the *now*."

"C'mon," I said, trying to break the awkward silence around Kenn's monologue. "Let's get this cassette back to the Replacements." Internally, I struggled with the fact that McCloy's manor was deserted and that we didn't have the satisfaction of facing him. Looking away from everyone, Rollins pulling himself up straight to his imposing stature, I reflected on what we had achieved, finally. Finally Kenn and I had got it right.

"You know, that was mighty gracious of you," Johnny Cash said to Kenn. "It makes me proud to see a big man to walk that line."

Kenn nodded distractedly and muttered, "Well, until you wear a rainbow every . . ." Perhaps he was thinking about returning the cassette that we now had, or reflecting upon our success, but maybe Kenn was ruminating on something else entirely. In that instant, I felt an overwhelming loss for Kenn. His isolation seemed so complete that even in victory he was alone—so haunted by his own ghosts that personal success passed by unnoticed like a silent shadow. There were lingering accolades and pats on the back for Kenn, but generally he was left alone.

It was Ice-T who grabbed Rollins and pulled him to his feet and led him down a hallway. "Yous best git outta here. Think about tonight, you jus' scored another chance. I'd say yous make best of it."

Anthony finally broke the tension. "Guys, this has been trippy. What a score! Flea, we're going to be talking about this forever, don'tcha think? Kenn, you guys got time to hit the beach and grab a couple waves?"

"Look," I responded, "that would be cool, but we really have to get going. We've still got road to cover. Maybe when you're up in Oregon next you can give us a call."

Flea chimed in, "You guys are on. This has been great."

"Anthony," Kenn responded, finally coming out of his reverie, "make sure you always check the dashboard lights in taxis. Never get in a cab without one of the engine lights on."

Flea and Anthony looked at Kenn blankly. Flea responded, "Are you OK? A little shock maybe?"

"Nah, it's true," I added. "Kenn has studied this, and it's a safety thing." I gave Kenn a wink and a knowing nod of my head. "Cabs are routinely used for nefarious ends, because of their ability to move around without drawing attention. The average cab driver barely makes enough to get by, so his car is always on the verge of complete disrepair; a well-maintained cab is a sure sign of trouble. Trust us."

Bidding everyone good-bye, Brandy proceeded to drop us off at the wharfs so that we could grab the train to the airport while she returned her roommate's car. Kenn lingered with Brandy as I took a last long look at the bay.

Reflecting later, I didn't really know what I would have said or done to McCloy, had he been there. Certainly I had been afforded the opportunity to say something in his basement but had failed to really engage him on the level that I thought I needed to. McCloy was wrong. Wrong about rock 'n' roll and wrong about what he wanted to achieve. But mostly wrong about his reasons. Surely I knew enough and had a sufficient understanding of history that I could convince him. Although Kenn and I restored music and saved the Seven, I still felt unfulfilled. Like I'd been denied something. I wished I had demonstrated the fortitude and resolve to face McCloy so I could have converted his thinking.

It could have been a moment that I would have looked back upon with pride and Kenn would have acknowledged as a success. A watershed experience capable of changing my life, re-charting a course to a long line of personal successes. Convincing McCloy would have brought more than just satisfaction; it have would brought validation to me and converted an adversary into an ally. McCloy as a supporter of rock 'n' roll would be a coup and could bring untold benefit, because after all, there is no antismoker more passionate than the ex-smoker. McCloy could have been rock 'n' roll's ex-smoker.

With the significant resources of John Denver helping us to find where the Replacements were playing, booking flights, and providing cash for travel, Kenn and I were on our way. Exhausted, I started falling asleep as the plane was taxiing and woke to blowing snow buffeting the windows as the flight attendants were announcing our arrival at O'Hare.

Within a few hours, we had tracked down MacLeslie and returned the cassette to him as he was conducting a sound check for the evening's show.

Did things turn out as I expected when we returned the tape to the Replacements? No, not at all. It was actually very strange. As anything that is strange, the outcome was totally unexpected. Kenn and I thought there would be a big shift as though everything had returned to normal, something seismic or tidal. You know, that the clouds would part and birds would sing, welcoming the sun out with us on parade as heroes.

But that didn't happen. We were met with a sort of shrugging of shoulders, an indifferent nod and grunt. MacLeslie didn't even offer to put Kenn and me on the guest list like he had promised back in Oklahoma City. Instead, he just looked at us like we were Martians. Martians who had saved rock 'n' roll, but aliens all the same. It would have been the very same if we had prevented him from being hit by a speeding bus by stopping to talk to him a block earlier, slowing his progress so that the bus would pass harmlessly along.

"So, what? That's it?" Kenn asked MacLeslie.

"Huh?"

"The cassette. We brought you back the bootleg from Oklahoma and you've got nothing to say?"

"Ah . . . thanks, I guess? Look, I'm sure it's great, but what do you want? I'm sure you guys went through a lot of trouble risking life and limb and whatever. I hear this story all the time, but I've got a sound check to do and the bus with the guys is late. So, sure. Thanks for the cassette. I'll make sure it's safe, but I don't really have time for a playdate." MacLeslie held up two fingers to the bar and continued, "Here, I've just told the bartender to buy you a couple of beers. Stick around and watch the show if you want. Just don't cause any trouble; you both look like you've been through meat grinders."

Kenn and I wandered over to the bar in stunned disbelief. "Here you guys go. I'm Joe; this is my bar. Drinks are on me tonight, but you guys look like you could really use a rest. You should have a couple and then head home. Seriously, you guys look like you've been left for dead."

And that's exactly what happened. Kenn and I finished our beers and headed out of the bar onto the street to figure our next move, but fortunately, as soon as we left the bar, we entered Kenn's house. Strange. Strange to finally be back.

We checked our music collections and they were intact, completely. Things were as they should be. Rock 'n' roll was on television again, commercials had jingles, and sports teams piped anthems to motivate their fans to motivate their teams. Still, an unease lingered; no relief or sense of accomplishment. No endorphin rush like completing a marathon or an exam. Strange, but not like the strange that we were getting used to; this felt like something else.

I guess it was just the end, just like that. No explanation, no fanfare, and nothing else to do, but the end. As much as I hate encores, they exist for a reason, and that reason is the same one as why you're asking me how it all ended. You're asking because people don't like to admit that the end has come.

But even this specific feeling of the end was different; strange, in fact. Something familiar, but still strange.

17

Strange

This is Sid at KQPL 90.1 FM at 11:50 in the evening. Sometimes I feel time slip. I enter off cue, like an anxious session musician. I know it's strange that I'm here before midnight, but there you go. Time doesn't always behave as it should.

Anyone who has a family understands that "strange" is relative. Strange is by its very definition extraordinary, so what's strange for one may be commonplace for others. In fact, you can even get used to things so that they're no longer strange, but transformed, changed into something familiar. Sort of like expecting me on the air after midnight.

This goes out to my uncle. Here's Galaxie 500 with "Strange."

FCC transcript KQPL 90.1 FM 04.07.2001 0153
Operator's comments: Strange. Time check incorrect.

Strange. Strange indeed.

"That bartender was strange," said Kenn.

"Strange? Which one?"

"The guy in the jazz bar, Joee."

"You mean the waiter? I suppose. Everything has been a bit off for a while, though, and I'm not sure I know what's right and what's out of place anymore." I sighed contemplatively and looked around Kenn's basement. "He did seem to think we had been through a lot. What do you think he meant when he said, 'he was always around to help us'?"

"Yeah, not sure. Pretty sure that's the first time I've seen him. Bartenders. They seem intuitive."

"He was a waiter. You're thinking about Brandy. But yeah, they seem to have a certain sense. So everything looks good here. I think I'm going to go home. I need to crash."

"Lock up on your way. I'll see you around."

I went home and found my music collection had been restored, just like Kenn's, and my place still smelled as fresh as it had when Kenn cleaned it. I set the iPod to play Mumford and Sons, making a note that we should cross to see them, eventually, hopefully in some sleepy little surf town. I couldn't imagine that Kenn was in a rush to cross; I certainly needed a break.

Fishing around for something to eat, I found proof instead. Proof that memories only fade but never depart. Proof of what Naked Eyes were thinking when they sang "Always Something There to Remind Me," staring with a mixed sense of despair and amazement, at the bottom of a bowl that I had planned to fill with instant noodles: There she was. Pyrah.

Pyrah was still in my apartment, or at least the backing of a single earring that she had put in the bowl to prevent it from getting lost. I threw the bowl and earring in the garbage, grabbed a mealy apple, and walked out of my house. I felt lost, exiled, and alone, but I had a plan. Now I was going to find a sandwich shop and then drop by the radio station to see if I could start my show again. Or at least make a start when they needed extra coverage. I would need a job soon, too. Perhaps Vinnie would let me pour coffee at Ka'Fiend.

It was strange. For everything that I had achieved with Kenn, all I wanted to do was return my life to the routine that I'd once eschewed.

Within a few days of crossing back from the Replacements adventure, Kenn and I returned to our routine of pizza and rock 'n' roll.

It was comfortable, familiar, but still parts of our escapade lingered like the stench of burned hair, taking us a long time to even consider playing Ice-T or the Red Hot Chili Peppers, not to mention the Replacements or Rollins. I never felt the need to discuss Pyrah's earring with Kenn.

One day, shortly after I arrived, Kenn announced that he had a plan. I was glad to know that we would be crossing again, part of the rhythm that our lives ran alongside.

"Hey, when you finish that slice, we're going to cross to see this great Canadian band. I know. Don't look at me like I'm crazy; they're crazy good. The story is that they're supposed to be a tight band and the lyrics are clever."

"Let's go. Just let's avoid any drama this time."

Louie Louie was set up, and off we crossed to see the Weakerthans. I don't know why Kenn didn't just tell me the band's name when he suggested crossing, perhaps to add flourish to the evening. Of course, we were familiar with their music and the complicated and clever songwriting, but just had never crossed to see them before. The time was now. The reports were that these gigs were always great, and we wanted to see firsthand.

I took a long swig of Dew and the room began shuddering. Light filled my mind as pressure started building in my head, and as the room began peeling away from us, I stumbled and felt my foot stick to the floor as though I had been standing on something tacky.

Kenn was slightly ahead of me, but once again, we had crossed into a live music venue. However, something was amiss. Looking around, I could see that the location was crowded but quiet. Rather than a stage, the scene was set with a low riser upon which John Samson, the lead singer and guitarist, and John Sutton, the bass player, were preparing to address the crowd. The house lights were lit and there was a conspicuous absence of instruments, amps, or other equipment. In fact the other members of the band weren't to be seen, either. Maybe this was just an acoustic set, with only Sutton and Samson performing. But even that appeared to be an unwarranted conclusion. It seemed that there was no gig at all, but rather just a meeting. There were no signs of rock 'n' roll, except for the presence of Sutton and Samson.

If you count attending live music as a must-do experience in one's life, then so too is arriving early. There are certain things that I can now say, looking back upon my life, that I think all responsible and civilized people should commit to doing. Arriving early to a baseball game in order to watch pregame drills and batting practice, where the players are rehearsing in relative calm; or attending the theater and enjoying the cacophony of the orchestra tuning and warming up their instruments. These experiences create a contrast, heightening the performance. The seemingly tactile din of the warm-up that gives way to the nuanced grace of the recital; a rawness that transforms into a polished performance. These experiences provide such stark contrasts that they enrich the event and always raise pimples on my skin faster than an autumn wind off the ocean. As much as I love rock 'n' roll shows, I relish the anticipation and blue-collar ethic of loading and unloading a band. It's like watching an artist painstakingly work through sketches, layers of paint, almost sculpting the painting into the finished work. Of course, it's always great to see the finished product, but one's depth of appreciation is in part dependent upon one's understanding the process.

But whatever was going on here, it wasn't a gig; this was something else entirely. Anytime you go to a gig early, if you can get in at all, before the doors officially open, there is a feeling. A vibe. The bartender filling his fridges, pouring buckets of ice into bar sinks, priming his kegs, and setting up his mixes. A soundman running cables and checking the speakers, roadies warming up amps and positioning mic stands or the low tables that hold the band's beer and bottled water.

Notwithstanding that, Kenn and I didn't really know, or even care, where we were; there were certain people who looked familiar. Not really a déjà vu, but more of a sense of recognition, but out of context, further contributing to the overall strangeness.

As you'd expect with time travel, strange had long since quit being strange for us. So, too, would the continual crossings to venues near and far, past and present. After a while you get used to the idea there is only really a finite set of people who will frequent CBGB's or L.A.'s Viper Room to take in a show. Rock 'n' roll is like that. It's not as though a tourist is going to roll into New York City and say, "What do you think? Should we go see something on Broadway after a day at the American Museum of Natural History or the Frick Collection? Oh wait, honey, the Hoodoo Gurus are headlining with the Lime Spiders at CBGB's. I know it's a dive, but . . ." Sure, it could happen, but not as often as tourists find their way to Yankee Stadium.

It's like the Louvre in Paris. Everyone knows it, but what about Le Bataclan? No, of course not. You would probably be surprised to know that it is a fifteen-hundred-person-capacity venue that has hosted the likes of the Velvet Underground, the Cure, Echo and the Bunnymen, INXS, and New Order.

But ultimately, because of the appeal of places like CBGB's and the bands that became their denizens, there is a good chance that when you continue to see these bands, you'll see some of the same folks. But again, this was different. This was strange. Stranger than we had become accustomed to and stranger than could be anticipated. There were no tables set up, or even having the appearance of being set up, to sell copies of CDs, special-edition vinyl in a cool colour (yeah, *colour* with a superfluous *u* because these clowns were Canadians; must be the cold that makes them want to do extra work to stay warm); no roadies busying themselves. Despite all the rock shows I'd been to by that point, there was nothing here that was at all familiar, except for Samson and Sutton. Strange.

Especially strange, given the reports we'd read that the Weakerthans were the very essence of rock 'n' roll. Their albums had a cohesion and continuity among the songs, and each song was always interesting. But like Kenn had said, it was their cohesion and presence as a live act that drew us across to see them in whatever cold, godforsaken backwater venue we were in. To go all this way for a show that seemed to be all sorts of strange, well, that was just plain wrong. Then we knew.

As we got closer to the riser, we could see that the people gathered around Samson and Sutton shared an appearance. Not fashionably punk like Brandy's roommate, but still something contrived. Like hipsters or mods; a certain look reflecting an identity.

While the audience couldn't be described as uniform, a sense of homogeneity filled the room. Manners, posture, dress. All slightly different but strangely similar, as though they were all screaming, "Look, I'm just as unique as you!"

Sutton was speaking to the crowd, handing out sheets of paper. "It's time we take a stand. Morality needs to be restored to music. What is being justified in the name of art and music—what's being done to our children—has to stop."

A chorus of agreement and support rippled through the crowd, but again with the same amorphous manner that mirrored the costume of the patrons. Nothing inspired, nothing contentious or challenging, just a bleating assembly seeking to be led.

Samson continued, "We're not doing rock 'n' roll anymore. It's simply wrong, and we need to make things right, starting with ourselves. We're calling on you to help us stop *Sesame Street* and Disney from using music to corrupt children."

They were handing out leaflets and denouncing rock 'n' roll. How could this be? Samson and Sutton had previously formed the punk band called Propagandhi, which was at once edgy, political, and against social repression of all forms. And what were they up in arms about here? According to the flier that I was looking at, all of this was about *Sesame Street*. Well, not *Sesame Street* as much as Katy Perry appearing with Elmo.

A crisis that had been and gone but left a stain as memorable as a failed rescue mission in Somalia. Ultimately, Katy Perry accepted that the episode wouldn't be aired, but she didn't accept it lying down. Based upon the little that I knew about her, she seemed tough. So in a typical rock 'n' roll manner, Perry accepted the decision and then flouted it. It was brilliant. Shortly after, on *Saturday Night Live*, Perry made fun of herself, of Elmo, and of the motivations that could have led to this wayward decision.

"What's the problem with the video?" Kenn asked the obvious question. A great question, in fact. I knew that there had been a brouhaha but never knew what the problem really was.

One of the Johns replied, "It's scandalous. Perry is simply not appropriate for children. Her dress, her values, her manner, and her image. It shows children that being an object of sexual gratification is cool."

Whoa, Silver, and where's Tonto? What had happened to these guys? Not a shred of who we thought the Weakerthans were was left anywhere with these two.

"Scandalous?" Kenn said.

"John," I said, not knowing which one was which, but knowing that they would answer either way, "seriously, what specifically is the problem? Sure, Perry is wearing a short dress, but sexual gratification? There was nothing even remotely sexual going on between her and Elmo. In fact, you can see more at the beach or in the paparazzi photos of Paris Hilton. Or are you saying that children shouldn't learn that women have breasts?"

"It's more than that," replied John. "It's subtle."

"You have to understand," the other John continued. "It's complicated."

Right, subtle and complicated. OK, well, Kenn had taught me complicated, and we had refined time travel and corrected history, so I figured I could handle *Sesame Street*.

"*Sesame Street* targets children by subtly subjecting them to subconscious inputs in order to corrupt their values. These values become the foundations of their morality, so if the values are deficient then their basic morality has no chance."

"What?" Kenn blurted out. I was inclined to agree with Kenn—this was the first that we had heard of a direct attack on *Sesame Street* rather than on Ms. Perry.

"So it's not Katy Perry but *Sesame Street* that's the problem?" he asked, both of us trying to catch up. Maybe I was wrong. This could be more complicated than I had anticipated.

"Well, really it's both. Rock 'n' roll, through Katy Perry, allows *Sesame Street* to make messages more attractive."

"Right . . . like the mendacity behind tricking children into thinking counting is fun," I retorted. "Maybe you should get those funny red cops who ride horses to arrest Feist for singing 'One, two, three, four.' I mean, what sort of devil worship is that?"

"It's actually more like Bert and Ernie and how they promote homosexuality," one of the Johns said.

Well, here we go. Back to this, are we? The long-standing argument on the sexual tendencies of Ernie and Bert. Were they merely roommates, or were they lovers? Why did it even matter? They always seemed decent to each other, so why meddle?

Again, I always found that the important questions were the ones that were missed. Presumably, Bert and Ernie were adults, as they were always on their own. In fact, as far as I knew, adults were never seen in their skits. Based on this logic, you've got a grown man playing with a rubber duck in the bath, yet we're all encouraged to watch; why do we find this acceptable?

What experiences had led Ernie to be so emotionally stalled that he insisted upon playing with children's toys in the bath as an adult? Shouldn't we be more concerned about this behavior than his sexuality? Shouldn't we be concerned about his childhood and what the toy duck could symbolize, rather than about a stable relationship between two consenting adults? Maybe *Sesame Street* wasn't about symbols or sexuality at all. Maybe it was simply about lessons. Lessons like having fun in the bath, personal hygiene, how to be polite in your local community, even to the surly neighbors living in trash cans (even if they shouldn't be trusted and are perhaps mentally unsound).

I laughed. "You're kidding, right? There is absolutely no chance that Bert and Ernie were or are gay. I can tell you this unequivocally."

"Unequivocally?" A hush fell over the room and all the attention shifted uncomfortably upon me. I had stood up to bullies before and had always been ready with an opinion, but this was a larger stage. Well, it was actually on the floor in front of a short riser, but figuratively I was on stage and this was a larger, more hostile (to my views) audience than I had been accustomed to.

"Look," I started, trying to gather momentum and confidence and perhaps even a bit of theatric flare. "There is no way that Ernie and Bert are in a homosexual relationship with each other. No self-respecting gay man would love another man who had one eyebrow. It's simply not going to happen. Groom or go. That would be the choice. In fact, I don't think that they let their straight friends get away with having one eyebrow. It's such a bad look."

"It's true," Kenn said coming to my aid. "We've been to San Francisco together a lot," he added, suddenly casting our conversation into a different light.

Silence. Disbelief. Or was it a lack of understanding? Clearly there weren't any gay men who were going to spring forth and bolster my conclusion, not that I expected support from that field, certainly not here. I would imagine that for anyone who happened to be gay, a gathering of forced morality that eschewed rock 'n' roll, artistic freedom, and homosexuality would be as popular an evening option as licking a frozen railway track. Hmm, what to do, what to do?

"Scandalous." A large, familiar-looking man stepped forward, breaking the trance that I had somehow managed to put the entire crowd under. "Absolutely scandalous. We're trying to have a serious discussion here, and you come in with flip comments and jokes."

"He was being serious," Kenn said in my defense. "Have you ever seen a gay man with one eyebrow?"

That-a-boy, Kenn; keep at it. You've got them on the ropes now, I thought.

"Scandalous. An abomination." The voice belonged to McCloy; we were face-to-face with McCloy again.

"Look, asshole, we got that part already," interjected Kenn, now losing the tenuous grip on his patience. "You can't be serious that *Sesame Street* or rock 'n' roll is the problem. Or even homosexuality. We're talking about adults and consensual choices."

"*Sesame Street* is about children," McCloy said.

Nausea spread from the back of my throat to my stomach, coursing through every nerve that I could have possibly had. There was a girl at his side who looked familiar, just different, and she gave me a look not of recognition but of ambivalence and revulsion.

It was Pyrah. Pyrah together with McCloy. No wonder I felt weak. Reaching for a folding chair that was nearby, I tried to steady myself, and then I simply sat down as I could hear Kenn pitching into a vengeful exchange with McCloy.

It was the sound of violence. Hatred, incapable of compromise. Without looking up, I knew the positions. McCloy coming to the aid of Samson and Sutton, leaving Kenn defending rock 'n' roll. Neither offering any quarter to the other. Both equally tenacious and strident; it was just that McCloy was wrong. As I sat there gathering my resolve and trying to manage the searing agony that the fresh and unexpected proximity to Pyrah was causing, I imagined Kenn and McCloy as wild dogs fighting over a kill.

I said, half to myself, "Years of evolution and we never change."

18

We Never Change

We never really change, do we? Or is it that we are constantly changing, but others change with us? You say, "She's never changed," implying that you did but without "her"; or you say, "He's changed," meaning that you didn't but that "he" was the problem. Maybe people change in a different direction, at a different rate, or in a different manner. But somehow, somewhere, something is lost between the two. This is the delta, the measure of that change. Is it change or the lack of change that is the problem? A chicken or an egg?

How has science failed to solve the chicken-and-egg riddle? How can science define gravitational forces between bodies, but not the attraction between people? Or the terminal velocity of certain objects, but not the speed of falling in love? With all the discoveries of science, has anything changed?

This is KQRL 89.9, I'm Sid, the program is Transmission, and it's nearly four a.m. Here's Coldplay with "We Never Change."

FCC transcript KQRL 89.9 FM 11.05.2010 0353

We never change. A problem without a solution is a result of an unwillingness to change, consigning the future to perpetuate the past. Kenn and I had discussed his ideas before. Just like many quarrels he pursued, he couldn't see there was nothing to be gained in arguing with McCloy.

"It's the Doppler effect." Kenn would explain.

"I don't think that the Doppler effect is what you think it is."

"Actually, I'm sure I know what Doppler is. It's a shift in frequency of a form of wave energy based upon where it's observed. Basically, things that seem like good ideas to me and come out of my mouth are perceived as bad ideas to those people who hear them. Sounds and storm energy work on the same principal."

Yeah, ultimately, that summed up what was wrong with Kenn and why he was socially dubious.

Had Kenn changed? Kenn had always been belligerent, but now at the Weakerthans gig, things just seemed more focused. If so, wasn't that a change? Perspectives change, but also perspectives are capable of changing views. The fundamentals could remain the same, but with different perspectives the result could differ. I had perceived changes in him since we started crossing, but maybe my tolerance had merely shifted. Maybe it was the Doppler effect all along. Kenn's voracious, competitive desire to better me was a change. Maybe he was just harnessing his frustrations or directing these emotions externally. Maybe the change was a manifestation of an existing, harbored irritation.

But whatever was going on, Kenn had seen and heard enough. Not just today, but for years. Kenn was tired of being kept at the end of his tether.

There was no question that Kenn was holding his own, arguing with Lon. Kenn was suddenly passionate, articulate, and compelling. Really, Kenn? Where did all of this come from? Kenn was becoming more brazen, more confident and engaged during the experience of crossing, but this display with McCloy was even beyond that.

Watching in fascination as Kenn and McCloy parried blows, what had started as intermittent support from me gave way to absolute detachment from my surroundings. Kenn and McCloy had both taken myopic stands, perfectly polarized from each other. The two combatants continued their circular arguments about various merits and countervailing points, neither allowing any quarter.

Kenn and McCloy were talking over each other, struggling to be heard, incapable of hearing the other. My mind filled with images of crusading armies marching across fields. Battalions of soldiers locked in pitched conflict. Swords and arrows becoming rifles and cannons becoming unmanned drones and missiles. Combatants locked in their own conviction of the infallibility of their views, inconvincible, while unaware of what the point was that was being advanced.

"Music is a form of art. The ultimate creative and personal expression."

"Sure, music is, but rock 'n' roll is vile. It's a canker on music by those without talent or insight into true art."

"You're talking about preferences now, splitting hairs."

"I'm talking about what's right." McCloy was as resolute as Kenn.

"Right?" I interjected, "Right is what's protected by the Constitution. The basis of what this country was founded upon. Freedom of expression is protected by the First Amendment."

"Artistic expression is protected, not obscenity. Rock 'n' roll isn't music. It's not art. It's obscene."

Kenn was back on the attack. "Why? Because you say so? All rock 'n' roll? Just because you don't like it? What about Christian rock 'n' roll? Music that makes reference to your God, that supports your beliefs in a God that alone shall judge?"

"Yeah, basically. Basically because right-minded people who have come together with a common view have banded together."

"Banned together is what should happen to the First Amendment rights of assembly that you and your hatemongers exercise for repression," I said. "Why does the First Amendment allow you to dictate what's right?"

"You might as well tell them how to pray," Kenn added. "You're bullying them anyway."

"There is only one true way to pray. One true religion, one true God, and one true way to honor that God," he said with zealous hatred and rage. "Anything else is . . . well, it's just an abomination." It was the final word that I heard the emphasis on. The words were almost spat out, and McCloy's complexion grew flushed, glistening with perspiration. "Abomination" was said with a conviction and contempt that were visceral.

With that word, I felt struck. Staggered, like when defending heavyweight champion Trevor Burbick was hammered by Mike Tyson. Smashed like Paul Simonon's guitar in the concert photo that became the cover of *London Calling*. It was as though I had been pinned and mounted.

Abomination. A word that seethes with revulsion and violent opposition.

Of course, violence is more than the physical. The mental aspect of violence also makes it traumatic.

Violence, violate, violet. In the color spectrum, violet was at the bottom, with the shortest visible wavelength. Bruises become discolored and bleed into purple shades, telling of a violation that is a base form of humanity.

Listening to Lon, I was realizing for the first time that change could occur, even when I thought it was impossible. Things not only unexpected but improbable. Kenn and I weren't just in peril of losing an argument. We were lost. Everything that we knew, or thought we knew, was wrong. More than anything else, we needed to extricate ourselves from this argument immediately.

Like the first time I stood up to a schoolyard bully, I understood that it was OK to combat violence if you were prepared, but here . . . today . . . now, I wasn't prepared. I wasn't prepared to see Pyrah. As much as I thought I wanted to, I wasn't prepared to have a confrontation with Lon. Seeing the Weakerthans changing their "colours" had surprised me. I thought we were going to a gig, not heading into battle. I failed to anticipate the past we were visiting.

I wasn't prepared to learn that I needed to change. A cool nausea fell upon me. I wasn't the solution; I was the problem.

"Kenn," I interjected, trying to regain some semblance of composure, "let's go. It's over. There is nothing that we can do here."

"Dude, I've got this," he insisted.

"Kenn, there is no winning here. We can't convince people like this." I sighed with some recognition. "We know the type, and there isn't anything to do but walk away."

"But—" he started.

"I know, Kenn," I interrupted. "I know you've got this guy. You don't have to convince me, but you're not going to convince him, either. We're just wasting our time here. Let's go."

Seeing the desperation in his eyes, I knew he needed to win. Not merely wanting to win, but physically needing to. Lon was just a proxy for Kenn; he was arguing with his parents. His parents he would never see, who had been dead for five years in our correct time line. His father who always told him he was an underachiever. No good. A waste. A father who could have been proud of him if Kenn had done something important with his life, something other than listening to rock 'n' roll. Parents whom he merely ignored rather than tried to talk to about his passions. A family whom he left disappointed, without time to make amends before they died. Back to a time that we rarely spoke of; only for a few weeks after the funeral. As far as I know, that was the first and only time that Kenn wore a suit.

I put my arm over Kenn's shoulders and guided him away in silence. When we were alone on the street outside, I said, "Kenn, you were awesome in there. It's just that there is no way to convince a guy like him, who is so zealous that his views are wrongly formed."

Of course, I recognized the type. He was a bully. His arguments were self-serving, carefully constructed on assumptions that were in turn carefully constructed in order to support his regime of beliefs. We had seen this before, and we called this type of practice "bullying the jukebox."

19

Bullying the Jukebox

This is Sid here at KQOR 89.9. We're looking at 1:17 in the morning. Perspective changes everything. Rebels are either freedom fighters or insurgents. Taxes provide a crutch or yet also cripple.

Belligerence is taking a stand. But usually there's a line to cross. Are you welcoming new teammates or perpetuating a barbaric hazing ritual? Is it just a joke, guys having a laugh and blowing off steam, or are they bullying the jukebox? Don't even get me started about group dynamics.

FCC transcript KQOR 89.9 FM 05.09.2010 0117
Operator's comments: Add to Watch List; Suspect [   ]

Bullying the jukebox. Just a harmless game. A game Kenn and I learned from a song. Harmless and fun. Hilarious, really, when you think about it. Except that it was symptomatic of something else entirely.

We had played bullying the jukebox before but not often, mostly for practical reasons. I mean, money spent feeding a jukebox could be better spent either on beer or on actually owning a personal copy of the music. This was only one part of the equation; the other, unsurprisingly, was all about the music.

Jukeboxes are known for their selection and ability to feed loose change to a bar owner, but Kenn and I usually went to bars only to hear *live* music. Not to play pool and certainly not to pay to listen to someone else's deficient music collection with crap acoustics. As a rule, jukeboxes suffer from years of misuse and the speakers are never set in a favorable location, but rather positioned to keep the floor space available and thus contributing to less than adequate sound.

Jukeboxes are still coveted by collectors as a metaphor of a romantic past. A beacon of a time remembered more fondly than experienced.

The game comes from the Bouncing Souls song of the same name. Bullying the Jukebox is the practice of exerting one's musical preferences over the bar by keeping the jukebox playing your selections. A game that, like most, ultimately goes too far and becomes a source of taunting and belligerence.

What if you replace musical preferences with something else, anything else, really. What about religious beliefs? Why not insert views on environmental protection or gender roles? Suddenly the story told is that because your views differ from mine regarding environmentalism, I'm justified in bullying you. This sort of behavior is more than inappropriate. It's obscene. Regardless of the justification or the context, bullying is bullying, and it has to stop.

There is no justification in saying, "I'm being a bully to stop other people from bullying." No, bullying is bullshit.

Kenn and I were imposing our views on everyone else. Bullying the jukebox because other people's taste in music sucked—just like the song. Rather than the heroes that we thought we were, we were the villains that we sought to vanquish. Crossing the line between defending an ideal and becoming belligerent in our views, we became bullies. No better than McCloy. Perhaps worse, because we thought we were better.

In the end, exploitation comes from malice, regardless of the form. Repressing workers, the environment, those with other religious views or a different gender, other societies or races, all arise from a belief or an understanding that the particular act is justified. An entitlement.

McCloy justified railing against rock 'n' roll because it stood against his beliefs. We justified defending rock 'n' roll because it reflected our beliefs. All struggling to flip the same coin in our favor.

Was it OK to subject women or other nationalities to hardship, exploitation, or violence because you could justify the end, a greater goal, or a better objective? Even saying that sounded wrong: It wasn't the means that mattered, but the end. We were fighting people who were evil, and evil we became.

I looked at Kenn in absolute shock, turning away in disbelief. I suddenly caught my own reflection. Kenn and I were glowing. If I looked closely, I could see that there was a hologram flickering on us; the sign that we had so easily noticed worn by others was now a cloak of shame upon us.

That's what this had all been about. There was no difference between rape, littering, racism, and xenophobia. These actions all started with entitlement. We let our prerogative drive our justification.

Suddenly that's what Kenn and I stood for? I suspected that our condition, the hologram and flickering glow, had always been there, but we had just lacked the perspective to see ourselves clearly.

Even once we had returned to Kenn's, he continued his rant about McCloy and how we needed to prevail over his Morality in Music.

"Kenn, stop, please," I pleaded. "Don't you see what's happening? What we've done? We're the same, Kenn. We're the same as McCloy, with different views but just as intractable."

Kenn remained silent as I explained my epiphany. Somewhere we had strayed away from the goals of being better. Goals of being heroes and leaders of men. Of having something that we rose above, that we had as ours, and that we enjoyed and were experts in.

No longer heroes, we became belligerents, as though pushed along by a lurking demon. The course of action never started as exploitation, but that was the result. It was never genocide or environmental degradation; those results were merely a side effect of the desired course of action or goal. Goals formed into words, words became phrases, and phrases became belief.

"We need those resources."

"Those people are a scourge."

"Relax, you'll enjoy this."

"Bon Jovi is an abomination."

Words that Kenn and I had used but now realized had come from our mouths with meaning and impact beyond what we had expected.

"Fuck," Kenn said, shaking his head. In fact, that was all he had been saying for about twenty minutes. The expression on his face indicated that he was close to vomiting, but the shimmer was fading, the hologram diminishing.

"Yeah, Kenn, big stuff. Time travel changed our world, giving us, I thought, a responsibility to make the right changes. I thought we were supposed to set history to how it was supposed to be. Wasn't it easy to go back and see what was wrong?"

"I thought so. We saved rock 'n' roll from dying. We stopped the apocalypse. Doesn't that make us right? We made things turn out right."

How were things supposed to turn out? We had averted the rock 'pocalypse but now stood in judgment for our actions, failing, just like our parents always said we would. Kenn and I were the bullies that we feared and despised. All we had left was our self-righteousness and the occasional radio spot I could scratch up in relief.

"Kenn. It's *us* that have to change in order to change history. Sure, both Sutton and Samson glowed at the Weakerthans show that wasn't, but you and I did, too. At first I didn't notice it, but now I recall seeing a shimmer and aura around you and me in the mirror behind the empty bar station."

It hadn't occurred to me that either Kenn or I would glow; we hadn't even thought to look for that on our other crossings. Had it happened before? Maybe. Maybe that's what happened when Kenn got Tasered in San Francisco. Maybe we were both glowing when we paid Mike Ness's cover to see Black Flag or when we first saw the Specials. Maybe all along it was us, not history, that needed to be changed. We could have been glowing when we saw Lemmy; it could have been our glowing that made him suspicious of us in Germany. OK, I suppose it was likely that

Lemmy would have been suspicious of us anyway, but still, our needing to change was a possibility that we hadn't even considered.

It had to be that we needed to change in order to make history better. That's how we were going to be heroes, by changing the only thing that we could control. We could make history better by our choices and actions, not just in historic gigs, but every day.

Of course, we are all entitled to opinions; that's the basis of art and freedom. People have preferences. Likes and dislikes. Some music is more accessible than other music. Really, was there any difference between Sammy Hagar yammering that "I Can't Drive 55" and the Cramps questioning "How Far Can Too Far Go?" or suggesting "Let's Get Fucked Up"? In fact silliness is just silliness, and like Baskin-Robbins, it comes in fifty-two flavors (or more). The only real difference was Kenn and I used our views to inflate our egos, and worse, to denigrate others who either didn't share them or lacked the knowledge that we had.

"What do we do now?" Kenn asked.

"I don't know, buddy," I replied, stunned with the revelations of the evening.

"We have to do better," Kenn sighed, "but how? What?"

"Maybe it's like everything else," I said. "Maybe the best answer is the one that takes the most work. We get it right, and if we fail, we just do it again."

20

Do It Again

Malcolm Gladwell says that repetition is the key to success. In short, if you want to do it right, do it again. Funny, my teachers would always get frustrated having to repeat themselves, yet I could have been contributing to their pursuit of excellence.

This is Sid, at KQSF 91.1 FM. My show is Transmission and I'm lucky to be here week after week.

I'm not sure if Gladwell has tuned in or not. It is 2:15 a.m., but let's "Do It Again" with a cover of the Beach Boys: here's Wall of Voodoo.

FCC transcript KQSF 91.1 FM 10.22.2015 0215

Operator's comments: License requirements clear.

"Do it again?" Kenn asked "Why?"

"Because, buddy, there are still things that need to be sorted out, and because we can."

"That's the same reason that a dog licks its own ass. Because it can. Not always good enough, but a reason all the same."

"It's good enough for the dog."

"But not for me. I'd need a better reason to lick my own ass."

"OK, but how about because we have an ability to repeat crossings, and this is how we change history. How we change ourselves."

"We should have really stayed with the *not* changing history idea, but I suppose you're right, and after all we've come this far . . ."

"That's the spirit. Nothing like resigned indifference to motivate the pursuit of excellence. Let's get back to the Weakerthans gig and focus our attention on rock 'n' roll and not McCloy. He's lost anyway."

"So you're saying we focus on our reactions, on who we want to be, and that will trigger the changes in us that we need?"

"Yup, see how easy that is? Logic, not science. Easy, even for me."

"You're a dick."

Returning to a crossing to retrace some steps but not others was a practice that we had developed along the same lines as how we organized our music. Searching for connections between artists or producers, anything that was of interest or tangible, could lead to more and more music.

For example, we'd cross again and again for Billy Bragg, and we'd go to see his shows and the acts that he'd bring along with him. For us this was one of the greatest sources of new music. Some were better than others, but it was always interesting. This was how we discovered Darren Hanlon, the Disposable Heroes of Hiphoprisy, and Kris Demeanor. It was also how we came to enjoy the Barenaked Ladies. While we had been familiar with the band, it was only in seeing them live that we discovered how good they actually were. But really, this was the lesson all along. That our judgment wasn't unassailable; it was merely an expression of our preferences. But at least in terms of the Barenaked Ladies, they went from being excluded to included in the subset of rock 'n' roll that we classified as "our taste."

Other crossings were different. Some of our interventions hadn't gone as smoothly as others, so we returned to tinker with them. The truth was that we'd tried to intervene in the Replacements gig a few times but never got it right. It should have been easy, but things never really do go to plan, do they? Why didn't we just swap cassettes, or wait and trip Mooseman? Yeah, we tried those things, and others, too, but the result was never the same. Perhaps the way that it worked out was the way that it was meant to all along. It was the history that was supposed to be, just with the details forgotten. Even Rollins was the same during the

Replacements crossing, as we called it. Rollins always played the villain during this crossing. Why? We never did find out. I suppose it makes sense, if history records life and certain things just can't be explained, that history can't explain everything, either, can it? Some things just are.

We'd cross to make sure that bands like the Offspring, Modest Mouse, Brad Sucks, the Black Keys, and Darren Hanlon were all doing what they were supposed to be doing and to make sure that the Cure, the Pixies, and the Specials were getting back together to take another swing through their ever-expanding fan base. We crossed to make sure that the schedules for Rancid and Jim Carroll were such that they would inadvertently overlap, allowing the boys from Rancid to meet literary icon Carroll so that ...*And Out Come the Wolves* was the album that it became.

Through these exploits, we continued to be amazed at how Brian Eno, Rob Younger, and Daniel Lanois continued to permeate through the art form. They continued to record their own original works or produce other bands, help set up tours, and exert a significant influence. I never understood what the concern over the Replacements cassette was about when an intervention aimed at the Velvet Underground, or at least Lou Reed and John Cale, or Brian Eno, would seem to have stopped a tremendous amount of creativity in its tracks. But perhaps that was attempted; certainly every imaginable distraction would have been thrown at Lou Reed, but maybe rock 'n' roll prevailed. Maybe there were some others crossing like Kenn and me, also being heroes and remaining unrecognized.

Fortunately, Kenn and I were able to learn from our mistakes, and although there was a certain amount of history repeating itself, as Shirley Bassey and the Propellerheads would collaborate to prove, we were able to make a difference. But the biggest difference that we made was in changing who we were and how we approached others.

Returning to the Weakerthans gig that wasn't, this time ready for what we'd see, we set our plan. As it turned out, the show was in upstate New York. It was a small community theater, Teatro's, I think, with a wide stage area that was more of a riser about two feet above the main floor. There were people milling around, but no instruments set up on the riser. Clearly, the Weakerthans weren't going to be taking to the stage anytime soon. The crowd was mixed, not unlike those at most gigs, but mostly made up of various anarchists and the self-proclaimed "enlightened" folks, people that collectively would be seen as unwashed and marginalized by society. T-shirts, caps, patches proclaiming support for Sea Shepherd, Amnesty International, Greenpeace, Occupy Wall Street, Anti-G8, the usual suspects. The only real diversity within the group was between those who understood the issues they were advancing and those who were in attendance looking for an excuse to caterwaul and throw bricks.

Scanning the room, I compared the inventory of the people assembled with my memory of the last time. Leaning against the frame of the emergency exit was a kid in a hoodie that looked to be covered in an oily residue of reddish soil. His face and head were submerged in the recess of his hood, but judging from the profile of his shoulders and his bony left hand, which was drumming on the door frame, he looked emaciated and more than a little disturbing. Close to the stage, I saw them, not the band, but rather McCloy and Pyrah, who I had suspected were both close to the source of trouble.

I anticipated seeing Pyrah, and while it didn't hurt any less, I was at least prepared. I thought that was half the battle. It might have been, but it was still half a battle I wasn't interested in and one I was drawn into against my wishes.

Pyrah smiled at me, and then I smiled. Then she smiled again and her eyes glinted, captivating me like always. As if the sacrifice could be worth it, wanting every day to be Valentine's Day and for Pyrah to be mine.

She appeared as she always did. Beautiful. Mesmerizing. Controlling. Her eyes didn't merely touch me. They reached through my rib cage and held my heart until it grew still. Her gaze held me with the comfort of a child's blanket, then her warm smile froze into a sneer and her hold upon my heart tore away like fingernails against a blackboard. I drew a shallow, wounded breath, but unlike last time I didn't falter. At least my anticipation had saved me this much. Steeling myself, I managed to say to her, "Is this really what you want to be doing? Tripping around trying to destroy music?" Although I tried to sound confident and suave, my voice quivered, taunting me as a liar.

"Really?" Pyrah replied. "You're still intent to follow your silly rock 'n' roll fantasy, thinking that you're making a difference, when all you really do is sit around listening to music? Dreaming up adventures with every new song lyric is a joke; that's not a contribution, it's delusional. Your radio show is over, you were fired from a volunteer position, and you can't even hold a job your daddy got you. Pathetic."

I'm sure she had more to say, but it didn't matter. The pain was absolute. Beyond the words that Pyrah used, it was that she had convinced me that we were in love. It was that I was vulnerable to her and continued to allow myself to be hurt by her. I thought that I had been cured of the heartache she'd caused, but obviously I was only weakened with a predisposition to her torments. I could have had yellow fever, or malaria, but instead this was an infection caused by a Harpy's talon. Interrupting, Kenn nudged me in the ribs, and we proceeded to the riser where John Samson and John Sutton were shimmering and handing out their leaflets to the gathering crowd.

"Hey," Kenn started, "you know, your music was really great. Both the time with Propagandhi and the Weakerthans, I loved that stuff, man. It spoke to me."

"Well," one of the Johns replied, "that time is over. We've seen the error of our ways, how rock 'n' roll corrupts. This is the important work for us now."

Calmly, Kenn continued, "Too bad. You know those songs, songs like 'Anchorless,' 'Leash,' 'None of the Above,' and 'Exiles Among You' inspired me."

Halted, the two Johns quizzically turned to Kenn, and one of them asked, "Inspired you how? What do you mean?"

"I mean, you have to seek answers that aren't obvious. Listening to your music, I'm moved to look for meaning, to take a measured pause, a fermata if you will, to reflect upon the world around me."

I chimed in, now composing myself from my interaction with Pyrah. "What we've always enjoyed most about your music, and really all the bands we've liked, is that you let us think about things. You share your interpretation but don't bully it upon us like a decree. Letting people make their own conclusions is a powerful way to affect them."

Continuing past the dumbstruck expressions of the Johns, I asked, "Isn't it that you guys want to make a difference, or do you just want to be in front of a crowd? Because all you're doing today is speaking to a crowd of converts. I'm sure it's gratifying, but you're not making a difference. You're simply talking to people who already believe what you think. It's like giving milk to a hungry baby. At least with rock 'n' roll, you're letting people see your experiences and giving them the opportunity to see if these experiences apply to them."

"John," Kenn said calmly, "you guys need to decide if this is the difference that you want to make. The activism of today will be the anthem of tomorrow."

Seeing the Johns were softening to the idea, I tried to put the whammy on them. "John, don't you want to live somewhere where love and justice shine? Somewhere where sappy slogans all come true? A place where cynicism sleeps and tyranny only talks to itself? Where fear and desperation starve?" I asked, seeking to find some resonance with them. Hoping that lyrics of theirs, from some time either past or future, maybe in an alternate reality, would find fertile soil to germinate in. Lyrics that I knew from "Confessions of a Futon Revolutionist."

"Is that what you're doing here? Are you making the world better or just throwing fat on the fires of ignorance?"

Watching the shimmering aura on Samson and Sutton fade away, Kenn and I made our exit without repeating the confrontation we had previously experienced. Although we were confident in our triumph, we retraced our steps, returning to the gig. Partly just to be sure, and also partially to enjoy the harvest of our success.

The next time we returned to the show, it was still a cold winter's night in upstate New York, but the Weakerthans lived up to their reputation for putting on a great live show. As a band they were tight and in sync with one another throughout the rhythm changes or outright stops.

"Look," I said to Kenn, pointing across the crowded floor. "I wonder what McCloy and Pyrah are doing here."

"Nothing good. I wonder if they can cross as well, or if they're only part of this time line."

"I suppose anything is possible, but I can't imagine they have a mixing table or a Guitar Hero console."

"Maybe there's another way, a way open to them. Isn't that what Rollins was searching for?"

"Yeah, maybe. Doesn't really matter, though; we're here, they're here. Some things just are."

Kenn and I drank a bit, danced a bit, and mostly sat back and enjoyed the show. There really were some great Canadian bands. I went to get more beer about halfway through the show, only to be jostled by a kid in a hoodie.

"Sorry, buddy."

He turned to me and hissed like a pipe of cold air, "You should be. I'm not your buddy. I've missed it all now. This is the end."

"What? I'm sorry. Look, just enjoy the band. I'm not here to start anything."

"No, you don't start anything. This is my ruin. This is the end."

Shaking my head, I walked back to find Kenn with the beer, now warm in my hand.

"What the hell took you so long? I thought you were going for a quick beer. You've been out for most of the set." He took a swig of his beer. "Let's go; the band's finished. This is the end."

21

The End

That was "In the End," by Snow Patrol. This is Sid here at Stanford University 90.1 community radio. I've been on the air since midnight. It is now shortly before six, so this is the end. Or near the end. Almost. The Doors are up next; for this week's show, this is "The End."

FCC transcript KQSD 90.1 FM 19.05.2011 0553

Operator's comments: Flag for escalation

The End. That was the end of the gig and the end of the feeling of being haunted by McCloy, but I would still find other demons to cloud my mind.

Returning to Kenn's, I noticed there was a strange acrid smell that lingered around me.

"Go have a shower; you smell like you've been wallowing in rotten eggs instead of your usual self-loathing."

"Fine. Get some pizza and I'll change."

Kenn was right, I smelled like a mass grave in the hot sun. Turning and looking at the reflection of my T-shirt in the mirror, I saw there was a reddish smudge on the back of a sleeve that looked like soot, but it was a stain, an oily residue that had soaked into the fabric as though it had its own will. Pulling my shirt over my head, I doubled over, retching. My sinuses revolted, filling my mind with images of anguish. I was unable to shake off the disorientation of crossing back to Kenn's; the vertigo remained. The light-headedness and blinding hot flashes accompanied an acrid smell that filled my nostrils as though a forest were burning.

Soaking the shirt at the bottom of the shower, I washed and tried to cleanse myself and dispel the lingering anxiety I was feeling. I scrubbed as though I were preparing for surgery, scouring myself until my skin was pink and sensitive, yet upon exiting the shower still the odor of decay lingered.

"Good jerk-off?" Kenn asked when I emerged from the bathroom. "Your pizza is cold. I called a couple of times but didn't want to open the door. I didn't realize you enjoyed the gig that much. I mean, it was good, but seriously."

I flopped into a chair and disregarded the pizza, instead holding my head and looking at the floor between my feet. "You OK?" Kenn asked. "I was just joking. Hey, you don't look so great. You were in the shower for a long time, maybe you're overheated."

"No. Yeah, I might just need something to eat. I think I have to throw that shirt out, though. I'm betting it won't come clean. I seem to be slipping time. You said I had a long shower and that it took forever for the beer run at the gig? It seemed so short, like I went right there."

"Time's like that, especially if you're masturbating. You want me to heat up the pizza? I'll get you a cold beer, too."

"Nah. Maybe, sure," I replied, picking up a slice and regarding it carefully before taking a small bite. "I bumped into that weird kid with the hoodie. Did you see him off to the side of the stage, the nihilist-looking kid? He was filthy. I hope he wasn't sick."

"Yeah, fucking people; not immunizing . . . You're probably fine. Remember all the times we crossed back after being roughed around at a gig? Or the beating we took from Pussy Riot?"

Kenn was right; rock 'n' roll was rough at the best of times. It was more than the rough jostle at the stage; we had endured beatings firsthand and never experienced long-term effects. There was some residual discomfort, but nothing like what we should have carried with us. Somehow, crossing back home had curative properties. Abstractly, it made sense, since years would have lapsed between the beating and arriving back at Kenn's.

"Still, there was something odd about the dude. Funny thing about rock 'n' roll; there's always something going on. He kept saying it was the end."

"Shocker. A brooding nihilist kid talking about Armageddon. You should have told him you've seen the end and it turns out differently than he'd expect. Someone needs to lock him in a room with Matthew Sweet. Maybe he'd get vaccinated at the same time. Here," Kenn said, handing me a beer from his fridge, "take another and hold it on your head. It'll help. Do you mean regular rock 'n' roll weird or really weird?"

"Hmm, thanks. Bit of both, I suppose."

This was the end, the end of the adventure that Kenn and I had with Guitar Hero. We saved rock 'n' roll. We became heroes by saving human expression and even the human experience through the arts.

There is a difference between the past and history. History is known, but the past is experienced, even if not recorded.

Kenn I still call "Junior" when he calls me "Dick," or to really piss him off, "Kenneth Preston Calvin Ramseyer III, of the Ramseyer family." Regardless of his name, Kenn finally went to college and put his trust funds and inheritance to the use that his parents had always hoped for. Sort of. Kenn enrolled in a university program based on musical history, theory, and business. He figured that if Flea from the Red Hot Chili Peppers could learn something about music, then so would he. I suppose how much he learned was an open question, but he attacked his schooling with the same zeal and resolve that was characteristic of his dedication to rock 'n' roll. Within a few short years, Kenn completed his program, as well as master's and doctoral degrees, and accepted a tenure-track position with a school in New York City.

Achievements coming at the expense of ending my day walking

through his door with pizza and beer, or receiving some lecture, or being part of some crisis, or even just listening to music together. We do stay in touch, but we're busy, and it's just not the same. I think of him often and miss the times that we were drunk or occasionally stoned or shaking with excitement over a new album or band.

It's true that his achievements and rise through the academic ranks have been modest. Kenn's efforts have produced no great discovery or opus, but that's OK. I hope he has come to recognize that he doesn't have to be great, he only has to be himself and be engaged. I don't know if that would have been good enough for his parents or not. As you know, history isn't so very certain. What he's done is good enough for me. I hope it's good enough for Kenn as well. It was good enough to have the restraints on his trust funds released, but he never really needed them.

Brandy left law school in a cloud of foul language and with a degree reading "First Class Honors" clenched in her resolute grip. She accepted a job with a prestigious law firm in the Bay Area specializing in business and entertainment law. Unfortunately for Brandy, she couldn't resist the temptation to play stand-up bass in local jazz sets, so as a result she was only barely making the grade at work. However, this shortcoming didn't last long, as during a client meeting she met a Canadian musician. It turned out that the guy was "Big" John Bates, who was trying to get local permits to set up an open-air show that combined rockabilly and burlesque. He was probably having trouble with the paperwork because of a penchant to spell things with extra vowels.

The supervising partners at the law firm would have never seen Brandy so engaged in a matter, but it wasn't the law that she loved. When Bates mentioned that he was also looking for a bass player to tour with his act, she unceremoniously threw him over her shoulder and carried him out of the law firm and off to audition. Turns out that Brandy, whose stage presence now included long, jet-black hair, eyelashes longer than her temper, tattoos, and a dress that was more burlesque than anything else, took our advice and started bringing more of an edge to her playing. After seeing Brandy beat, shake, and seduce her bass, Bates gave her a local contract and she became a regular fixture in a L.A. in a band called Kitten Heels.

I've seen Brandy's band play a couple of times and have to concede that they're good. She's still hell on wheels. They're as loud as a '72 Nova without mufflers, with a beat that pounds like a toothache. Unabashedly stealing the concept from Big John Bates, they make the rockabilly and burlesque combination work as well, invoking an earlier time where things were more primal and rebellious. You know what I thought of Brandy mixing drinks, so you can imagine what she's like pounding on a bass during a raucous gig. Of course, her being scantily clad doesn't hurt the aesthetic, either.

Brandy and I have stayed friends, but she and Kenn are closer. She usually stays at his place when she's in New York, and, not one to let a joke die, always offers a handjob. Brandy has retained her hard edge, but her wit has ripened with age. Of course, she's as smart as she is quick, but it's her relentless attack that always leaves me flatfooted and flummoxed. I'm not sure if Kenn feels the same, but I suspect that he would. Brandy is a handful and more. I may have a clever response for her from time to time, but Brandy is out of my league in so many ways that she makes my joints ache.

As for me, well there have been a number of changes in what has become mostly a madras patchwork of things that I now call my own.

Although not entirely resolved, I addressed the historical rift with my own parents. I've made it as clear as I can that I'm not a socialist, a vegetarian, or a homosexual (well, at least not for sure). That I'm not a recluse (also not for sure) or antisocial. But that even if I was, they would be my choices and my circumstances, that they could either accept them as part of me, or not. Since then, I've conceded that I'm somewhat antisocial but not an anarchist (well, at least not for sure).

There hasn't been a lot of further discussion about this, so I guess we'll see. Maybe you do have to travel through time to change history, and maybe some histories can't be changed. At any rate, I've found peace.

More interesting (or at least more positive) is that I've since moved to San Francisco and started a couple of different projects. I'm running a blog and a radio show at Stanford that allow me to maintain a certain degree of antisocial and derisive behavior, while still working within a most comforting personal environment. But now I'm trying to do so with more of a tongue-in-cheek style than a true judgment. Most of the time, I find that I'm making fun of myself, so I'm still judgmental. Just more self-deprecating.

Rather than joining the troll-gazing hordes of critics who decried albums like *Lulu*, the collaboration between Lou Reed and Metallica, I've just let it be. Everyone should give *Lulu* a listen, just because. I've tried three or four times now but I still can't tolerate it. Not much of a surprise, having never been a Metallica fan, although I like the mash-ups that people have made with their songs, such as "Enter Sandman" versus "Hot N Cold" by Katy Perry.

Music is different for everyone. Even without the crossings, I still find that I hate whatever David Bowie puts out, at least until seven or ten years later, with the only exception being *The Next Day*. So what does that say? Probably that Bowie is still years ahead of me; hopefully he'll continue making music now. Perhaps *Lulu* is the same thing. Different times, different perspectives. I think that there is room for all of it. Even if *Lulu* remains inaccessible to me, lots of collaborations have failed: Sonny and Cher and Ike and Tina are two that spring to mind. Oasis is another one, but like Ike and Tina, that might be because the relationship was characterized as much by violence as it was by music.

I have changed, I have learned.

For instance, I played a Bon Jovi set of originals and covers the other night. Yeah, I know, Bon Jovi, but it was their 2010 world tour that changed my opinion of them.

It wasn't the tour alone that was interesting. Bon Jovi elected to run a contest in conjunction with their tour, and that captured my imagination.

Their contest encouraged local bands, with a previously limited exposure, to compete for the opportunity to open for Bon Jovi and have a video produced for one of their singles. What the bands would later make of this opportunity was up to them, but the fact was that Bon Jovi left city after city on their tour with more than just their music, having given a local band a break like none other. If for nothing else, Bon Jovi deserved props for changing the future for various local bands.

The contribution that I have become the most proud of is called Breaking Rocks, an outreach program for street youths to teach them skills and music. While I still can't hum a tune or clap a beat, even in a crowded stadium, I organized the program, arranged funding, and hired people with the necessary musical talent. I've unashamedly taken the idea from Billy Bragg's "Jail Guitar Doors" program and unimaginatively lifted the name of my program from the documentary on Billy's program, but then I have always said that art, life, and rock 'n' roll is an iterative process. So Billy Bragg inspired me, just like Joe Strummer inspired him. Of course I inspired Billy to be inspired by Strummer, so we're good.

Breaking Rocks is proving to be generally successful in redirecting what might otherwise be lost souls. As you might imagine, we cater to a vulnerable lot, so success is relative but failure is absolute.

Often I use tickets to shows or spots on my radio show as a reward to encourage the kids to achieve some type of goal or objective with Breaking Rocks. The current initiative is Goal or Gaol, where they have to bring an original perspective to a piece of music about either jails or goals, and then perform the music, orate an opinion, or present a multimedia creation. Then as a group we vote, and the winner goes to the show. My idea is that everyone will be capable of winning, and some of the contests favor some more than others, but this is part of the lesson, too. In life, there are winners and losers, but no medals for participation. Some bands make it and exceed all expectations, like the Ramones or Coldplay, while others like Died Pretty or Lloyd Cole seem to go relatively unrecognized for their magnificence. Is it good or bad, or fair? I suppose it just is.

Breaking Rocks is a good program; I'm making an effort and trying to change our world.

However, like Billy Bragg said, he needs help to save the youth of America, to save them from themselves. Well, I suppose he said it after Kenn and I, posing as angels, suggested it to him. But I'm trying to help turn these kids away from a bleak future of crime and poverty to something else. What else? Well that's up to them; I'm just giving them an option for something different. If after it's all done I've helped one of these kids become a Clash fan, or even a music fan for that matter, and to avoid a life of crime, then I'll be satisfied.

And in fact, this is every day's goal. I think about the Blasters gig that Kenn and I came back from before we had learned to cross. We were out later than we had anticipated and found the window on his front door broken and the house in utter chaos. Lights were broken and knocked to the floor, glass and dishes broken; everywhere things had been thrown around violently. Looking at the house, you couldn't be sure that things were even at right angles or that everything wasn't twisted sideways. We learned later that his parents had interrupted a burglary committed by drug addicts looking for easy money.

Kenneth Preston Calvin Ramseyer II was a successful industrialist who had moved his family away from Portland, "away from the crime and base influences." Ramseyer Industries, of which Kenn's father was the CEO and controlling shareholder, included interests in mining, timber, and shipping. His relatively significant wealth and exceptional business acumen allowed him to run the interests from his home, notwithstanding that he traveled a significant amount of time, tending to these interests. It was the wealth of Ramseyer Industries that resulted in Kenn's home becoming a target of junkies.

Although the addicts were eventually arrested and jailed, they had forever taken most of Kenn's CDs, his amp, his parents' lives, and any hope that Kenn might have had mending his relationship with them.

Kenn replaced the amp, but he never bought a CD again. Of course, we rarely spoke of that night; there was the latent pain that Dave Alvin or the Blasters would later rekindle. Kenn carries these scars every day. I'm sure that there are others, too, who share the same sense of loss. I still remember looking across the house in disbelief. It was more than the mere appearance of chaos; it was a feeling that hung in the air. Something had been disturbed, upset, defiled. Looking at Kenn, I was unable to help him. I was frozen in place. Caught out by the violence, the loss, and the violation of it all.

Kenn had fought with his parents earlier that night about wasting his life. Nothing new for a night of rock 'n' roll; in fact I had a similar story that may have occurred that night for me as well.

Kenn was a child of financial privilege but emotional disadvantage, both created through an inescapable obligation. Because Kenn shared his name across three generations, because prior branches of Kenn's family tree had borne fruit, Kenn was consigned to a future he didn't want. Kenn was enrolled at Princeton but failed to attend the first day. Family holidays in the Swiss Alps that he would sneak away from, instead scouring the local record stores. Really, the consequences of the successful history attached to the Ramseyer name was that Kenn 3.0 was expected to march to the same drum as that of his father, and anything less than that would be a failure.

Suddenly the arguing was swept away. Everything became still and quiet, but so loud, like being caught inside a wave of breaking water. There was the broken glass, the furniture knocked over, muddy footprints, and the acrid smell of blood drying in the carpet and still pooling on the linoleum.

Kenn was still catatonic when the police arrived. I was marginally better. They took our statements, provided us with a place to stay, counseling, and some warm coffee. Warm coffee and counseling. Was that what Kenn needed? Probably not, but nothing would have made a difference at that time.

Later, when we returned to Kenn's, we went downstairs to the basement and locked ourselves in it for days with nothing but pizza, Dew, and of course, music.

Will programs like Breaking Rocks stop crime in America or even in the lane behind my studio apartment? Will it stop people like Kenn from having to suffer? Probably not, but it won't stop me from trying, either.

I've also learned, following Pyrah's betrayal and Kenn's moving away, that I need human contact. This is harder for me to find, but I'm working on it. San Francisco still feels new, full of discovery, although I've been here a few years now. And without Kenn near, my need for contact takes different forms. Sometimes going to a show or a movie is enough. Just to be in the crowd. Sometimes it's dinner with a colleague or even a date.

People say you can't change history, or that you can't change the future, but they're wrong. People also say that time travel is impossible, but it isn't. Even if it's not to the same degree that Kenn discovered with MC5 and Guitar Hero, we all travel through time. We experience other times, other periods, and other places through art.

We change history and the future every day with every decision or inaction. Today's action results in tomorrow's reaction. These events become history. History is made, manipulated, and changed every day; you have to be careful.

Regrets? I've had a few, but then again . . . right, that's Sinatra, not me, but yeah, I've had some. I regret not telling my parents where I was at earlier than I did. I regret not finding love yet. I regret saying hurtful things to Kenn about the CDs at my place. Also, I never did manage to see the Clash in a park with chips and a beer. Maybe there's still time.

I'm also doing some writing, primarily rock 'n' roll based, for various publishers. I'm an occasional contributor to *Spin* and *Rolling*

Stone, mostly small pieces and some reviews, all fairly modest. There has also been a call for contributions in the re-release of rock 'n' roll literature, as all the young punks become old folks, who into their forties have more disposable income to purchase things that were out of reach earlier in life. This has been fun for me, because I've been recruited to write the "proposed book club questions" that are so popularly appearing in books. My publisher tells me that I've got a unique perspective on it all, which I suppose is true.

Is this the end? Well, of course. It's the end for now. That's the fun of it all. Rock 'n' roll will never die and history will never stop being written. What this is the end of is Kenn and me being tourists in our lives. Judging rock 'n' roll from the sidelines. Being spectators, offering our opinions of rock 'n' roll—what it was and what it should be—or, worse, imposing our opinions on others, was over for us. Sure, we still had our opinions and stuck to them vehemently, but we had softened our stance a little, too. Rock 'n' roll is bigger than all the bands. Bigger than my views. Bigger than Kenn and me, and bigger than history. It is our history, our present, and our future. Rock 'n' roll is a reflection of the human condition.

So, this is the end. Unless of course there's an encore.

Encore

Encores. A practice that I'm not partial to, but one that I understand. We all want things to continue; we eschew an end. Crowds feverishly chant for an encore, not because they are trying to get their money's worth, but because they don't want the night to end. It's natural.

We cry at funerals. Lament over photographs from holidays and miss loved ones. Memory doesn't take the place of the immediate, and nothing can carry on forever. Unfortunate, but true.

I'm Sid and this is KQOO 90.9 FM at 3:30 a.m. And while I wish things could last forever, this is the last set of the night. I will be back next week, but tonight there will be no encore.

FCC transcript KQOO 90.9 FM 04.04.2003 0330

Operator's comments: redacted

"Hey, Kenn," I said into the phone. I was in a taxi leaving JFK, having arrived in New York about twenty minutes earlier. Kenn had invited me, as he had been doing four or five times a year, to guest lecture with him about the cross influences of art and rock 'n' roll. A series of lectures he designed that we were both unexpectedly enjoying.

Not only did the students find themselves inextricably engaged by the subject, but also the lectures had a real rock 'n' roll feel: unprepared, freeform, unpredictable, and accessible to all. Even the notes that Kenn posted on his blog site and the Baruch College whiteboard site were called "set lists."

"I'm just in the cab now, yeah . . . no . . . the cab's fine. Right, I checked for De Niro … we're all good." I glanced forward to watch the alarmed-looking cab driver starting to search around his seat for something unseen. I held up my free hand, indicating to him that I was confused, too, and then made the universal "crazy person" sign of circling my ear with a single finger and then pointing to my cell phone, suggesting that Kenn was the problem. A practice I had developed over the years.

"Sure . . . yeah, right. I should be there in about twenty, twenty-five minutes. Yes, the taxi has a functioning GPS, so I won't get taken for a fare. Fuck, buddy, this isn't my first time out of Kansas. Do you need anything on the way? Right, of course, beer. Pizza, sure. Where from? *Elegante*? OK."

Predictably, when Kenn moved to New York, he elected to live in Rockaway Beach as his tribute to the Ramones. This also meant that he was consigned to a train on a daily basis, but he liked the commute and adjusted his routine. It was during this time that he conducted his research, with a loaded iPod, or a Kindle, or an iPad, or whatever device he was now using to listen to music or to read, or both, while in transit. Kenn simultaneously found harmony with his world while being indifferent to his environment. Insisting that New York City was too big for him, he would lie and say he yearned to be back in Oregon; we both knew better. Kenn would never return to Oregon. Oregon was gone for both of us, and even if there were things there to go back to, home is never the same as you left it.

New York was great, but visiting with Kenn was always the highlight. We had become aware, acutely aware, of the importance of history, as well as our own actions in shaping that history. In learning this, we had seen our relationship strained and then strengthened. Now thousands of miles apart leading busy lives, we were rarely together, but when we were, it was just like being back in his house. More often than not, since I was visiting him, I would show up with a couple of pizzas and some beer. He and I would listen to rock 'n' roll and catch up on the scene until the early hours of the morning. In addition to the staples of Mountain Dew and Frank's RedHot sauce I was used to seeing in his fridge, I would also be astonished to see real food: milk, produce, meat, and an assortment of condiments as well. Kenn told me that he was starting to actually cook for himself, but I wasn't courageous enough to see firsthand.

Sometimes we would go to a show in Manhattan, or just walk by the storefront that was temporarily occupying the space that had been the epicenter of independent music—CBGB's. We would pause in solemn silence, thinking of all the shows that we had seen in the filth and decay that was the bar. We would think about the Replacements gig and the other cities that we had seen great shows in and bars that were no longer part of the scene. Kenn and I would reflect upon but rarely discuss the recording that we recovered and how we'd changed not only the world, but ourselves, too. Eventually the moment would pass and we would comment on how the space had changed hands yet again. History marches on. CBGB's was replaced by John Varvatos, which was replaced by a Guess boutique, which was later replaced by a bath and soap shop for a few months and now Coach handbags. At least Varvatos had a connection to the original landmark, but again, history tends to lose focus with time. I suppose we all do.

We've all seen enough change over time and enough time itself to know that change happens every day, and that if CBGB's couldn't last, then nothing else will. On second thought, I suppose rock 'n' roll will, but probably because it doesn't really require real estate, just imagination.

"Oh, yeah," Kenn said. "Just bring lots of quarters. Did you download the 'Through Space and Time and Air and Cable' single, I told you about?"

"Of course."

"Look, just bring the quarters. Say, fifty bucks' worth." Before I could even ask why or what was going on he continued: "Dude, I bought an old British-style phone booth that I've tricked into taking American quarters."

"So?" I asked. With that, I could feel pressure building in my temples. Internal pressure or external pressure I wasn't sure. Intuitively I knew this sensation had nothing to do with the transcontinental flight I had just finished, but rather a sense of foreboding mixed with pensive anticipation. There was always something with Kenn. Some conspiracy. Something to rush for, an emergency or something. Some real, some imagined, but always something.

"So?" he broke the silence. "So, dude, I just had a cigar with Castro." Kenn was still talking about something else in the background. Something that he would undoubtedly repeat when I arrived with the pizza and beer. I was getting the vague sense that this was about historical phone calls, time travel, and international commerce conspiracies.

"Driver," I said with a heavy sigh, "I need to stop and grab some pizza at *Elegante* and also beer on the way. Can you suggest someplace? Also, do you know where I can get some change? I'm going to need some silver. A Laundromat perhaps," I added hopefully. "Yes, of course, you can keep your meter on . . ."

My phone started to ring again almost as soon as I had set it down. I sighed; the ringtone was the drum lead from the Ramones "Do You Remember Rock 'n' Roll Radio?" It was my updated ringtone for Kenn. I thought that I was in town for a lecture series; I really wasn't sure that I was ready for this again.

"Yes, what else?" I answered.

"Hey, dude, just messin' with you about Castro . . . but get the quarters."

Acknowledgements

Travelling through any project requires the support and assistance of many. Accordingly, I owe a great debt of gratitude to those who've assisted along the way.

The endless support and re-re-reading by my wife Nicole; Fil and Dee from Paladar Fumior Salon, who kept me caffeinated in their shop in Brisbane while the story was being written; Matt and Zoe from Emmalou's Macaroons and Café, who kept me caffeinated in their shop in New Plymouth while the story was being edited; C. Emery who continues to provide input and feedback; D. Youles, S. Marchand, N. Deyell who've offered feedback, ideas and laughs along the way; Steve from DoddMusic who provided professional answers to all my amateur music questions; M. Zablocki who has continued to provide ideas, support and web tutoring; McNeill who fell in love with the original story and spurs me along to finish; Paul Carter who has always offered me his support; Peter Wyse who's imagination and amazing art continues to captivate; and the readers who've enjoyed the first book and reached out to tell me as much.

Thank you all. Your support has made this fun.

www.ingramcontent.com/pod-product-compliance
Lightning Source LLC
Chambersburg PA
CBHW051843180726
48284CB00007BA/2026